ROOSTER

Rooster © 2024 Madison Hamilton

All Rights Reserved. No part of this book may be reproduced in any form or by any electronic or mechanical means including information storage and retrieval systems, without permission in writing from the author. The only exception is by a reviewer, who may quote short excerpts in a review.

This book is a work of fiction. Names, characters, places, and incidents either are products of the author's imagination or are used fictitiously. Any resemblance to actual persons, living or dead, events, or locales is entirely coincidental.

Printed in Australia

Cover and internal design by Shawline Publishing Group Pty Ltd

First printing: June 2024

Shawline Publishing Group Pty Ltd

www.shawlinepublishing.com.au

Paperback ISBN 978-1-9231-0199-9

eBook ISBN 978-1-9231-7110-7

Hardback ISBN 978-1-9231-7122-0

Distributed by Shawline Distribution and Lightning Source Global

Shawline Publishing Group acknowledges the traditional owners of the land and pays respects to the Elders, past, present and future.

 A catalogue record for this work is available from the National Library of Australia

HE'S THE CLUB PRESIDENT, SHE'S HIS MINX,
AND THEY'RE BOTH ON THE LIST

MADISON HAMILTON

ALSO BY MADISON HAMILTON

The *Black Alchemy Motorcycle Club* series
Book one: *Rooster*
Book two: *Gunner*

To the weird girls

DISCLAIMER

This book is meant for readers 18 and over. Some content may be unsuitable for some readers. Due to the nature of this book, there are some heavy topics discussed. Please find the list of trigger warnings below.

- Rape
- Murder
- Serial killer
- Loss of a parent
- Reference to alcohol abuse
- Explicit sex scenes
- Knife violence
- Fighting
- Gun violence
- School shooting
- Sexual assault
- Torture
- Death

PLAYLIST

Closer by Nine Inch Nails
That Don't Impress Me Much by Shania Twain
Every Rose Has its Thorn by Poison
(I Can't Get No) Satisfaction by The Rolling Stones
Too Lost In You by Sugababes
If You Want Blood (You Got It) by The Police
Hold the Line by Toto
This Kiss by Faith Hill
Can't Help Falling in Love by Elvis Presley

PROLOGUE

Under the cover of a peaceful North Carolina night, a figure shifted from deep within the bushes surrounding one of the unassuming properties along the quiet, sleeping street. A monster with the face of a man waited among the shadows. He watched the upstairs window as the silhouette of a woman moved about her room. She undressed, grabbed a towel from the cupboard, and proceeded to get ready to turn in for the night. Innocent enough, she seemed, but he'd hunted her well enough to know better.

From all the days he was keeping her in his sights, one night was all it took to show that she was unclean. He'd watched as she subjected herself to a night of debauchery: drinking, flirting and fucking that biker. It made her the perfect target. Steam fogged up her bathroom window. The monster chuckled under his breath. As if a shower was going to wash her sins away. He shifted closer to observe as she retreated deeper into the room, out of his sights.

The monster ran his hands through his thick hair. He knew he shouldn't be there, but he couldn't deny the urge inside him any longer. The monster had tried to resist before, but it had only increased his desire. It was hard to control himself so close to perfecting this game he loved to play, so close to winning his prize.

His hunger burned within him at the thought, the taste he imagined hovering over his tongue. All the planning, all the practice.

She would be worth the wait.

He blinked away the memory of his ultimate prey from his mind. Keeping his breath steady, he focused on the beautiful target waiting above, just for him. He loved the way she swirled her mid-length curly hair away from her neck only to let it swing down her back a few moments later. His prey had a little more meat on her bones than he envisioned, but that wouldn't matter come sunrise.

He crept forward, the leaves brushing his hoodie, as he started toward the house. He knew that this woman would be alone; she was always alone. Well, except for her small, white dog, but that mutt wasn't going to be an issue anymore.

The monster stepped over the lifeless white mop of fur he had taken care of and carefully avoided the creaky board of the front porch as he made his way to the front door.

Just like every other door in this godforsaken small town, it was unlocked. His prey obviously felt very safe.

She was stupid.

As he stepped inside the cookie-cutter house, the monster took in the simple, almost bare rooms. The walls were painted a cream colour and there were boxes lining the walls. She hadn't completely moved it, but she had been living in Bryson City for a few months now.

He listened as the woman's husky voice travelled down the staircase and the evil inside the man roared with delight as he slowly moved closer to the sound. There was no more running water, just the sound of her husky laughter.

With a peak around the corner, he noticed the girl with her cell phone to her ear. He wondered if she knew that this would be the last time she spoke to anyone, the last time her name would be used without being tied to his moniker. The Bryson City Slasher was what the papers had been calling him. He didn't hate the name. He hadn't come up with anything better to send to the press anyway.

The monster listened as his prey said her final goodbyes. He was in the shadows of her bedroom door. He snuck a glance inside and watched as her silhouette stalked closer to his hiding place. He slid into the spare room, keeping the door cracked open enough to hear her lock the front door and check that the doggy flap was operational. The monster held his breath as he waited for the woman to find her mutt bloody on the front lawn. His dead heart raced at the thought of the chase; it wasn't part of his ritual and it would ruin the entire experience.

When no scream came, he crept into her room, pulled the closet door behind him and watched for his pretty to come back. It was like they were playing a deadly game of hide-and-seek, but only he knew they were playing, which made the game that much more fun.

He heard a loud sigh as she moved back into her room. It was almost time to feed.

The monster watched as she slipped under her blankets, the tank top she wore riding up slightly, showing her plain cotton underwear. The man bared his teeth at the sight, the only thing that was keeping his anger to a simmer was the knowledge that he had his favourite matching bra and panty set from her drawers.

The monster couldn't wait to take the ripped lace; he could already see them covered in his pleasure and her blood. He just knew that this prize was going to be one to remember for a long time to come. It had better be, his urges were growing stronger with each kill and he didn't know how much longer he was able to hold out for.

He reached into his hoodie, grabbed his now small roll of duct tape, and ripped off a piece loudly. The monster stilled when he heard the woman whimper in her sleep. He didn't want his prey to know about his presence yet. He still had a few more things to get ready before he woke her up.

He was laying out the lingerie set when he caught her fidgeting in her sleep. The monster fought his groan. His whole timeline had been ruined because this woman was a fucking light sleeper. He waited for her to turn over and used the tape he had pre-cut to slap over her mouth. Her blue eyes opened. A scream caught in her throat behind the sticky gag and fear was laced in her eyes.

'Hush now, my sweet, it will all be over soon,' he whispered in her ear. The monster guided the knife down her body and cut the fabric away from his prey's skin. 'Put on the bra,' he ordered.

Her eyes shone with tears and his cock sprung to full mast. She was terrified and that fact alone thrilled him. Excitement buzzed through his veins when he saw his prey glance at the door once, like she was thinking about escaping or planning her next move. He knew exactly what she was thinking.

'I wouldn't do that if I was you, sweetheart,' he whispered huskily. He helped her up and strapped the bra onto her body. The monster threw her back down on the bed and secured her hands above her head to the iron headboard.

The monster moved the knife up to her face, gliding the silver blade down her cheek. He watched the skin come apart, crimson blood oozing out. The woman whimpered. The man swore he could feel his insides vibrating, the adrenaline rush overwhelming. It gave him the energy that he craved.

'I'm going to have so much fun, my dear,' the monster whispered as the woman gasped in rasping breaths through the tape. He could feel her body tremoring, and her tears were creating a delicious mix with her blood. The man licked at the dripping liquid and groaned low in his throat.

This was going to be his favourite one by far.

He stripped her out of her offending plain cotton underwear and replaced them with the silk and lace pair. The monster stood back for a moment and admired his work, needing to remember this moment, this feeling. He pulled out his burner phone and snapped a picture, making sure that her terrified eyes were staring straight at him through the camera.

His cock swelled in his pants.

It was finally time to feed.

The sun was peaking its head over the mountains surrounding quiet Bryson City when the monster was finally satisfied, and the man resumed the life of an average Joe. His prey now lay dead in her bed, the sheets a mess, her body bruised beyond recognition from all the fucking he had forced her to enjoy.

The man glanced at his burner phone and enjoyed the last photo he managed to take. The morning sun had cast through her blinds, creating the look of fire around the woman's body. Her bra was askew and her breasts red with welts and cuts. Her ripped panties covered in her blood and his pleasure sat in the Ziplock to preserve the smell for when he needed another hit. The man knew that once the smell was gone and the monster could no longer be contained, he would have to feast again, but for the time being he was satisfied.

The man's gait held confidence as he walked back to his rental car. He knew that he wasn't going to get caught. He was above suspicion, and he knew that no one was going to stop his urge to take as many women as he needed to.

He needed to feed the monster inside him. Who knew what would have happened if he hadn't found this outlet. The man's confidence continued to grow as he pulled away from Main Street and the people starting out their day in the small town. They knew there was an evil among them, but no one would guess who he was.

That wasn't just his arrogance talking. It was a plain fact.

CHAPTER 1

Boots stomped on the worn wooden floors of the chapel and ring-covered fists shook in the air. The celebration in the small room was deafening, forcing a smile to spread across Rooster's face. His father's old presidential patch was being sewn onto his cut while his brothers continued to party.

At twenty-six, Rooster would be the youngest president in the history of Black Alchemy. The motorcycle club was in Rooster's blood and the presidency was always going to be his. He never thought he would get it until his pops stepped down, but instead of Patriot enjoying his retirement with Queenie, his father was being prepared for burial.

Rooster knew that his pops had plenty more years left in him, but they were cut short only days ago. The gunshot that had taken down his old man still rung in Rooster's ears, and burned behind his eyes was the way his father looked at him when he realised what had happened. Rooster had no idea what possessed Patriot to trust their life-long enemies, the Jokers Ace MC, but everything that went down at that meet-up thrust the BAMC back into a deadly war. They had been at an unstable peace for years thanks to Patriot, but as soon as that bullet was fired from the shorn off shotgun, the BAMC and Jokers were back at each other's throats.

Black Alchemy had been the product of his grandpop Huey and his Vietnam buddies missing the brotherhood that the army produced. According to the stories, Huey, Bass and Grizz were the only three left of their squad. When they returned to civilian life, things weren't the same for them. It was that way for many of the other Vietnam vets, but in 1975, Black Alchemy was founded in the small town of Bryson City, North Carolina. The creation of the club came with rivals who wanted to continue their expansion, and so the way with the South Carolinian Jokers Ace was born.

Now the war was his responsibility, as was the rest of the men and woman who lived the BAMC lifestyle.

Rooster's heart pounded against his chest wall hard enough to be painful as his pop's best friend and fellow brother Dice approached him with his cut and new presidency patch. He knew it was not the time to think about those fucking Jokers. The club needed to let off some steam before someone did something really fucking stupid, causing more than these last three funerals to attend. Rooster knew why Dice and the other executive board members called for this emergency vote – it was the perfect excuse to let loose and get messy.

Slowly he slid the worn and familiar leather over his shoulders and turned to his brotherhood. Rooster proudly showed off the new patch on his chest, and his brothers' voices rose. He sucked in a breath through his nose when his eyes threatened to prickle with tears and a thickness settled in his throat as his father's face came to his mind.

Thank fuck he wasn't expected to make a speech.

Rooster knew that his father would be proud of him, that Patriot would have been the loudest of his brothers cheering and celebrating

Rooster's new post. It was a bittersweet moment that he couldn't wait to end.

'Time to fucking party!' Grizz's alcohol-damaged growl rang out. The old man raised the beer he had snuck into church, and the rest of the brotherhood followed suit with their fists. 'To Rooster, the youngest president to hold the gavel!'

Rooster's lungs expanded to their fullest through a deep satisfying breath, but then the tightness in his chest returned with a pain in the back of his throat. His pops wasn't even cold in his grave, and now Rooster was the head of his household and the leader of the Black Alchemy Motorcycle Club. Everything was happening so quickly and he didn't have a chance in hell of processing his new life.

His brothers continued their cheering as they exited the chapel and spilled out into the clubhouse. Rooster followed the wave of bodies. A beer was pushed into his chest and he grabbed it, but he didn't want to drink it.

How the fuck was he supposed to celebrate when his old man was killed only days ago? He should be grieving, not drinking his sorrows away. Rooster scanned the room. Some of the club girls had already started making their rounds, their heavily made-up eyes scanning over his patch. Rooster's skin crawled as he fought the urge to cover what was now a trophy challenge to them.

Rooster sighed and kept on walking toward the bar. Maybe he could sit with some of his brothers and shoot the shit for a while, spending some time with the boys before he could sneak away.

Happy with his plans, Rooster continued through the clubhouse. Brothers would slap him on the shoulder congratulating him, making Rooster want to slam them and remind them why he was the new president, but he held in his anger and grief. He needed to prove that he was ready for the challenge and they needed the release.

Rooster spotted his best friend Gunner leaning against the bar, a beer sat on the wooden slab, calling out to him. He would have obliged his brother, but a blonde ponytail captured his attention as she leaned over and spoke something to her friend. She didn't belong in the clubhouse; her tight pencil skirt and white button down screamed professional, but Rooster was intrigued.

He turned on his heel and made his approach.

***

Mila Rice knew she should never have agreed to go to this bizarre biker party with one of the teachers from her new job. As soon as they pulled up to the gate, Mila knew it was a bad idea. She should have tried to convince her fellow teacher to do something else as soon as her 'friend' mentioned wanting to go to the Black Alchemy clubhouse for some fun. She hadn't been in town long, but Mila had heard about the BAMC before. The run-down schoolhouse had peeling yellow paint and tinted windows. It should have been her first sign to run for the hills, but she wanted to make friends in this new town. So, she put on a brave face and followed her inside.

The interior was entirely different. After showing their ID to prove they were of legal age, they walked into what looked like a surprisingly clean bar. It was crowded with men in leather and smoke swirled around people moving about. Mila knew she should have cut her losses and left then and there. She didn't belong here. Not to mention, she was insanely overdressed, literally, if she was comparing herself to the other woman walking around – which she wasn't.

Mila scrunched her nose up and leaned away as yet another biker invaded her personal space. This one planted his hand on her back as he grabbed his drink from the bartender. Mila turned to say something, but something stopped her. This was not a place for her to let her mouth run. She had to fight the urge to slap the man for daring to put his hands on her, but no one would come to Mila's rescue. Even her 'friend' was four shots in and too trashed to back her up. Instead, Mila adjusted in her seat to lean as far away from the biker and watched her co-worker lean further over the bar toward one of the men with light blonde hair and a smirk on his face that she could only describe as practiced. She watched as the blonde biker glanced down to the top of the physics teacher, her breasts practically falling out of her unbuttoned teacher uniform.

Mila shook her head slightly and caught the attention of the young bartender, who she guessed wasn't much older than eighteen. 'What can I getcha?'

'Just pour your best whiskey into a glass,' she spoke. The bartender shot her a grin and did as she asked. He didn't ask for cash but did nod at someone behind her. Mila downed it as soon as it was sat in front of her and she motioned for another as the burn continued down her throat and into her chest. She would sip on the next one; she wasn't going to end up like her 'friend' who had now gathered an audience.

Mila wanted to tell her co-worker to slow down, but she knew she would just brush her off. The woman mumbled something into the biker's neck, the words turning into a slur. She was on a mission and Mila knew there was nothing to stop her.

Not wanting to remain at the bar, she turned to move from her spot. She didn't have the guts to go wondering around this den of debauchery, but she did take inventory of the men and women in various stages of intercourse. She watched one couple who were going at it finally come up from their passionate lip lock to breathe. The man's tongue licked at the corner of the woman's mouth. Another couple was sat at a random table and the woman did nothing to hide her pleasure as the biker's hand disappeared under her skirt.

This place was so overwhelming that Mila's mind screamed at her to leave, to go back to her respectable life and forget about this disaster of a night, but her body was shamelessly enjoying the show. So much so that Mila yelled for another order of whiskey, this time a double.

'Now, you don't look like someone who would frequent a dirty place like this,' a guy said from behind her.

'And how would you know how dirty I am if you've never seen me around before?' Mila's loose alcohol lips moved on their own. Her words sounded flirty and she wanted to bury her head in her hands from how cringe worthy she sounded. She turned to her conversationalist to apologise when all the air in her lungs left her.

Her body shivered at the sight on the man in front of her. Mila's experience with bikers was minimal, but she had always imagined them to be old, fat, heavily-bearded guys that paid for the death machines with their retirement funds.

The man in front of her did not fit that description.

His dark brown hair was cut short to the sides of his head, while the top looked windblown, the strands coming down in front of his hazel eyes. For a moment, Mila was bewitched by the honey-brown pools, framed by thick eyelashes that made her jealous compared to the blonde ones she had to coat in mascara. Her eyes travelled down to his full lips lined with stubble that she knew would leave marks if she kissed him.

Those lips turned into a smirk, and Mila blinked out of her gaping.

This guy knew how attractive he was, the grin on his stupidly handsome face not holding back his cockiness. She ignored how the small upturn made her stomach drop and her body warm. Mila knew she shouldn't get involved with a biker. Been there, done that, got the t-shirt. This wasn't her scene anymore, and a guy like this was bad news.

Her cheeks flared up, and she blamed the whiskey again because it definitely wasn't those captivating eyes travelling over her button-down shirt and her respectable pencil skirt that got her a little hot under the collar. She hammered the nail in her wall of bravado – she didn't like the way her skin tingled even though he wasn't touching her.

'Can I help you?' Her hand landed on her hip, but it felt awkward. Mila knew she needed to stop talking to him. Hell, she needed to stop looking at him. His hotness combined with the alcohol she had consumed didn't spell a recipe for a quiet night. So why was she still sitting at the bar waiting for his reply?

'I'm sure you can darlin'.' The biker winked. Mila's lip curled and her nose wrinkled. She would have thought that the crude comments and suggestions would stop after she graduated college. She should have turned around and gotten off the stool but not only did he have her trapped, his gaze made her freeze.

Caught in this weird stare off with the biker, the elastic of her hair tie burst, freeing the ponytail she had painstakingly pulled her blonde strands into that morning. Mortified, she reached up to tuck it away, but he beat her to it. Oh so casually, he swept it behind her ear.

'What the fuck do you think you're doing?'

Okay, now it was time to leave.

'Hey, where are you going?' he asked as she jumped down from the bar stool with a disgusted huff. She pushed her hair away from her face as she stormed toward the exit. She knew her friend had no plans of coming home with her. Mila continued to ignore him until he quickly beat her strides and stood in front of her. His arms crossed against his impressive chest and that damn smirk played on his face. 'You know, I don't usually chase women… but for you, baby, I'm willing to make an exception.'

'Then I must be one of the lucky ones,' Mila replied, sarcasm dripping from her as she pulled her hair away from her face again. There was a fucking reason she liked to have it up. She scanned the room, looking for an easy escape route.

'To get the attention of the club's president. Yeah, baby, you're one lucky woman.' The biker stepped closer to her, completely invading her personal bubble.

'Okay…' Mila said, putting her hand on his chest. She ignored the way it heated her palm as she pushed him, or at least she tried to. Her blood was boiling in her veins at his comment. 'Who the fuck is this president… and who gave you permission to talk to me like that! You fucking rude asshole!'

'The name's Rooster.' He uncrossed his arms and held his hand out, waiting for her to shake. Mila looked from him to his offending appendage. She didn't know what she would do if she touched him again. Not wanting to give into temptation, she crossed her arms over her chest, but it only managed to make her cleavage more prominent. That caught Rooster's attention, causing his crooked smirk to grow wider. Mila shook her head at the fucking audacity of the man.

'What the fuck kind of name is Rooster?' she asked, regretting her question immediately. She should have just walked the fuck away.

'Well…' Rooster's lips pursed and his eyes looked at the ceiling for a moment. Mila could see that he was fighting his smirk as he pretended to think. 'What's another name for a Rooster, babe?'

Mila's mouth hung open as the biker winked. The loud sounds of the room muffled like she was wearing earplugs. She closed and opened her mouth, completely at a loss for words. How did she ask a man why they were named after their penis? Why did she even want to know? A blush crept up her cheeks and she didn't know where to look.

It was time to leave.

'I have to go!' With a final huff, Mila turned away from the president and made a hasty exit. She cast a quick glance back and noticed Rooster hadn't moved after her, but he still had that fucking smirk on his face. Guess she wasn't as special as he originally claimed.

Good, she couldn't risk getting sucked into this life.

Now it was time to forget about this night and those honey-brown eyes that were so insanely gorgeous. Mila questioned if they were real. She could almost convince herself that Rooster was a figment of her imagination, but his leather scent hung around the cab of her car. Mila was just glad that she never had to see him again.

CHAPTER 2

Light from the morning sun streamed through the window, demolishing Mila's dream of honey-brown eyes and a smirk that she wanted to smack from his beautiful face. She groaned and rolled over to avoid the blasting sunshine. She wasn't ready for the day, or reality.

Squinting against the offending rays, Mila checked the time on her phone. A surge of panic raked her body when she saw that all of the alarms she set were for pm… not am. If she didn't get her butt up now, she was going to be late.

That shot of adrenaline was better than any caffeine Mila had in a while, but it didn't hang around like her favourite macchiato. So it was no surprise that in her weak brain the man she met at the bar forced his way to the front of her mind.

Mila rubbed her hands down her face. She had not expected to meet the cockiest, most self-righteous biker in the whole damn world. It didn't matter how good looking he was, or that her body responded in a way that made her slightly embarrassed. She decided that her body's response was a result of the whiskey straight. Rooster was not the man for her, and Mila knew that.

So why the fuck did he keep popping into her mind… and without the help of alcohol!

Mila knew she had to get on with her life. What good was it to dwell on someone who wasn't going to be part of it? She stretched her arms above her head, trying to loosen up her stiff and rigid muscles, a heavy sigh leaving her lips.

Reluctantly, she slid out from under the duvet, showered and stood in her walk-in wardrobe. A lot of her clothes were strewn across the floor since she had been in the middle of a clean-up when something had distracted her over the weekend. Thankfully, her pencil skirt and white button down was still hanging. She dressed quickly and moved around her small cottage, pulling her hair into its signature ponytail, ignoring the memory and the audacity that the biker had taking her hair out.

She moved over to her jewellery box and pulled out her father's chunky class ring. Mila hardly ever wore it anymore because she didn't want to risk losing it like she had once when she was in college. She never wanted to make that mistake again.

Her mind drifted back to the weekend. She never should have agreed to go to the Black Alchemy clubhouse with her co-worker. What in the world had made that biker approach her? The question had been plaguing Mila all weekend, but she still couldn't put her finger on the answer. It wasn't like she looked anything special. She stood out like a prude compared to the other women who, no doubt in Mila's mind, threw themselves at Rooster after she left.

She passed the mirror in her doorway and wrapped her blonde ponytail around her fingers. She imagined him slipping the bond out to release it. Mila squinted at her reflection and wondered again what made the biker so interested. She shook her head at the image in front of her. Mila wasn't the type of girl to throw herself at a boy. She hadn't done that since high school.

Mila hated the way her mind kept playing on how Rooster had singled her out. It dominated her head space and she didn't have the energy or motivation to think about it when she still had classes to teach. Mila scooped up her car keys and left her white cottage, vowing not to think about Rooster, the president of Black Alchemy.

Bikers were nothing but trouble.

Monday mornings were always predictable. Her senior students filed in slowly after the first bell, some of them even resting their heads on their desk hoping to catch a few more seconds of sleep. Mila always walked in with a coffee in her favourite mug and a lesson plan in her hand. Her seniors hardly ever shocked her anymore but she was surprised when the final bell rang and her best student was missing.

Trying not to show her surprise, Mila instructed her students to take out their copies of *Animal Farm* and crouched down next to a teen.

'Ivy?' Ivy sat back, surprised by Mila's close proximity.

She understood her student's apprehension; she was still a new teacher and even though she had been teaching for a few months, her students were still unsure about trusting her.

'Where is Daisy today?' she whispered. 'It's not like her to miss my morning English class.'

It wasn't like Daisy to miss any of Mila's or any class according to her other teachers, but Mila didn't want to mention that.

Ivy glanced around and Mila bit back a smile. She was probably making sure no one was listening to her. Especially if it was going to get one of her fellow classmates in trouble.

'Her brother is dropping her to school later today. Her pops died over the weekend.' Ivy shot a tight smile toward Mila.

Mila hung her head at the sudden news and had to actively fight back the rise of pain in her heart. Her heart sunk for poor Daisy Bates.

Mila blinked quickly to stop her hot eyelids from dropping. She still had to remain professional even though her heart felt like it was going to fall out.

She should find out who Daisy's brother was and have a talk with him. Maybe she could even give him some advice on what the next steps for Daisy's mental health might be. Mila didn't know much about the young lady, having only started at Bryson City High six months previous, but she knew this grief and what it did to a person. Mila wanted to make sure that the teen felt safe and free to grieve her father.

With a plan in mind, Mila nodded her head and placed her hand on Ivy's arm for comfort. 'I'm so sorry, Ivy, that's very sad news. If you need a place to share, I am here for you.'

The loss of a parent can be hard for everyone around the child, not just the child themselves. Mila made her way back to the head of the room and started her seniors on a simple task.

The rest of her morning went by fast, but Mila was still pressing her palms into her eyes as the shrill of the school bell announced lunch. She was immediately thankful that she hadn't been scheduled for cafeteria duty – she had a date with her latest book, a large cup of coffee and a salad at the café down on Main Street.

Mila marched herself down the school hallways filled with lines of dented and scraped lockers and the colourful handmade posters for school events adorning the walls. Her ballet flats squeaked on the scuffed floor, and the sounds of students talking, laughing and shouting out greetings to friends surrounded her, but Mila was so engrossed in the back cover of her latest purchase that she ignored all of it.

That was until she walked face first into a brick wall of leather and denim.

'Watch yourself there, darlin''.' A deep drawl broke through Mila's concentration. Warm hands steadied her from falling backward in front of the filled hallways and a surprising zing of electricity lit up her skin. She dropped her book to her side and took in the man before her.

Large biker boots and dark blue jeans frayed over them. Thick thighs and an enticing bulge filled out the crotch of his pants that had Mila blushing at the thought. Then there were the black tattoos that swirled around muscles protruding from the worn-in leather vest – a vest with a patch sewn in with the word 'President'. Mila mentally cursed herself for looking at his unfairly handsome face, he was even more so now in the daylight. His amazing honey-brown eyes drew her in completely, but she refused to allow this man to know how much he affected her.

Mila cursed the fire that started to rumble in her belly, blaming it on her lack of food and not the fact that no other man in her life had ever looked at her like he wanted to swallow her whole.

She hated to admit it, but she liked it.

A lot.

'You?' she stammered out. 'What are you doing on school property? Are you freaking stalking me or something?'

The biker raised a single eyebrow and looked slightly amused. He opened his mouth to retort when a girl poked her head around his bulk.

'Hey, Miss Rice,' Daisy Bates said, her normally bright smile dimmed. Mila wanted so badly to hug her, but that would immediately get her fired. Daisy tucked her foot behind her leg and focused on the ground. 'I don't know if anyone has said anything, but I just wanted to apologise for not being in class this morning. I've been dealing with some family issues and…'

'You don't have to explain yourself to me, Daisy. Ivy did inform me and I am so sad for you and your family,' Mila interrupted. She glanced at Rooster who was watching the girl with an intensity that should have been terrifying. 'You take all the time you need, sweetheart.'

Daisy raised her head and nodded slightly. She turned to the biker and thanked him for her ride. Mila watched as Rooster's curved lip morphed into a scowl when Daisy gave him her own version of his smirk and waved.

'See you at Mom's later, big brother!'

***

Rooster watched his youngest sister's retreating back down the school hallway. Daisy had been putting on a brave face since learning of Patriot's death. Rooster had been waiting for her inevitable breakdown, which was why he originally didn't agree to her going to school that morning, but it never came.

When Daisy finally put her foot down, literally, Rooster had been ready for an argument, but their mother – ever the voice of reason – stopped him just as he opened his mouth. If Daisy wanted to be around people her own age and distract herself from her grief then who was he to stop her?

Rooster silently thanked his father for encouraging his protective instinct. Yes, it drove his sisters and mother crazy, but if it hadn't been for his insistence on driving Daisy to school, he might not have run into the mystery woman from his presidential celebration. Rooster was still dumbfounded that she not only dismissed him entirely but straight-up ran off before he could really turn on his charm.

Now was his chance.

He adjusted his cut and turned to at least wrangle a smile out of his sister's pretty teacher only to see that she was repeating her actions from the weekend and was speed walking down the hallway while he was distracted.

'Whoa there, little minx,' Rooster said, loud enough that he knew she would have heard him, but his sister's teacher didn't slow her ass down. Damn, what a nice ass it was too. Rooster was positive that if they had teachers that looked like Miss Rice when he was in school, he would have shown up a lot more… for her classes anyway. Whatever it was she taught.

'Where are you going?' he asked and chased her down. Rooster strode easily next to the scurrying woman. His legs ate up the distance between them easily.

'Lunch,' she puffed and even tried to speed up a little more. 'Look, if it's got nothing to do with Daisy, I don't really want anything to do with you. So can you please just leave me alone?'

Rooster was taken aback for a moment. No woman had ever been this candid with him. He hadn't been turned down by a woman since he was a teenager going for a college girl because he liked the way her hips moved.

He let his smirk glide across his face as he stuffed his hands into his pockets. 'Nah… Actually, now that you mention it.'

'Excuse me?' Miss Rice spun on her heels. Her hands landed on her hips and her blonde ponytail landed on her shoulder. Goddamn, she was the whole fucking package. Rooster wanted nothing more than to dig his fingers into her luscious hips while he brought her to the edge of pleasure and back again over and over. He wanted to drive this sexy teacher insane.

Jesus, he needed to get his shit together. He was standing in the middle of his old high school hallway. Rooster didn't need any more weird looks than he was already getting. He had barely stepped foot through those doors when he was a student here, but now all he wanted was to prolong his time with Miss Rice as much as possible.

'I mean you're heading to lunch. I know a great place and maybe we could fit in some dessert afterward.' Rooster smirked and wiggled his eyebrows. He watched as the woman's face turned bright red. He wanted to feel the heat of her pink cheeks beneath his lips. Rooster leaned down so that he could whisper in her ear and he could feel her blush just as the scent of something fresh and yet somehow creamy caught in his nose. 'Listen here, darlin', once I know I want something, I damn well get it, okay, so are you thinking about dessert first, or do I have to warm you up to the idea?'

Miss Rice stared at him and Rooster enjoyed the way her cheeks continued to redden. He watched as her ocean-blue eyes went from swirling seas to a storm. She was pissed, but instead of laying into him, the woman huffed and walked out the doors without a single word to him.

Rooster chuckled and followed after her. She unlocked a beat-up cage and threw her purse into the backseat. He could see that she was actively avoiding meeting his gaze and acknowledging that he was on her tail.

There was no fucking way Rooster was going to get in that cage, not unless he absolutely had to. Like when the snow occasionally stuck to the ground. When he told Miss Rice as such, her response pulled at his smile.

'That's good,' she said, 'because I didn't invite you into my car and I definitely didn't agree to have lunch with you. Let alone give you a fucking ride…'

Rooster opened his mouth to say something, maybe try and convince her to change her tone, but that blonde wasn't finished.

'… and while you're at it, drop the whole macho attitude. It's not only boring, but it's downright disrespectful.'

The little minx climbed into her car and left without another word.

Rooster watched the tail-lights of her car speed out of the school parking lot. His smirk had turned into a true grin as he mounted his own bike and kickstarted the beast. He pulled his sunglasses down over his eyes and pulled the bandana up around his mouth. Rooster wasn't going to let her get away so easily again.

His grin grew when she pulled into the newly opened café. The MC had been discussing looking into a new restaurant on Bryson City's Main Street and this had been on the list.

Rooster pulled up next to Miss Rice's beat-up car, enjoying the way she glared at him through the driver's side window. He yanked his bandana off the bottom of his face and sent her a wink and withheld a chuckle when she turned away. He wanted to know what she was thinking, but he had a good idea that she was cursing him out in her head.

Rooster dismounted his Harley, and leaned against it, waiting to see what Miss Rice was going to do next.

She didn't seem intimidated, and he liked that about her.

Rooster offered his hand when her door swung open, but it was quickly rejected with a stern glare. She stormed off toward the door, only he was faster than she was. He reached it before she did and opened it like a real gentleman. The teacher was forced to look up and she thanked him. Rooster caught the small glimpse of her reluctant smile.

He had to take a moment to regain his breath before entering the café after her. Rooster was immediately hit with the whining croon of a singer over the speakers and the smell of stale coffee.

This place should be brand new but, by the looks of things, the owners really didn't give a shit about this place. That was good information for Rooster to use later.

He knew he should have been focusing on more recon for the café, but Rooster was man enough to admit that he was distracted by the way the pencil skirt curved around Miss Rice's ass. He was focusing his entire attention on the woman's amazing asset, and he didn't realise who was serving them at the hostess stand.

That was until he met the familiar gaze of his other sister.

'Angel…' he greeted. 'Didn't know you were working today.'

He had completely forgotten that he had his sister apply for this job to see if this place was worth the club's involvement. He glanced at the lovely Miss Rice, trying to gauge her reaction. She was meeting more of his family than he ever wanted to introduce her to.

'What are you doing here, Rooster?' Angel's eyes travelled to the woman standing next to him. 'And with someone I've never met before?'

Angel extended her hand, leaning over the hostess stand. Miss Rice complied without hesitation. The corner of the woman's lips turned up a bit and Rooster was struck again with breathlessness. How could a small movement brighten the teacher's already gorgeous face?

'I'm Angel. Rooster is my older brother.'

'Mila.' The woman smiled back. 'I'm Daisy's teacher.'

Well damn, if Rooster wasn't in trouble before, he sure as fuck was now…

CHAPTER 3

Rooster sped through the weathered gates of the clubhouse, the dirt road flying up around him as they swung open without him having to brake. The prospect stationed in the shitty watch-shed that one of the brothers had built years ago saluted him as he sped past. The familiar yellow building with burn marks from past bombings came into sight and a feeling of home spread through Rooster's chest.

The refurbished schoolhouse had been Rooster's family since his grandfather and the co-founders of Black Alchemy landed in North Carolina. He spotted recognisable spackle covered bullet holes from when the Jokers thought it was a smart idea to open fire on women and children during a birthday party. The yellow paint was peeling in places and mismatched in others when the brothers decided to add extensions to the clubhouse. Through it all, Rooster's second home was still standing. He couldn't say as much about his family, something that made his chest tighten and tears to prickle his eyes. He blinked them away; he couldn't let them fall.

His grandpop Huey, along with Vietnam vets and best friends Bash and Grizzly, founded Black Alchemy in 1975, two years after the pointless war ended. They had watched too many of their army brothers die for a meaningless conflict. The originals didn't want to lose any more of their men. So they made sure that no other club had any kind of territorial claim over North Carolina before they set up camp.

The Jokers Ace had held the state of South Carolina since the early sixties and they had been buying to take the north as well. Huey found this out, and he suggested that they take action. According to the stories, Bash agreed but voted against doing something that would make them an enemy so early on. So they sat down with the Jokers, and it was decided that they would keep the south and Black Alchemy would continue setting up in Bryson City.

Everything was going fine for the first few years. BAMC had negotiated a deal with the local police department, agreeing to keep the hard A-class drugs out of the county in exchange for free passage when making gun runs. Mama Bear became the first ol' lady of the club and Pipsqueak, or Miss Pippa as the younger generation referred to her as, became the second. Things were going really well for the club – they were even getting a fair number of men wanting to join after their own stint in the armed forces.

As the story goes, Huey was riding through their territory one day. Something about clearing his head and making sure that everything was right within their state when he noticed some Jokers Ace members. Their bottom rockers claimed them to be holders of the North Carolina region.

Needless to say, the original Black Alchemy members were beyond pissed, which resulted in the BAMC retaliating. Everything escalated in the late seventies and early eighties, clubhouses were bombed, and shoot-ups and drive-bys became commonplace. It placed all the ol' ladies and children right in the thick of the conflict.

But the rivalry didn't reach its peak until 1985 when Bash and his ol' lady were out riding. They had been cornered by some new Jokers Ace members. Chopper and Rookie took chase and Bash was killed when he lost control of his sled at high speed. Miss Pippa survived but she had physical and mental scars. She didn't last the year.

It wasn't much of a surprise when Huey took the death of his brother the hardest. Rooster's grandpop had always been the one with the shortest fuse. Huey murdered the Jokers that killed his brother and landed himself in jail.

Years later, Grizz's oldest boy was arrested for taking revenge.

The two of them had gotten life with no chance of parole.

Patriot had been way too young to take the gavel, so it went to Crow, but the man didn't want that kind of responsibility. He waited until he felt Patriot was ready. The story that Crow used to tell before he died from the Big C was that he couldn't wait to get rid of the gavel.

The war with the Jokers only got worse when Patriot met Queenie. Rooster's mother, Queenie, was once the Jokers Ace princess. Her father, Bulldog, was and is the vice president of their rival club. Rooster's parents met at a biker rally, he couldn't remember which one, but they exchanged secret letters for months. Neither of them had any idea who each other was until their clubs faced off at Sturgis months later. By the end of the rally, Queenie had escaped her father's control and left with Patriot back to Bryson City.

No one had been very welcoming toward the JAMC princess, but over the years Queenie had proved her loyalty again and again. No one in the BAMC questioned her devotion now.

The role of president went to Patriot after that, and things with Jokers Ace didn't get better but they definitely didn't get worse. In the many years that Patriot was prez, there had been no bombing of the clubhouses, and no shooting of the weaker members and associates. Rooster's father managed to sort out a truce of a sort, even going so far as giving the Jokers a piece of North Carolina. It was only a small piece, but it was land, nonetheless.

The truce lasted about five years, and it was violated again by the Jokers when they set up a chapter in Black Alchemy territory. They were continuously pushing the fucking limits of the truce and Patriot finally agreed with his brothers and sat down with their rivals.

The Jokers arrived at the warehouse for the meet up with loaded guns.

There were no hellos or greetings of any kind. Just gunfire.

Now Rooster was president, and he planned to not only end this fucked up war that was back on track but also figure out who was killing the women associated with the BAMC.

He shook his head as he parked his bike. Now was not the time to get emotional, he had shit to do. Starting with new posts for some of his brothers.

Rooster spotted his best friend, Gunner, leaning against the peeling paint of the clubhouse wall. The six-foot-seven bulk of a man had been his most trusted confidant since they were kids. One of the sweetbutts stood in front of Gunner, her heels too high or she was already drunk as she wobbled in her spot.

Rooster watched as Gunner brought a joint to his lips, before he blew out the smoke, shotgunning it into Candy's awaiting open mouth. Rooster had appointed Gunner as his vice president of the club over the weekend. The previous VP – who just happened to be Gunner's own father – had taken off with his ol' lady after Rooster's party.

Dice and Flash were currently speeding toward California, enjoying their retirement according to Gunner. Rooster had gladly granted the request of absence from the club; he knew better than anyone that Dice needed it.

Rooster's decision to make Gunner his VP almost went without saying. They had a lifetime of trust and friendship together and were both directly descended from the Black Alchemy founders. The club was in their blood. Rooster knew Gunner loved it as much as he did, and Rooster trusted no other like he trusted his right-hand man.

He grabbed the roach off Gunner, leaned against the wall next to him, and took a long pull. The smoke filled his lungs as he passed it back to his friend.

For the first time in almost a week, Rooster let himself take a moment. He knew what he needed to do, he just needed a fucking moment to think. The sweetbutt rubbing her ass against his leg was more annoying than anything else.

Candy's pastel-coloured hair hung dead from the hours she spent colouring it and she had tried to mask the overpowering smell of chemicals with perfume that made Rooster want to fucking choke. That mixed with the scent of the weed wasn't a good combination.

'Beat it, Candy,' Rooster said and watched as the sweetbutt pouted for a moment before she stumbled back into the clubhouse. Hopefully, she would annoy some other desperate brother for a while.

'Did ya have to do that? I was gonna have a good fucking time with that one. You know what she's like if you get her high enough,' Gunner complained, watching the sweetbutt stumble into a brother on his way out of the clubhouse.

Rooster just rolled his eyes. Gunner might be a hulk of a man standing at six-foot-seven, but Rooster was never intimidated by his friend. They both knew their roles within the club and they respected the hell out of each other. Perks of being raised by fathers who were born into the club, he guessed.

'I need to call a church,' Rooster said, eyeing the joint. He desperately wanted another hit, but he knew it would mess with his head too much. He needed to be as clear minded as possible.

His VP nodded and went off to do his job, pinching the end of the joint before tucking it away in a tin. Rooster nodded his head and rested against the peeling wood, his finger tracing the outline of a bullet hole. He took much needed breaths of fresh air and looked out at the playground his father had built for his children.

He could see himself and his sisters playing on the monkey bars. Angel begging their father to push her higher on the swings while Rooster and Gunner would sit at the very top of the equipment and tease Daisy and Tank about not being big enough to climb to the top as they were.

Later, he and Gunner would sit in that very same spot and smoke weed. This was before they were presented with their prospecting patches at eighteen.

Even now, Rooster could hear his father's laugh from the upstairs window when he was in the middle of a particularly gruelling task given to him by one of the other brothers.

This clubhouse, the club, all of the problems that came with it were all Rooster's now. He had to protect the ugly yellow building and the people inside of it from any kind of harm. It was all on his shoulders now.

Rooster took one last look at his father's legacy and headed inside.

He passed by the bar, ignoring the prospect that was asking if he needed a drink. Taking the stairs two at a time, he avoided looking at the random collection of photographs that lined the walls. He knew they were all haunting last photos of brothers and ol' ladies that were lost to the violence caused by the Jokers. There were even haphazard mementos nailed to the walls. Mostly street signs that were important to the originals.

Rooster had been avoiding opening his father's office door since the day he was shot. Rooster stood in front of the door and felt like every weight in the world was on his shoulders. He turned the handle and cracked open the door. Dust floated around like snow, and almost choked Rooster.

At least that's what he told himself when his eyes started to water.

The room hadn't changed since he was a kid. Rooster remembered days when he would sit with his father as a toddler and play with his little toy bikes. Sometimes, his sisters would fall asleep on the comfortable couch that sat against one of the walls. Rooster fought the urge to sit and run his hands over the worn fabric. Instead, he walked to the door on the opposite side of the office.

The door connected the presidential office to chapel. It sat behind the desk that was covered in more papers than usual. The gavel sat in its usual spot, surrounded by photos of Patriot's family. Rooster's eyes landed on the one in the middle. Patriot and Queenie on their wedding day, both dressed in leather, looking just as happy as they were a week ago.

More photos of his siblings growing up and reaching big milestones in their lives surrounded the large one of his parents. Rooster thought about the other moments his father was going to miss now because he was six feet in the ground.

Angel's wedding, Daisy's graduation, Rooster proving himself to be more than just the president's kid. Patriot would miss all of it.

He didn't want to disturb the room any more than he already had, the dust was messing with his eyes again. Rooster grabbed the gavel and made his way to church.

Their meeting room was a bit of a dingy-looking place. It was dark, the windows had been blocked out since Rooster was a kid when the Jokers had shot through the glass during church. Lights above the custom table his grandfather carved were the only source of brightness. The club's executive board were already sitting in their assigned seats, their black cuts adding to the darkness of the room.

The rest of the club stood shoulder to shoulder in the small room. Rooster had to fight his smile, he was pretty sure his grandfather never imagined how crowded their church would get all these years later.

Rooster hesitated at the head of the table. This had been his father's seat, and even though he was wearing his presidential patch, he didn't feel worthy of the chair. Three seats remained empty.

Along with his father, the treasurer and the road captain had been gunned down at the 'meeting' with Jokers Ace. The positions needed to be filled, and because the club was a democracy of sorts, the club needed to vote for the new members of the executive board.

Rooster reluctantly took his seat and the room immediately fell silent.

Clearing his throat, he glanced at Gunner. His VP nodded his head offering his silent support. Rooster adjusted his ass in the seat. It felt cold and all fucking wrong. 'This is an emergency church to decide the new treasurer, road captain, and VP. Dice has taken an extended leave of absence and has made it real fucking clear that not only does he want to give up his seat, he wanted Gunner to take over… Any objections?'

The silence continued.

'Now treasurer. Does anyone want to put forward a brother for nomination?'

'Creep.' Diablo, his enforcer, spoke. 'The fucker might be quiet, but he knows a thing or two about money. He's been helping Hawk, Sleave, Hammer, and Ghoul with their books for years now. Creep can make dirty money come out cleaner than a fucking virgin.'

Rooster turned his head to the man in question. 'You want the job?'

Creep held Rooster's gaze for a moment, like he was considering all his options, before finally nodding. Rooster smirked at his brother and turned back to the club.

'Objections?'

Still nothing.

'Okay, Creep, you are the new treasurer. Go and see Queenie or Mama Bear about your patch when church is over. Last one boys… road captain. I would like to ask Rubble to take over from Dawg.'

Rooster watched his future brother-in-law – the man's face was priceless. It was obvious that he wasn't expecting the promotion. 'You've been helping the old dog out for years with the runs and now it's time. You want the position?'

'Fuck yeah!'

'All those in favour of Creep, Gunner, and Rubble's new roles within the club?' The room burst into 'ayes' and thumping fists on the wooden walls as Rubble and Creep joined the officer's table.

Slamming the gavel on the table, Rooster dismissed everyone. The celebration and hollering continued out the doors of church and into the main room of the clubhouse. He knew he should join them for the fun that was inevitably going to occur, but Rooster couldn't bring himself to move from the still uncomfortable chair.

He scrubbed his hands down his face, Rooster had no idea how to be the president. Even though leadership was quite literally in his blood, Rooster had a feeling he was going to screw everything up. He needed to figure his shit out soon.

If he didn't, he could get someone killed.

CHAPTER 4

Rooster's palm slapped on the desk in front of him as he stood from his chair. Papers jumped and his computer shook under the force, the newspaper clutched in his hand crumpled as he shoved it in his VP's face.

'What the fuck do you mean you know her?' Rooster yelled. He really didn't have time for any of this shit. He had enough on his plate already.

'We fucked once.' Gunner defended himself in a low voice, steeling Rooser with his blue eyes, and crossed his arms over his chest. 'She wanted into The Blind Hog and honestly… every citizen around her knows that's our roadhouse. I had no idea she would be fucking killed because of it.'

Rooster rubbed at his temples. A headache had been forming since he woke up. He didn't need any of this crap on his doorstep, and yet here it was again. There was a guy out there targeting women, killing them brutally, and now the papers were trying to link the murders together. It wouldn't be long before they concluded that the girls were related to the club somehow.

The first two girls had just been some leather chasers that some of the brothers had seen around a clubhouse party or two. Nothing seriously concrete, but now with the confirmation of Gunner's involvement with the newest murder, it was only a matter of time before the papers would start pointing the finger at Black Alchemy. Someone was messing with the girls who came looking for a good time with his brothers.

Rooster didn't like it one fucking bit.

'Did you fuck her at the clubhouse?' he asked his best friend. Rooster's fingers pressed into the creases of his eyes.

'No, she's not a regular hang around. I followed her to her house, but I was wearing—'

'Your cut,' Rooster finished for his VP. It was written in the bylaws that a BAMC member must always fly his colours when riding. Rooster just wished for once Gunner didn't listen to the rules that both their grandfathers wrote.

'She's the third to die at the hands of this fucker,' Rooster said as he threw the paper down on his desk. 'The fucking pigs are going to figure out sooner or later that these women were connected to us. Stick with the sweetbutts for a while. We can't have any more citizens in danger.'

He watched as Gunner ran his hands over his face and scratched at his shortly trimmed beard. His friend nodded in agreement and left Rooster in his now sour mood.

He slumped back in his office chair and ran his hands through his own hair. Rooster's mind had been on this fucking sicko for weeks. He had been worried that he would strike again. He had originally hoped that the first two women were just an unfortunate coincidence.

But now... Rooster was tempted to call a full lockdown and bring all the club member's families into the clubhouse to keep them safe. Especially the women, but he didn't want to cause that kind of hysteria. Plus, calling for kids to be pulled out of school and businesses to shut down would pique the badges' interest. Rooster didn't want to give them any excuse to start sniffing around the clubhouse.

Fuck, who knows what those assholes would find if they got a warrant to raid the compound. None of the brothers did drugs, except for the premium weed. There were some ex-cons among the membership that would have firearms hidden around the clubhouse somewhere. That would land at least Crash and Diablo back in jail if they were caught.

Jesus, Rooster needed to clean this place up. His pops had done a good job being the president, but Rooster wanted to guarantee his brothers stayed free and not behind bars.

He grabbed his phone and texted his sisters and mother, deleting and retyping a few times before he was finally satisfied with his message. Fuck, Rooster hated texting, but it seemed to be the only way the women in his family communicated nowadays. They had a family group chat and everything.

His thumb hovered over his father's phone number when he got a notification that Angel had replied. She was already on her way back to the clubhouse, assuring him that Rubble was going to take her to and from work.

Rooster slumped further back into his chair as relief came over his body. Even though his pops didn't originally approve of the relationship between Rubble and Angel, Rooster was happy that his sister had someone to look after her.

His phone buzzed on the table again. This time it was his youngest sister, Daisy. His blood started to boil slightly as he read over her words. Her best friend Ivy was going to drop her around the clubhouse after cheer practice and not a second before.

Daisy was the baby of the family and used to getting everything she wanted. Rooster wanted to demand that she come to the clubhouse as soon as the final bell chimed but he also knew how much his youngest sister needed normalcy in her life.

Rooster let out a breath and slumped in his chair. He was going to let it go, at least for now. Daisy was going to have to get used to a new way of life, where she couldn't bat her large blue eyes and get away with murder.

***

'Miss Rice!' a familiar voice echoed through the empty school hallway. Mila turned to see Daisy Bates running toward her.

'Hello, Daisy.' She smiled, running her eyes over the girl's face for any sign of distress. 'What can I do for you?'

'Oh well, I was actually wondering, thought, hoped that you might be able to help me get somewhere after practice today?'

'Practice?'

'Yeah. Cheer practice.' Daisy smiled and patted her Bryson City High duffle bag on her shoulder.

Mila raised her eyebrows. She had no idea how to respond to the teenager's request. It wasn't exactly a usual occurrence, Mila wasn't even sure if she would be allowed to help out her student.

'I just need a lift, it's only a couple of minutes down the road. I would walk but my brother doesn't want me alone, and Ivy's car is in the shop. I'm only asking because my mom is helping out at the clubhouse and Angel is working until late this afternoon.' Daisy's large blue eyes somehow grew larger. Mila hid her giggle. It was obvious that this girl was used to getting her own way.

Mila was happy to help out her student, but she needed to make sure that she followed protocol first.

'I will need to get permission from a parent or guardian, then I can drop you to where you need to go.' Mila grinned when Daisy's smile widened. Damn, it felt so good to help out.

The teenager squealed and bounced on the balls of her feet.

Mila wondered if Daisy wanted to hug her but before she could even process the question Daisy was scampering off into Mila's classroom, just as the final bell sounded. She followed after her student and watched as the girl settled herself next to Ivy and Clark, a boy who was obviously smitten with both the girls.

Mila wondered if the boy knew that his puppy love was unrequited. That neither of the girls were remotely interested in him beyond a friendship.

She shot the boy a smile and turned to her white board, a collective groan sounded as Mila wrote the name *Shakespeare*. She didn't care if it was cliché, he was her favourite playwright of all time and she was going to teach these kids about the man behind the fancy words.

By the time the lunch bell rang, Mila had decided to eat in her classroom. She didn't have any kind of cafeteria duty and none of her students had wanted to stay behind and speak with her.

So, for the first time in a while Mila allowed herself to relax.

A newspaper from this morning's issue lay closed on her desk. Staring back at Mila was the latest victim of the psycho who was raping and killing the girls around town. Just the thought of it sent a shiver down Mila's spine and she tried to remember if she locked her front door in her usual rush that morning.

Mila had left Charlotte and moved to Bryson City because she thought it would a safe town. If a crime was committed, it was more than likely a teenager doing something stupid. Although, now that she knew about Black Alchemy, Mila was regretting not doing more research on the town before packing up everything and moving away. Not that she really had anything left in Charlotte anyway.

Her mother saw to that.

Mila blinked back the tears at the thought of her mother and glanced down at the paper. The heading was clear and bold.

Another Young Woman Slain.

She took in the photo that had been provided to the *Bryson City Bugle*. It looked like it might have been a school photo, a smiling brunette with a sparkle in her eyes that had been extinguished by a crazed man.

Mila sat in her chair and opened the paper to continue reading the article. According to an anonymous source, the police had connected this woman's murder to two other women in the area.

How had no one found this guy yet? Surely someone would have noticed a man creeping out of this woman's house in the early hours of the morning. She might not have been a morning person, but Mila was sure that someone would have seen a suspicious person walking around covered in blood.

Her skin started to crawl, and she glanced over her shoulder. All she could see was the courtyard where students were sitting in their cliques. None of them were looking her way. Mila could have sworn that she felt eyes on her. She shook her head at her unfounded fears and flipped the page to another story, something more light-hearted.

It's just the papers, they have you spooked, she reprimanded herself.

Even though she reminded herself of that fact, Mila was still tense for every period that followed. Sure, the rest of her day went off without a hitch, Daisy even produced a text message from her mother, but Mila and the principal insisted on a phone call. They wanted to make sure that they weren't getting tricked by the teenager.

Mila was pleasantly surprised when the voice on the other end of the phone was soft and motherly. Nothing like the stereotypical raspy cigarette-smothered voice she was expecting.

The principal, who was very familiar with Marie-Anne, or Queenie as she corrected Mila, decided that she was happy with the permission given. It was also good timing since Mila had a meeting with the poetry club while Daisy finished up her cheerleading practice.

Mila was juggling multiple papers in her hand when she spotted her new passenger standing by the teacher's parking lot and it wasn't long before the two women were driving down the highway. Mila's student babbled the entire time, thinking that she needed to explain some of the rules of the MC life. What Daisy didn't know, and something that Mila wasn't going to divulge, was that Mila already had first-hand knowledge about the outlaw lifestyle, and she had no desire to get involved with a biker again.

In between breaths and the biker rundown, Daisy instructed her teacher on where to go. The teenager said that using a GPS was useless since the clubhouse was fairly hidden from the public eye.

The further they travelled toward the edge of town, the more the uneasy feeling in Mila's stomach grew. She could also feel a headache behind her eyes forming.

God, she was fucking stressed.

'You might want to slow down a bit, Miss Rice. The driveway can be a bit tricky to see if you don't know where it is.' Daisy leaned closer toward the driver's side.

'Do you live out here, Daisy?'

'No, my brother, Rooster, the one you met the other day, texted and said that he needed me at the clubhouse...' Daisy admitted as she glanced down at her hands, and redness spread across her cheeks. Almost as quickly she snapped her head back and shouted, 'Turn right!'

Startled, Mila turned the wheel of her car and heard the scrape of bushes against the paint. Daisy wasn't wrong, the driveway was basically undetectable, and she almost missed it.

Dirt from the unpaved pathway flew up around Mila's car as they sped toward the large gate and a young man standing by it. His arms were crossed over his leather cut.

'You'll need to wind your windows down,' Daisy said, a smile spread wider across her face. Especially when the young man at the gate leaned down and lay his arm over Mila's driver side door.

'Hey, Tank,' Daisy called out. Mila scrutinised the boy as he took her in. He couldn't be much older than eighteen, and that's when she recognised him. Mila was sure that this boy had been in one of her classes at the beginning of the year before he dropped out. She was sure that she saw him and another young man sitting with Daisy and Ivy at the back of the classroom.

'Daisy? What the fuck are you doing here?'

'Rooster wanted me here this afternoon. What's going on? He never wants me around the clubhouse.'

Tank's eyes grew suspicious, she could see that he was trying to figure out why the hell Mila was driving the president's sister. Then he turned back to Daisy.

'You know I have no idea what's going on, Dove.' He flashed his *Prospect* patch toward them. 'Lower than pussy still.'

'Nice, Tank,' Daisy said with a large, obvious roll of her eyes. Mila didn't have to ask if the teen was used to the language, her reaction answered her question.

'Who's the woman?' Tank growled, ignoring Daisy's comment completely. His dark eyes kept hold of Daisy's making the small cab of the car a little uncomfortable.

'She teaches at Bryson City High, don't you remember her? She's giving me a lift 'cause David has Ivy's car in the shop. No way he was driving me to the compound.' Daisy rolled her eyes again. She definitely had some attitude on her and Mila had to admit that she admired her for it.

'Does Prez know about this?' Tank asked, his dark eyes switching from Daisy to Mila and back again. She knew that he was trying to figure out if she was trouble or not, and normally she would be offended by this, but Mila had to admit she was impressed with how seriously he was taking his job.

'Does Rooster know about me coming to the clubhouse? Sure! I already told you that,' Daisy huffed. Tank raised his eyebrow.

'Does he know about the woman?'

'Well…'

'Damnit, Dove!' He groaned, but something behind him caught his eye and, before they could say anything else, Tank turned away from the car quickly and opened the gate, a phone to his ear.

Mila took that as a sign that she could continue, but Tank's hand shot up and stopped her. Daisy just shrugged when Mila glanced her way, but the smile on her face told Mila that she knew what was going to happen.

A loud roar of bikes broke through the quiet and about half a dozen hogs came screaming past her as they entered the clubhouse parking lot. The gates quickly closed in front of Mila's car again.

Mila glanced at Daisy and watched as her cheeks reddened again. The girl's eyes kept peeking at Tank.

'Who is he, Daisy?' Mila found herself asking.

'That's just Tank. He's prospecting to be a patched member of Black Alchemy,' Daisy stated very quickly, making Mila raise her eyebrows. It seemed like a very rehearsed answer.

'He called you Dove.'

'Huh?'

'That young man, he called you Dove.' Mila looked over to the boy still on the phone. He was definitely tall for his age, as young as he seemed, his arms already covered in tattoos. One full sleeve, the other only half. She inspected his tattoos, until one caught her eye. A beautiful white bird, in mid-flight with a daisy sitting in its beak. It seemed like a fairly feminine tattoo for the young prospect.

Mila glanced back at Daisy and then Tank one more time. She put two and two together. Not only had he called her Dove, but the tattoo with the daisy was a dead fucking giveaway. Mila opened her mouth, ready to say something but Daisy beat her to it.

'Don't tell Rooster! Or even my mother! They don't know, and we want to keep it that way.' Daisy's pretty blue eyes were wide with panic and Mila had to wonder if she was worried about her or her secret boyfriend.

'Daisy, what is going on? Why can't your family know about you and this young man being in a relationship?' Mila asked, and her student's eyes went straight to her hands again.

Oh dear. This couldn't be good.

CHAPTER 5

Mila sat in her car with Daisy and waited for her student to answer her question. She didn't know what she was expecting to come out of the teenager's mouth, but Mila knew for sure that whatever the girl was going to say could end with her being in some serious trouble. 'Daisy, what is going on with you and Tank?' Mila prompted one more time. The teenager let out a resigned sigh and twisted the little crown ring on her finger.

'Before, when my pops was still around...' Daisy's breath hitched slightly but continued. 'He didn't approve of how my sister Angel was claimed by her man before she even went to college. Pops didn't want that for me. So he made a rule that I was not to be claimed by a member until I had a degree. Tank has been prospecting since he turned eighteen at the beginning of the year. So he can't technically claim me anyway. That, and if Rooster ever found out, Tank would never be patched in at all.' Mila watched Daisy as she spoke, worried about how this girl spoke about herself. No woman should ever be the property of a man.

'Why are you so worried about Tank getting patched in?' she wondered out loud. As soon as the words left her mouth, Mila worried she might have stepped over the line. She didn't regret it though.

'Because of his dad, Grizz. Well, his adopted dad. Grizzly is an original, like my grandpop was. Tank has always wanted to prove himself to his family and the club, so he's been talking about patching in for as long as I can remember.' Daisy still didn't look at Mila as she spoke, focused instead on the ring around her finger.

'I promise you, Daisy, I won't say a thing. I'm not saying that I like it, but I won't say anything to your brother.' Mila took hold of Daisy's wringing hands. Her student finally raised her head and flung her arms around Mila's neck. Not knowing how to handle the situation, Mila just patted Daisy's back until the teenager pulled away.

'Thank you, Miss Rice.'

'Rooster wants to see you.' The deep timbre of Tank's voice broke through their moment. He stuck his head through the car window, as Daisy started to get out. 'Both of you, Dove.'

The gate slowly opened as Daisy and Mila looked at each other dumbfounded. Tank was impatiently waving them inside, so she slowly rolled to a stop at the front of an old schoolhouse. Glistening in the sun were about twenty chrome bikes, and men were hanging around talking, smoking, and tinkering with bikes. Some had girls at their sides, squeezing asses and breasts for everyone to see.

Mila turned her head to Daisy to ask if she was sure she wanted to stay there, but Daisy was already out of the car.

'You're going to need to stick by me,' the girl said, as Mila got out and caught up to her. There was no way she was going to leave Daisy alone. 'You don't have a property patch, so you're fair game. They seem to have started early this Friday. Then again, as soon as the sun is halfway down…' Daisy trailed off with a shrug. 'Just stay close to me.'

'But you don't have a property patch either,' Mila pointed out, sticking close to Daisy as they walked into the schoolhouse she had occupied only a week before.

'You catch on quickly, Miss Rice.' Daisy smiled and kept on walking. 'I am, however, the former president's youngest daughter and the current president's favourite sister.' Daisy grabbed at Mila's hand and led her through the men who congregated around the front door.

'Rooster's favourite sister?' a busty woman in a leather jacket said with humour lacing her voice. 'Puh-lease, Daisy, I think you'll find that I am his favourite.'

Mila blinked through the smoky haze, immediately recognising the woman in front of her, and not because of the patch on her breast that claimed her name.

Although that definitely did help; Mila wasn't always the greatest with names.

'Come off it, Heather,' Daisy muttered over the loud music. 'You know that I'm Rooster's favourite.'

'Whatever, little Dove.' Angel waved a dismissing hand, but her smile was one only a sibling could give her. Mila had to wonder just how many people in this club knew about the nickname Tank had given Daisy.

Silence fell upon the three of them. Angel turned towards Mila and her bright smile faltered for a moment, her eyes studying Mila thoroughly. She wondered if she should have worn something other than her pencil skirt and a white button-down shirt.

God, she felt so out of place.

'I know you.' Angel finally smiled.

Mila just nodded her head and returned the grin. She couldn't help it, the woman was infectious. Then Angel crossed her arms and cocked her hip, the smirk on her face was similar to her brothers.

'Ma did say that Daisy was going to be dropped around by her teacher. Didn't know that teacher was you, Mila,' Angel said and suddenly Mila felt eyes on her from everywhere. Her skin crawled under all the attention. 'Come on, I'm sure Rooster would want to speak to you.'

'Oi, Angel!' A booming bark introduced a man taller than she had ever seen before, blocking their path toward the staircase. His hair was cut close to his scalp and tattoos roamed over every surface of skin that was on display, which was a lot considering the biker wasn't wearing a shirt under his cut. 'Who's your friend, babe?'

The man's arm slung over Angel's shoulders, his eyes dark and penetrating down to Mila's very soul. He looked like he wanted to eat her alive. She tried to fight the shiver but there was something about him that made her feel uneasy.

'Oh, fuck off, Ranger, she's not here for you.' Angel pushed the big man away and grabbed Mila and Daisy's arms. She pulled them up the stairs leading them to the second floor. Newspaper clippings and mugshots of men of all ages decorated the walls of the hallway. One photo, in particular, was blown up in a big print. Three men stood arm in arm with each other and a bike behind each one.

Mila looked at Angel and Daisy, her curiosity getting the best of her, and was about to ask who the men on the wall were when they stopped at the closed door.

'Hasn't he moved into Pop's office yet?' Daisy asked Angel, sharing a look that made Mila long for siblings of her own. Sometimes, she really hated being an only child.

'Nope,' Angel said bringing Mila out of her self-pity party. 'He's refusing. Says that it's disrespectful or something like that.'

'So, no one is in there?' Daisy asked as Mila brought her hand up to her now aching neck. Watching these two converse was like watching tennis.

Daisy reached across and knocked firmly on the door.

'What?' Rooster's deep growl echoed through into the hallway.

'It's your favourite sister,' Daisy said and smirked at Angel when Rooster replied.

'Come in, Daisy.'

The teenager threw a look at her sister, who waved her off with a single finger salute and again Mila's heart burned to have family in her life.

They left Angel out in the hallway, and Mila and Daisy entered the surprisingly neat office. A large desk sat towards the back of the space, with a high-end computer set up around piles and piles of papers. A bookshelf sat on the wall to the right of the man's chair while a couch was the first thing to greet them on the left.

Motorcycle memorabilia hung from the walls along with a couple of framed photos. Rooster sat behind his desk, but he had yet to raise his head in greeting. As soon as the door closed behind them, his eyes met Mila's and he finally greeted her with a smile that almost had her dropping to her knees.

'Hey, big brother, what's going on?'

'I need you to hang around here in your room for tonight. Shit's going down and when Tank said that a woman who wasn't Ivy was driving you into the compound I had to make sure that you were safe, and that she' – Rooster pointed to Mila with a pen – 'was trustworthy. Something I still plan on investigating further.'

The man's intense, burning honey gaze broke right through and tingled in the bottom of Mila's stomach. There were so many promises in those irises, promises that Mila was nervous to see if Rooster could keep.

'Well…' Daisy said, breaking the connection and bringing Mila back down to earth. Even if it was just for a moment. 'Now that you've seen that I am okay can I go into Pop's office? I want to be near him.'

With a nod, Rooster threw his keys at his sister. Like a practiced art between the two of them, Daisy was able to catch the jingling metals in mid-air while scurrying out of the room at the same time.

The wooden door shut with a thud, causing Mila's heart to jump in her throat. She could feel his gaze on her skin, leaving gooseflesh in the wake of his wondering eyes.

'Now, you,' Rooster said, pushing away from his desk. In two long strides, he was standing in front of her. Mila had to crane her neck slightly just to meet his bewitching stare head-on. His hand landed on her collarbone and for a moment the electricity sparked through her bones and made her dumb.

She desperately wanted to get closer to him, but where in the hell did this guy get his kicks from? There was no way she would ever allow any one of her dates to turn her on like this and yet, when it came to Rooster, there was nothing she could do to stop it.

He had her under some kind of spell.

Mila's bottom lip slipped between her teeth, and she swore she heard the man in front of her groan softly. What was it about this guy that made her crazy? She knew she was losing her goddamn mind. She should have left when her student did.

'Don't bruise those gorgeous lips, baby. If anyone is going to do that, it's going to be me.' Rooster's gruff timbre rolled around her. She wanted to open her mouth to tell him where the fuck he could put his macho man attitude, but before she could speak he dipped his head, his eyes locked solely on her lips. His mouth fused with hers. In a flood of energy, she felt his lips soft, warm…

What the fuck?

Mila pushed both hands to his chest, whether to push him away or pull him closer, she wasn't sure. Rooster however wasn't in the mood to have anything between them. His hands circled around her wrists and brought them up his hard chest and around his neck. He pressed her closer to his hard, muscular body.

'Shit,' he said when he broke away from her for just a moment. 'You are the most infuriating woman I have ever met.'

Dizzied by lust, Mila was crushed against him again when his hands grabbed her waist and pushed her against the closest wall. There was no way for her to escape, she was literally between a rock of a man and a hard wall.

Mila looked up at him, and her breath hitched as Rooster's eyes grazed over her face. Slowly his gaze went to her mouth, his calloused thumb rubbed her bottom lip.

Rooster inclined his head, and his lips came down on hers again. Only this time he devoured her, and she let him as shivers ran through her body. Rooster must have felt it and in response his kisses grew more savage.

And Mila couldn't get enough.

Neither of them were fighting the desire. Rooster's tongue invaded Mila's mouth. He grazed her lips with his teeth, igniting a fire in her centre. His kisses left her hungry for more, weakened by the need he invoked, she hated to admit it, but she fucking loved it.

Without a thought in her head, Mila grabbed a handful of Rooster's hair and tugged, needing him closer to her body. His hands went to her ass, kneading and squeezing the firm globes. One of his hands moved down to her thigh, running up the seam of the pencil skirt.

'You're so needy, baby, I can smell how badly you want me. Your pussy is begging for me, isn't it?' Rooster's growl rushed the blood to her cheeks and turned her ears red.

His crude words snapped Mila out of her passionate, fogged up brain. What the fuck did he just say to her?

'Stop!' Mila's hands wedged between the two of them and, with a shove, she finally broke away from Rooster's lips.

'What the fuck do you think you are doing?' Mila asked, her

breathing heavy as she tried to figure out how she got herself into this situation.

'Nothing you didn't want me to, babe.' Rooster smirked and winked.

Mila ground her teeth and she felt heat rush through her body. She had never met a man who could make her so angry in such a short amount of time.

'You're such an asshole,' Mila hissed, before she patted her clothing down, trying to make herself feel more presentable. Shit, she needed to get out of this fucking office. She turned back to meet Rooster's heated gaze and his stupid amused smile. 'I want to leave immediately,' she demanded.

Neither of them said a thing, but Rooster led Mila through the rowdy clubhouse. Many of the men called out and cheered. About what, Mila wasn't sure. All she knew was that she wanted the hell out of there.

She walked ahead of him, he followed her to her car, opened the door when she fumbled with it then left her without another word.

She sat in her car for a good minute trying to figure out what had just happened, when a tap on her window caused her heart to jump in her throat.

She was so surprised to see a monster of a man with blonde hair pushed back with a black bandana invading her line of vision.

'What?' she yelled through the glass at him. The smile on the giant's face grew wider. He motioned for her to wind down the window. Mila opened it slightly.

'Hey, I'm Gunner. Saw Prez leaving you alone out here, just wanted to make sure that you're okay. He can be a bit of a dick sometimes.' Gunner squatted down and leaned his arms against her door.

'Yes, he can,' Mila agreed, blinking back tears furiously as she started her car. She was a little bit embarrassed with herself and completely furious with Rooster. Sucking up her emotion, she tried to smile at the face peering in the window at her. 'Thanks, Gunner. I'm Mila.'

He stood and she lost sight of his face, her window was filled with his bulk. He tapped a knuckle on the top of her car. 'I guess, I'll be seeing you 'round Mila.'

She watched as he strode away with a deep rumbling chuckle.

Mila drove home with the same thought on her mind. There was no way she was going to be seen by the members of Black Alchemy. She needed to keep space between her and Rooster.

Storming up to her front door and slipping inside, she made sure she heard the satisfying click of the lock behind her. In the safety of her home, she took a moment. Even with the lock activated, there still wasn't enough of a barrier between her and the heat she felt in his office, the feeling on his lips on her. Leaning against the wood she covered her mouth as she tried to steady her breath, trying to wipe away the memory of his kiss.

Jesus, what had she gotten herself into?

CHAPTER 6

The hairs on Amanda Cooper's arms tugged against the duct tape as she struggled against the headboard. Her pulse quickened as the same truth embedded in her brain. She was trapped. Her arms ached above her head. She had tried to close her legs to the cold but even her ankles were tied up. Her muffled pleas alerted her attacker. It earned her a backhand to her cheek. Another groan of pain muffled under the duct tape over her mouth.

Tears streamed down her cheeks. A smell of smouldering skin burned through her nose as the monster lit and extinguished another cigarette on her body. She stifled another scream, but it was no use. She could see how much her pain excited him. The cut on her cheek stung more thanks to the salt from her tears mixing with the blood.

The monster had been at her for hours, alternating between torturing her and raping her repeatedly. Every time he entered her a piece of Amanda's soul died, and she wasn't sure she had much left.

She felt his weight on top of her again and Amanda cried out, hoping that someone in her apartment building would hear her. If it wasn't for the loud music in the apartment across from hers, Amanda might have a chance.

'Shh, sweetheart.' The monster stroked her dark hair away

from her face. 'Remember what I said about making any kind of noise? You have to be quiet, okay? If you ruin this for me, I will have to go in search of someone else, and your mother would be the easiest victim.'

His calm tone made the blood in Amanda's veins turn to ice. The threat of bringing her ageing mother into this nightmare worked. She turned her head as the tears flew down her face faster and thicker.

Amanda knew at that moment that she was never going to see the light of day again.

She still had so many things she wanted to do. She wanted to go back to college and make something of herself, move out of this run-down apartment that took most of her wage at the diner a town over. She wanted to fall in love, have a family, and maybe even try and fix the rift between her mother and brother. Amanda just wanted to live the rest of her life.

None of that would ever happen now.

The attacker pushed more of his weight on top of her, his skin against hers. The welts and bruises were even more painful with the added pressure and she could feel the burns oozing mixing with all the other fluids he pulled from her body.

The monster ripped the fabric of her favourite panties, leaving nasty burns down her thighs. He sat up and moved them over her body, gathering all the blood from her skin, rubbing the oozing liquid into the lace. Amanda watched in horror as he brought the ruined delicate fabric to his face and took a deep breath. She heard him groan low in his throat before he landed on top of her again.

She turned her head, squeezing her eyes shut as she felt him push against her centre. Her eyes sprung open and they landed on the one and only photograph she had of her older brother.

Richard stood in a frame beside her bed, his arms crossed against his army regulation uniform and his hair cut short to his scalp.

Amanda stared back at his stoic gaze, while her own younger grin from ear to ear was almost foreign now that she was facing her own death.

Amanda teared up, she had always been proud of her older brother. Richard had done everything in his power to provide for his family, even going so far as joining the armed forces to help bring money to the household. He stood up as the man of the house when their father left them for a younger woman.

She hadn't seen her brother since he left for basic training. She remembered the emails and letters she got from him while he was overseas. He didn't say much about his experiences, but he did talk about the men that he met while deployed, and in particular about one man who was going to join the local motorcycle club in his hometown when he returned. Her brother mentioned joining the club after his last tour in passing once, and their mother completely lost it.

Their mother hadn't spoken with Richard since then. Amanda was ashamed to admit that she took her mother's side in this situation. She went years without hearing a word from her brother, and she soon came to realise that she was wrong. So, Amanda finally reached out to her brother to catch up. She hadn't seen Richard since he turned twenty-one and joined the Black Alchemy Motorcycle Club against the wishes of everyone.

The one and only time they caught up for coffee, Amanda was pleasantly surprised and impressed by the man he had become. His hair was only slightly longer, but still cut short like the day he shipped off. The thing that was different from the brother that she grew up with was that he was quiet. Amanda remembered a time when Richard would tell her stories to pass the time, now he listened.

She missed her brother.

Rough hands encased her jaw and jerked her back to meet his terrifying black eyes. They gleamed with excitement at her fear. There was no coming back from this point on.

***

Rooster glared at the newspaper in front of him. His elbows rested on his desk while his head was in his hands. Another girl had been killed, this one even closer to home for one of his brothers than just a random hook up.

Creep's sister was the latest victim and even though the man hadn't seen his family since he prospected for the club, at least to Rooster's knowledge, his brother was taking it fucking hard.

Creep was well known around the club as the quietest of all the brothers. If there was a stealth mission assigned to the club or even a protection run that required more of a subtle touch, he was the first on Rooster's list to send. The man was so light on his feet, the target wouldn't even realise that he was being followed until there was a blade pulled across his neck.

Rooster ran his fingers through his hair as he tried to calm the rage circling in his blood. He had no idea who was doing this to these women, but he needed to find out who it was.

Some MC's had a bad reputation of treating their women roughly. Black Alchemy was not one of those clubs, the ol' ladies and families of the BAMC were strong and respected. Not only did they command as much but they earned it. So the fact that some of them were being attacked and killed was a real fucking kick to the balls for Rooster.

Without a word to any of his brothers, he walked out the front door and mounted his bike. He needed to get out of the clubhouse. He needed the wind against his skin and the open road at his feet.

He needed to think, and a ride was always his go-to remedy to clear his mind.

Rooster sped through the normal looking neighbourhoods. Houses passed by him in a blur, and even at the speed he was taking, he caught a glimpse of the blonde teacher sitting on her wrap around porch with a mug in her hands. The white cottage was surrounded by a garden. Her denim shorts hugged her legs perfectly and her breezy tank made her seem like she was some sort of mythical creature trying to lure him into her trap. Goddamn she was not only gorgeous, but she was also fucking temptation on a stick.

Rooster liked the way she looked in her teacher outfit with the tight skirts and the innocent ballet flats, but this weekend look was just amazing. It almost had him turning around to see what was underneath.

But he kept on going. He had priorities to the club, and the club always came first.

CHAPTER 7

Mila didn't know what to do with herself. That kiss with Rooster had just about shattered her every thought and consumed her every waking and unconscious moment. She had been actively ignoring the mountain of reports she had to grade, and the week's laundry had been piling up, but Mila couldn't bear to be stuck inside.

The spring day had a cool air to it, but the sun was warm. She breathed in the sunshine as she stepped out onto her front porch. Mila touched her father's class ring that she had hung on a necklace that morning, grabbed her gardening tools and plonked a hat on her head. She plugged in her headphones and cranked up classic music her dad grew up listening to.

Mila was determined to drown out the rest of the world.

Seeing a bike drive past during her morning coffee on her porch and knowing it was Rooster was messing with her head. She needed to think, and the best way for her to do that was to start pulling weeds.

Her cottage was surrounded by a white picket fence, flower beds running along the fence line. Mila spotted a few weeds, squatted to her knees and started pulling as The Rolling Stones crooned about not being satisfied.

She couldn't help but smirk at how fitting the song was.

Mila was adjusting her gardening gloves when a shadow hovered over her. She inwardly groaned when her heart spiked at the thought of Rooster coming to visit her, that he made the effort to find her. Like it wasn't enough that he sped by on his bike and had been consistently on her mind.

Her inward groan escaped from her lips when she raised her head, it wasn't Rooster above her.

It was Foghorn.

God, why couldn't this asshole just leave her alone?

Mila had stupidly gotten involved with the biker from Jokers Ace MC when she was still in college. Red flags had been waving since she met him at the dingy college bar, and now he still wouldn't take 'no' for an answer. Foghorn was the one boyfriend that Mila would always regret. She was childish and rebellious when they got involved, she had been grieving in the wrong way and it was still biting her in the ass.

'Hey there, sweet thing. How's my woman doing?' Foghorn leaned over the fence, his grubby hands leaving black marks on the white paint. Mila couldn't even count on her fingers how many times she had asked him, and sometimes downright demanded, that he leave her alone.

'I'm not your girl, Foghorn. I'm not anybody's anything!' Mila tried to stand up, but he pushed his hand on her shoulder, forcing her back onto her knees, and marked up her favourite gardening shirt.

'I like you down there, baby, where you belong. You know who you belong to, don't you, sweet Mila? No matter how many bitches I fuck, they ain't you, baby.' His hand smeared more black smudge over her cheek and down her jaw as she clenched. She had to wait for the perfect moment to strike. He must have sensed her fury because he said, 'I think you need to be reminded of that, you need to be taught a fucking lesson.'

Foghorn's grin made her skin crawl, his teeth were yellowing and, from the smell coming from him, rotting in his head. The smirk on his lips caused a shiver to run up her spine.

'You can't even keep your eyes off my lips, I know you want a taste.' Foghorn licked his disgusting cracked lips and grabbed a handful of her ponytail. 'And since you're down there…' He thrust his hips towards her, hitting her fence. A wince came from him, that made Mila chuckle a little under her breath. He noticed because his grip tightened again.

'Actually,' she managed out through gritted teeth, 'I was wondering when you would need to get fitted for dentures, 'cause those teeth of yours don't look like they're going to be around for much longer.'

'Aww, listen to you, babe. Worrying about your man, like a good ol' lady.' Foghorn finally released her hair but grabbed her arm instead and pulled her to stand. Mila took this as her chance and started to squirm, she didn't want to be anywhere near this man. The smell from his breath alone was enough to trigger her gag reflex.

'Let me go, Jye!' she cried out as she pulled at his hand on her arm. An unexpected squeal escaped her when his hand came into contact with her cheek.

'It's Foghorn, baby, you would do good to remember that. It's going to be the only name on your lips as I fill you up the way you like.' Foghorn's hand slipped down to hers and pushed it over his jeans. She felt his excitement and she was sure it wasn't just because of the image he was painting. The few times they did have sex, Mila had ended up covered in bruises.

'Stop it,' she cried out and looked around trying to spot any of her gardening tools, but the heavier ones were at the other end of her front yard. The rest of her neighbourhood was empty, but she hoped that someone would see what was happening and come to help her.

Utter hopelessness fell over Mila as Foghorn continued to tug at her. She closed her eyes, trying to think of something else, when the rumble of a Harley broke through the quiet. Her eyes ripped open for fear that more Jokers Ace members had come to back up Foghorn, but then she caught sight of those honey-brown eyes and the man dismounting from his giant machine.

'Well, well, well, if it isn't Decay's little lackey, so far away from home and all alone,' Rooster growled, his hands buried deep in his jean pockets as he leaned against his bike. The anger came off the Black Alchemy president in waves, and even though there was absolute rage in his amber-like eyes, Mila wasn't afraid.

'What are you doing with Minx?'

'Who?' Foghorn's grip on her wrist tightened.

'That woman you're holding. She's Minx.' Rooster pushed himself upright and stood in front of her. 'And she's mine.'

Minx? Where the hell had that nickname come from? Mila wanted to hate it, and glare Rooster down, but her lips turned upwards slightly.

She kinda liked it.

Plus, he was rescuing her.

'What are you doing here, Foghorn?' Rooster continued his stalk forward. Mila noticed his bicep tense up when he crossed his arms.

'I'm having a conversation with my woman, that's what I'm fucking doing here. What's your excuse, Chicken Shit?' Foghorn's grip on her wrist tightened and he pulled her closer over her fence. Her wince didn't go unnoticed by Rooster.

'If she's your woman, then where is her patch and why was she at the BAMC clubhouse not just this week but the week before that?' Rooster's gaze fixated on Foghorn's grip. Mila knew from experience that it was going to leave a gnarly bruise.

She hated that Foghorn's dirty fingers were branding her arm for at least a week. Rooster finally raised his gaze and steeled her with a look that made Mila question a lot of things, her sanity included, when heat pooled between her legs. Rooster quirked an eyebrow, daring her to say something, giving Mila the confidence to stand up for herself again. She wasn't fighting this alone anymore.

'I'm not his fucking woman,' Mila spat. 'I'm not his fucking anything. I knew him when I was in college and looking for a bit of danger.'

'You definitely found it,' Rooster commented, his hands rubbing his chin. 'Well? You heard the lady, she's not your anything. So, fuck off back to Decay and your rotting clubhouse – while you still have the chance.'

Mila watched as Rooster hurdled over her picket fence, landing with a thud on the soil and missing the flower buds that were just starting to peak out.

'Hey there, Minx,' he said completely ignoring the asshole who still had her arm in his grip. Rooster's smile was directed at her. Mila's own lips quirked slightly, and a feeling of smug camaraderie came over her.

Rooster grabbed Foghorn's wrist hard, mimicking the way he was holding her. Foghorn let out a small but hearty whine before the dirty biker let her go. Finally using what little smarts he hadn't smoked away.

Rooster placed his hand at the base of Mila's spine and guided her away from her ex-boyfriend. Standing her behind him, Mila allowed herself a moment and grabbed onto his cut. She held on like it was her lifeline, and immediately Mila felt safe.

She watched as Foghorn glared at them both, but still moved toward his bike, mounted it, and rode off. The glint in his eyes told Mila that this was nowhere near over, but at least he was gone.

'Thank you.' The words slipped out with her sigh when his bike was out of sight. Her hands were still gripped on Rooster's leather cut, the menacing skull over red fire stared back at her and she let herself enjoy the feel and smell of real leather and something completely Rooster.

She was safe.

'You okay, Minx?' He turned and cupped her bare shoulders with his large hands. Mila nodded and breathed in deeply, black coffee and motor oil filled her senses.

'Just, thank you. I don't know what would have happened if you hadn't driven past.'

'I wouldn't have let anything happen to you, Minx. You'll be safe now. He knows you're under my club's protection,' Rooster promised. Mila wanted to question his vow, it wasn't like he was going to be with her every day...

Right?

CHAPTER 8

She missed him.

She fucking missed him.

How the hell could she miss him?

Mila hadn't seen Rooster since the day he helped her with Foghorn. Rooster had sent a prospect over to her house when he left after he got an emergency call. She'd asked Rooster what was going on but all she got back was the words 'Club business' and that she was to stay safe.

Her mood to garden now tainted, Mila went about the rest of her weekend chores, but each load of laundry, each paper she graded was bombarded by the thoughts of Rooster.

Why was the guy always on her mind?

Yes, he had helped her with Foghorn but other than that all Mila knew about him was that he was the new president of a local biker club, he had two sisters and a mother. He was also the most arrogant asshole she had ever met, the things he said and did drove her insane. Yet, she couldn't get enough of him.

God! She was becoming one of those biker groupies again! When the fuck was she going to learn?

Mila's weekend certainly didn't improve when she received an email from the head of staff at the high school informing them that there would be an early morning staff meeting to discuss some issues happening around campus. Probably about the increase of biker activity on the school grounds.

So, when Mila's Monday morning alarm blared in her ear, she groaned. Normally her mornings would be surrounded by her seniors, but they were all getting ready to graduate. Her mornings were wide open again, unless there was a pointless staff meeting that really could have just been an email.

Mila mindlessly went through her morning routine, and even managed to consume two coffees by the time she arrived at the school parking lot. As soon as she opened the car door, the cold morning air hit her like a freight train.

'Fucking shit, it's cold,' Mila blurted out, thankful for once that it was so early and none of her students were in the courtyard. She didn't want to deal with some of the younger freshman boys making fun of her swearing.

'Mila.' A male voice called out and her heart leapt at the thought of it being Rooster, but the timbre wasn't deep enough. Fuck, she hated the way her body reacted to even the possibility of him chasing her down. Too busy chastising herself Mila didn't realise that Jason Wright was walking briskly over to her.

The maths teacher had been sweet on her since she started at Bryson City High. He was nice enough and she had even thought about accepting one of his many invitations for dinner or even just a simple coffee. He just didn't have that spark about him, definitely nothing on the sensation that she got whenever she was around Rooster.

Fucking hell, why was her mind always going back to him!

'Hi, Jason, how are you?' Mila smiled kindly. He was handsome enough, his light brown hair slicked back and flicked slightly behind his ears. He was clean cut, respectable and probably her safest option...

'I'm good, thank you. Sad to be seeing my seniors go, but I'm happy to have my mornings off again. That is... when we don't have meetings.' Jason returned Mila's smile, it was sweet, but it didn't reach his eyes and it didn't make her tingle like Rooster's stupid smirk did.

Shit! Why couldn't she get her mind off this biker!

'I know what you mean about mornings,' she said and looked into Jason's brown eyes. They didn't have that honey golden shine like Rooster's, but maybe that was what she needed.

Someone nothing like the BAMC president.

'Did you want to grab a coffee after work today?' she asked before she could stop herself. It was time to move away from the bad boy, and Jason had shown genuine interest, he would be the perfect guy for her to do that with.

Mila watched as Jason's face turned white and, for a moment, she was worried he was about to pass out. But when words seemed to finally hit his mind, his head nodded so viciously, Mila was worried it might bruise his brain.

'I'd love that, Mila, should we go in my car?'

'No,' she said a little too quickly. 'No, I would prefer that we take our own cars and meet there.'

'Sounds like a plan.' Jason smiled as he stepped forward and opened the front doors for her to walk through. Mila nodded her thanks and smiled as they both walked down the empty hallways. He was good, a good distraction from Rooster and his loud, distracting Harley. But damn, it was a beautiful Harley.

As the meeting droned on, she could almost hear the engine revving of that glorious machine, the president's strong hands twisting the throttle. Mila's fingers twitched against the books in her lap as she remembered the feel of his leather cut. She pulled them up to her chest, imagining the heat of his body against her if she were to ever feel that roar of the motorbike between her legs, among other things.

She shook the idea out of her head. Mila wondered if her move from Charlotte was a mistake after all. She left her toxic alcoholic mother and past transgressions behind her to start anew, only to become completely intrigued by a man in leather and denim.

Mila really needed to get her head back in the game, she needed to focus on fixing her life. She tuned back into the head teacher's drones and immediately wished that she hadn't.

Just as she predicted, the meeting could have been an email. The rest of her morning dragged on although some of her classes were better than others. The sophomores and juniors were handfuls as per usual. Her freshman classes were always on their best behaviour, Mila did enjoy them the most. They were all still new and hadn't been around the older students long enough for them to be corrupted, Mila always wished that they would stay so well behaved but, come the next year, most of them would come back with an attitude, fuelled by hormones.

By the time the final bell rang for the end of the school day the football jocks and the extracurricular students were standing up. Usually, Mila would be running the poetry club, but since the year was coming to an end, Mila had dismissed them all early.

She spotted Daisy stretching and warming up with the rest of the cheer squad. Mila couldn't stop her grin. No one would have pegged the MC princess to be a pom-pom girl but, then again, she should have never stereotyped her. Daisy was a sweet girl with her whole life ahead of her, it didn't matter who her family was.

She watched Daisy as she did a full jump into the splits, feeling a sense of pride, far more potent than she felt for any of her other students. That girl was definitely going to have the time of her life away at college.

Reaching her car, Mila felt the hair on the back of her neck stand up. She looked around the parking lot sure that she could feel eyes on her. Her hand went to her neck as she turned, eyes searching for something – anything – that would explain her weird reaction.

The vibration of her phone started in the pocket of her skirt, scaring the absolute shit out of her for a moment.

Jason: I got us a table :D

Mila almost rolled her eyes at his eagerness. It shouldn't be a bad thing, but *god* the guy was just too excited about some coffee and conversation. Something inside her screamed to cancel but she ignored the voice, pulling herself back to her senses. Mila wanted – *needed* – to get Rooster out of her head and Jason was just the guy to help her.

At least she hoped that was the case.

***

A buzzer sounded behind Rooster, and a click of the door alerted him to the man that was about to be in his presence. The cream-coloured room with brown trim was the only place Rooster could see anyone from his father's side of the family.

His grandma Emma passed away when Patriot was born due to complications, while his grandpa Huey was fighting Vietnam. The old man came home to no wife and a seven-year-old son he didn't know. Rooster's father had been raised by his grandmother and even turned into a good ol' American boy. Grandpa Huey wasn't ready to be a father without his Emma, so he drove away with his army brothers to start up Black Alchemy.

When Patriot was sixteen, his grandmother passed away and he went in search of his father. He found him, and he found the club as well. He prospected, earned his road name and a place to call home.

For a year.

By the time Patriot re-joined his father and the brothers of the BAMC, the war with Jokers Ace had been going on for almost ten years and the other side was due to strike.

It was only weeks before Patriot's seventeenth birthday when Bash laid down his sled with his ol' lady on the back. The original was murdered in cold blood, gunned down by two fuckwit Jokers Ace members who wanted to show how fucking tough they were.

The murder, coupled with the fact that Bash had survived 'Nam only to die on the back of his bike doing what he loved with the woman he loved had sent Huey into a violent rampage.

Revenge sent Huey to Central Prison, North Carolina and that was where Rooster sat, waiting to speak with his grandfather – a man he had never met in person – ready to face the presidential tradition.

Huey didn't smile at his grandson as the old man approached, but Rooster could still see that he appreciated his visit. The original in front of him made Rooster think of Patriot. Their faces were so similar, only Huey's sported a few more wrinkles and two tear drop tattoos under his left eye. That pain in Rooster's chest returned, his father would never look like this, he would never get the chance.

Rooster rubbed at the pain in his chest and picked up the plastic phone. He held it to his ear and for the first time in his life, Rooster heard his grandfather's voice as he took in what Patriot might have looked like during retirement. 'Well look at you boy. All grown up I see. Your pop's been showing photos of all you kids for years. Never actually expected one of you to greet your grandpa in prison. How is your pops going to handle this?'

'You didn't hear?' Rooster asked before he thought about the words. He had just fucked up, badly. He watched as his grandfather's weathered face turned sour.

'Hear what, boy? Got thrown in the fucking hole again. Something about not shivving a member of your enemy club or some bullshit like that.' Huey shrugged his elderly shoulders. Even though the old man had developed some muscle definition, his age was showing in his wrinkled face and white hair that tumbled past his collar.

Rooster spotted multiple tattoos on his grandfather's arm. Numbers specific to the Vietnam platoon that he lost, a large red heart with Emma inscribed on a scroll and a bird that Rooster thought to be an eagle was unfinished.

'Whatcha doin' here, Dylan? Where's your pop? He's not due to visit for another few weeks.'

'I hoped that someone would have told you already.' Rooster braced himself for his grandfather's rage – which was legendary within the club – as well as the pain of reliving the worst moment of his life. 'Patriot was killed by the Jokers about a month ago, in front of me.'

'Are you fucking kidding me!' Old Man Huey screamed and slammed his palm against the glass separating them. He dropped the plastic phone and stood up abruptly, causing the chair to collapse behind him.

'Inmate. Sit the fuck down,' the guard behind Huey muffled, his voice sure but his posture giving away his fear. A few of the other inmates visiting family members jerked their heads at the outburst but promptly ignored the old man, who was clearly still well known for his temper.

'You want to shut the fuck up bull. My son died!' Huey said as he turned his reddened face, glaring at the guard. Rooster was slightly amused by the fear on the young man's face, but it didn't take away from the pain.

Picking up the headset again, Huey barked through the glass.

'Rooster, who's president? Who's taking care of the club and your ma?' His grandpa's face held more of a tortured look than when Rooster first saw him.

'I've got the presidency, Grandpa. I'm taking care of everything.'

'So that's why you're here. The traditional passing of the guard. Have you seen Bash?' His grandfather's eyes turned murderous in front of him. Even after all these years, the murder of his friend and brother was painful and created a reaction from him.

'Had a shot at the cemetery.'

'Good.' Huey leaned back in his chair, the phone cord pulling. 'And Grizz?'

'You know that old coot never wants any kind of responsibility, but he did make the argument that the president should be from the original three bloodlines.'

'What about Bash's boy, Dice? Where is he?'

'Dice and his ol' lady took a leave of absence. I think after Pop's death they wanted to live their lives to the fullest. Last I checked they've stopped somewhere in Texas.'

'I'm gonna tell this to you straight Rooster. I already saw this coming, Dice was never a man ready to take responsibility. Has a lot to do with his pop's death, I think. Are you sure you're ready to take on the club boy? You're still young. I'm sure there are some other boys who would look after the club until you feel ready.'

Rooster was taken aback by the question. His grandfather was asking him something that no one had bothered to ask yet. Something he himself was questioning. Was he really ready to take on the club and the obligations? Did he have enough years under his belt? The club certainly thought so, Grizz looked as proud as the old man could when Rooster put the new patch on his cut.

'Do you trust me with the club?' Rooster finally asked. Huey chuckled.

'Y'know, when I wound up in this slammer, Crow asked me the same thing…'

Crow was the only BAMC president not born from the original bloodlines, but he was an original of the club. Rooster remembered an old man with the long grey hair and even longer beard who always sat with Old Man Grizz, up until the day Crow died of liver failure.

His grandfather turned down his gaze and cleared his throat. He wiped his face to conceal a sharp sniffle, then looked up at Rooster. He couldn't read his expression, but something about his question changed the old man's demeanour. 'Your pops did too, when it was his turn.'

Huey tightened his grip around the phone, his face returning to the tough veteran with the same eyes of his father.

'Rooster, I trust you with everything. From the rides, to the women, to the club itself. Take care of Black Alchemy, and yourself.'

With that, the old man nodded his head toward Rooster. He got up and waited for the pigs to escort him out of the room, handcuffs jiggling as he walked.

Rooster watched him go, vowing to not only never end up like his grandfather, but also to take care of the club just as he was trusted to do.

CHAPTER 9

As the May sun turned warmer and June rolled in, the end of the school year approached. Mila's weeks had consisted of trying to keep her student's attention, spending time with Jason and making sure that her garden was going to survive the summer. She tried to keep busy while the sun was still high in the sky, but her nights were when her mind would fill with thoughts of Rooster.

It didn't matter how many dates she went on with Jason, or how many times he kissed her, Mila was never able to remove the thought of the Black Alchemy president.

She remembered Rooster's lips as soft but demanding. He definitely knew what she needed before even she did. It was honestly so fucking annoying but it was also pretty impressive and Mila couldn't stop her mind from imagining sex with Rooster and what it would be like. Especially when she was relaxed.

His mouth and his tongue promised wicked nights in bed, and his demeanour said that he wouldn't be lying about that. Mila hated that she couldn't stop thinking about how he called her his woman in front of Foghorn. Was that just to make the Jokers Ace member leave? He'd given her a nickname that she should hate, but honestly Mila didn't. She smiled every time his husky voice wondered out from the corners of her mind and whispered *'Minx'*. She had to keep reminding herself that he was still the president of an outlaw club. She shouldn't even be entertaining the idea of a single night with that man, but her body's response to those thoughts... she couldn't stop them.

Mila groaned and threw her arm over her eyes as the light streamed through the gap in the curtains. Her tank top was sticking to her skin with sweat, whether it was from the heat seeping into her room during the night or because of her dreams, she wasn't exactly sure.

'I'm going to hell,' she said into the empty room to herself, as she tried to ignore the ache right in the centre of her core.

It was Friday and Mila was debating whether or not to go out on another date with Jason. The past few dinners he had started to become a lot more possessive and had been pushing the idea of them spending the night together. He was always trying to sneak a feel and had recently taken to running his fingers up her thigh when she did agree to travel with him. Mila was increasingly becoming more uncomfortable with the man, but he was the better option, the safer option... right?

He *had* been commenting a number of times about what she was wearing and the attention she was receiving. He'd even mentioned how she was looking for someone else to replace him.

Mila didn't like the words that came out of his mouth, she didn't like the way he made her feel even when she knew the truth, but she had dealt with a lot worse in the past. Other than those snide comments and the occasional glare she would catch him giving some man who glanced her way, Mila had to remind herself that he was nice, and that he wanted to date her.

Not just fuck her once and ruin her for other men.

But, he's not Rooster, her brain supplied unhelpfully. Yes, Jason wasn't anything like Rooster but that was a good thing... wasn't it?

Mila dressed quickly in her weekend attire of a breezy tank top and her shorts. She needed to spend some time in her garden, needed to get her head together before she started to get ready for her date.

She skipped down the stairs of her porch. Walking toward her flower beds, the sun was streaming through her sunglasses. For a moment she enjoyed the quiet moment with her face toward the warmth.

A tree branch snapping brought her out of her trance. Mila watched as a shadow ran away out of the corner of her eye. It was there one minute and gone the next. She searched her yard for any kind of sign of the shadow. The shape was a man, she was sure of it, and it wasn't Foghorn.

A tall, slightly thin man, but a man nonetheless. Mila felt her airways narrow.

Someone was definitely watching her.

She considered calling the cops but had no desire to. She knew there wasn't much they would be able to do for her. Instead, she debated whether she should call the club or Rooster. Even though she wasn't part of the club or even knew a way to contact them, Mila was really tempted to find a way to get the help she needed.

She rubbed her hands over her arms, she didn't know why she was trying it again when it didn't work last time. It wasn't doing anything to calm her raging heart.

Mila couldn't stand being out in the open any longer. She gathered up her gardening tools and raced back inside. To busy herself, she started to get ready for her date with Jason.

Mila pulled into the parking lot of the local Italian restaurant and the first thing she noticed was the number of bikes parked in front of the building. It almost rivalled that of the clubhouse or even the small café that Rooster had followed her to not so long ago.

Mila scanned over the parking lot, as if her eyes were trained to find him. Rooster's honey-brown gaze caught the ocean-blue of hers. There was a wildness in his stare, a happy lift at the corner of his mouth, and it gave her image upon image of late nights in his bed, staring into those eyes as she pulled him closer to kiss her. Mila's breath hitched. He started strutting over toward her.

She just couldn't keep her eyes off him. There was something about the way he swaggered, commanding the attention of everyone around him. It was a complete turn on for her, something that surprised Mila.

Suddenly, her car door flung open and she came face to face with Jason. The smile on his face might have been handsome but there was something sinister underlying in his eyes. It caught Mila off guard because she hadn't really seen it before. Her eyes travelled down his clothes, and she was disappointed that he was dressed exactly like he would if he was at school.

Brown slacks, light blue button-down shirt and sports jacket.

Mila gave him a kind smile and accepted his hand out of the car.

'Hi, Mila,' Jason said, bringing her closer to his body. He placed a sweet kiss on her lips, which she did return but she was acutely aware of Rooster's eyes on her. Risking a brief look, Rooster stood in place in the middle of the lot. His eyes burned as he watched her with Jason.

'Hi, Jason.' She smiled after she pulled away, trying her best to ignore the piercing gaze from behind her. 'How are you?'

'I would be much better if that biker behind you wasn't checking you out so much. Did you have to wear such a skimpy shirt? And what about those pants? They look like you painted them on to your body,' Jason criticised, making Mila blush with embarrassment. She liked the way she looked, so why the fuck didn't he?

Her heart rate picked up when she caught Rooster appreciating the way she looked. His eyes travelled over her black jeans that hugged her legs and thighs in a way that should have been sinful, but still looked classy on her. She had paired them with a shirt that would probably look better in a nightclub in Charlotte than a small-town restaurant. Her boots, even with the slight heel, gave her some extra height but not enough, since she was still a head shorter than her date.

Mila looked up at Jason, opening her mouth to defend her outfit but the way he glared back at her, daring her to talk back to him made Mila shut her mouth and tilt her head down. She hated that this was her response. It cemented in her heart that this wasn't going to work out with Jason. She'd known it from the beginning, she just didn't want to admit it.

She couldn't live up to his expectations, and she wasn't going to even try. Especially since there was a man who, while dangerous, wanted her for who she was.

Mila was officially done with Jason Wright.

***

Rooster watched Mila's head drop at the words the asshole spat at her. He hated the idea that this guy even had the fucking nerve to say anything that would hurt the woman's feelings. He didn't know why he cared so much, he shouldn't. He didn't even know the woman that well, and yet he still found himself walking toward her and putting his hand on her delicate bare shoulder.

Rooster took a good look at the douchebag who had his hand on the small of Mila's back. He seemed familiar, but Rooster couldn't put his finger on the name. Being from a small town, everyone knew everyone, but Bryson City was just large enough for names to be forgotten from time to time.

'Whatcha doing here, Minx?' he asked when he got closer. He

could never forget this woman's name, but he couldn't stop calling her *Minx*. The name suited her, and he liked the blush that bloomed on her cheeks.

Rooster admired the way her hair landed on her shoulder as she turned. It hung down her back in golden waves and Rooster's hand wanted to run through the strands. He liked how the blonde locks looked in the ponytail she always wore, but the way it hung down her back had Rooster itching to tuck a wave behind her ear, letting his finger linger down her jaw.

God, he fucking wanted her.

He kept the asshole in his peripheral, noting his hands on her and the way he glared Rooster down. This was something that Rooster would never stand for from any of his brothers, this fucker had better respect him. It didn't matter that he was a citizen, everyone in Bryson City knew who Black Alchemy was and which current brother held the gavel.

'Did you miss me?' he smirked as he turned his attention back to Mila, watching the asshole's frown deepen only increased Rooster's enjoyment of the situation.

'What makes you think that she even knows you?' The asshole, as Rooster had officially dubbed him, who thought that he had a right to this woman, spoke up.

'I think you should pay attention to who you are talking to and watch your mouth.'

Now that Rooster was close enough, he recognised just who this guy was. Jason Wright, only son of one of the richer families in Bryson City. He and Rooster's older brother Steven were good friends back in the day, when Steven had still been in town.

Jason Wright had been the captain of the football team and a kid who thought because his daddy was rich, he could own the school and everyone who walked the halls. Rooster had heard rumours that asshole Jason had returned to Bryson City and had started teaching at the same high school he terrorised.

'How dare he talk to you?' he heard Jason mutter under his breath toward Mila. Rooster watched as her gorgeous body tensed up, what the fuck did she even see in this guy?

Rooster had to hold himself back, he wanted to go over and pound the motherfucker into the ground. Instead of making himself look foolish over this girl he turned to his Minx and said, 'You look fucking smoking, enjoy your night… if you think that's possible without me.'

He turned on his heels and joined his brothers at their bikes, shaking out a fist. As much as it would satisfy him to punch the asshole in the face, Rooster knew Jason was one of those citizens who would press charges and bring more attention to the club than what was necessary.

'What are you doing with your sister's teacher?' Rubble asked around his cigarette.

'What are you doing smoking?' Rooster retorted. 'Angel's going to smell that on you the second you get your ass home.'

Rubble puffed a ring of smoke. 'Doesn't answer my question, Prez,' he teased.

Rooster shrugged, he actually had no idea how to respond to his brother. His mind drifted back to the clubhouse to the pile of paperwork on his desk, but he preferred to stick around for a few more minutes and shoot the shit. Rubble passed over a flask and Rooster took a long swig, his future brother-in-law always had the best whiskey.

He was actively facing away from the restaurant, he couldn't bear to watch Mila walk in with fucking Jason Wright. He was almost tempted to say fuck it and climb on his bike, get the hell away from the shit show in his head when cat calls and crude remarks came from some of his brothers.

Rooster turned to see his Minx strutting toward him. He smirked as she walked right up to him and for a moment stood there silently. He could taste her apprehension. He could almost hear her questioning herself.

'Ah, fuck it,' she said and wrapped her hands around the back of his neck and pulled him down to meet her pink lips. She kissed him long and slow, rolling her tongue against his, saying in no uncertain terms what and who she wanted.

The crude comments, cat calls and other shouts got louder as Rooster cupped the small of her back in one hand and the other cupped the back of her neck. He wanted to keep her against him for as long as possible, but the woman in his arms didn't stop. He pulled her flush against his chest, growling his approval at the way she felt against his hard chest.

Rooster finally admitted to himself that he wanted Mila Rice desperately, and he let her lead him down the road to ruin.

She wanted him too.

Thank fucking Christ!

CHAPTER 10

The monster knew this woman.

He knew all the women he had taken from this world, in one way or another, but this woman… she knew him just as much as he knew her.

This one was different from the others, she was the mother of one of those fucking Black Alchemy members, but not just that. She was a crack whore and had been known to shoot up a huge amount of heroin into her body, even at family events.

He remembered this woman from his teenage years, in his fantasies she had long brown hair, wavy and full. It used to swish as she walked around the clubhouse grounds on family picnic days. Her face was always beautiful, sometimes it was lightly covered in makeup, otherwise it was clean, unmarked. Her eyes were always a bright blue and wide, lined with thick black lashes and she always smelled fresh and flowery.

Looking at her now, the man couldn't believe that this was once the bright woman on the compound that he used to lust over as a young teen. Her hair was thinning, sticking up in every direction, greasy and even falling out in clumps in some places. She had dyed it blonde over the years, but there were still large clusters of brown where it hadn't taken properly.

She had obviously not been eating regularly, she was nothing but skin and fucking bones. The man could probably serve soup in her clavicle, or even just break it.

That was a satisfying thought.

The idea of breaking this whore's bones made the man inwardly groan. God, he would love to feel that power under his hands.

The monster couldn't believe that the crack whore didn't recognise him. Not that he wanted her to, it wouldn't matter in the long run.

She would be dead come the morning.

But still it hurt, how come he wasn't memorable enough for this woman to know who he was?

'Hey there, handsome, did your car break down again?' the crack whore slurred. The monster had been using the excuse of an old shitty car for the past few weeks while he watched the women of the club. Some of them, like this crack whore, were easier to get to, most however weren't. He could get to them eventually, he just had to wait for his moment. 'You really need to get a better car, honey.'

The woman swayed as she leaned seductively against the entry way. The man noticed the fresh track marks along her bony arms. He wouldn't be surprised if it had only been moments since she shot up.

'Not this time, I came to see you,' he said leaning in closer to her, trying not to gag at the smell of her body odour. It was pretty clear that she hadn't washed in several days.

'Me?' The man fought the urge to roll his eyes at her fake, high-pitched voice, but he needed her to believe that he wanted her like nothing else in this world.

'Yes, baby, you. You are making me think of a whole lot of bad things.' He inwardly cringed at the bad lines he was throwing out. God, he really needed to step up his game.

If the monster was honest with himself, he had hoped that she would be too high to understand anything he was saying properly.

He didn't want to knock this one out, it would be too easy. He didn't even know why he targeted this woman – no, that was a lie. He knew why he did, the fantasy of the woman from his younger years kept playing through his mind.

But she wasn't the same as the woman who stood in front of him now. She was so fucking drugged up that she let him inside and didn't catch a glimpse of the danger that was brewing inside him.

'Well, come on in, sugar.' The crack whore momma batted her clumped eyelashes, ones that used to frame her bright eyes. Now they just made her look cheap.

He didn't wait for her to step aside to let him in. He shoved her out of the way and had her up against the nearest wall, his hand around her throat blocking off her air supply for a moment. She started to moan and make lots of fake noises like a porn movie. That pissed him off, he hated the fakeness that surrounded these women.

'No!' he snapped. 'You don't make a fucking sound. Not unless I allow you to.' He squeezed the hand around her throat tighter, holding her dulled gaze as she finally understood the danger she was in. He walked her toward the back of the house, having memorised the layout in his previous visits. He had his favourite bra and panty set in the pocket of his hoodie and the rope he bought recently. He had to switch up from the tape since the last time.

'Bedroom,' he growled into her ear before he let her go. He watched as she scampered down the hallway with him stalking behind her. His anger brimmed under the surface. He wasn't going to let it out just yet, he needed to be patient.

He needed to make this feeling last. His last kill was beautiful, but it wasn't satisfying him like it used to.

'I'll give you what you need. Just don't hurt me,' she begged and stripped out of her filthy robe and undergarments. He followed quickly behind as she tripped and stumbled over thin air.

He needed to get this over with, fuck being patient. She was ruining the fantasy he had created, the one he needed to be right for him to be completely satisfied. The monster dropped the bra and panties in the plastic bag on the floor and threw the whore on the messy bed, the sheets stained with blood and other discolouration he didn't want to focus on. They were rumbled from recent use.

His hand went to her throat again, with her laying on her back. He moved over her naked, pock-marked skin. He couldn't stand to look at her sunken or torn apart face, his fantasy wouldn't allow him to. He flipped her onto her stomach and frowned when he saw that her ass was sagging slightly.

The man should have left, but the monster was too far gone. He needed to feed.

His hand came down with a stinging spank.

The sound alone was erotic, for only a moment.

'Did I fucking tell you to strip, whore?' He pulled at her hair and spanked her again. This time making sure that the skin turned red under his palm. He wanted it to fucking hurt.

'Ow… baby, can you not hit me so hard?' The crack whore lifted her head up for a moment to look at him, but he scrunched his hand into a fist and whacked her in the back of her skull.

'I told you not to fucking speak,' he growled. The crack whore's instincts jumped in at that moment. He felt it immediately. She started to wiggle, trying to loosen his steel trap grip.

'What the fuck are you doing slut? Don't fucking move!' He tried to get her hands together, while reaching for the knife in the pocket of his hoodie. The whore took the opportunity to move, elbowing him in the stomach quickly.

He let out an *oohf* and she saw her chance, getting out from under him. The whore ran to her door, clearly unbothered by the fact that she was naked. The man charged after her, he knew she was in a well populated area, and he couldn't let her get out to one of her neighbours. His mission wasn't anywhere near done. The monster knew that he should have just cut his losses there, but the crack whore had seen his face. He wasn't going to be caught because some bitch was stupid enough to try and escape him.

Her chipped nails and bony fingers wrapped around the doorknob as a primal scream came out of his throat, and he tackled her to the ground.

The woman's dead eyes stared back at him. The cut on her cheek was now becoming the 'Slasher's' signature, something that gave him the uniqueness that was his killing spree. That's what the papers had been saying, he had been front page news for weeks now.

He looked over the woman, she was completely naked, the cuts on her body were still oozing blood and, in some places, pus from the infected marks on her skin. He hated that he wasn't able to complete his ritual, because she stripped before he told her to. He didn't even get to see how she looked in the set he had picked out for her.

This had been a messy killing. He had to use some of her dirty pantyhose to shove in her mouth to shut her up, and the rope he used to tie her up wasn't tight enough for her thin wrists and ankles.

Her blood was dirty, it was the only thing that was making him feel a bit better that he didn't try to gather it up in a pair of the used panties.

His pleasure was abysmal, he was going to have to find something. Another to satiate his need before he killed her.

This crack whore did nothing to cure his hunger.

The man didn't know how much longer he was going to get away with the killings, let alone doing one in a single night. Hell, he didn't even have another woman lined up for his next one.

There was the pretty blonde teacher, but she wasn't going to be home tonight, and he didn't know her schedule well enough to get away with it. He hadn't witnessed any transgressions on her part, but she was getting awfully close to the new president. He hadn't even picked out which set he liked the best from her collection in her drawers. She wasn't going to be wasted on a whim. He wanted to take his time with that one.

His ultimate prize wasn't going to be wasted on a whim either, he planned to take his time with her, to punish her for allowing herself to be pulled into the biker lifestyle. The monster wanted to teach her a lesson, before making sure she was pure.

His hunger was so wild in that moment he would have just taken any woman and ruined his plan. It was out of control, dangerous. The urge to pick a girl off the street and kill her was almost overwhelming. But he couldn't blow this on just some random slut, or on account of a filthy crack whore fail.

He was thinking through his list of women, he still had many girls to punish before he came to his final prize. He wasn't ready for any of them, when a girl who looked like a biker chick version of Dita Von Teese strutted past him, throwing him a sultry look as she stepped down from the sidewalk. Her black hair was pulled up in a burlesque style hair, her lips stained red, and she even had a small beauty spot.

She was definitely pretty... for a used whore, and the fact that her jacket claimed her to be a club girl for Black Alchemy.

The night had started to look up.

He couldn't believe his luck. He had no idea that they even let their whores out in the public.

This was just fucking perfect.

CHAPTER 11

Mila pulled away from Rooster. He had just given her the best kiss of her life and her mind was running with thoughts that she might have fucked up. She looked into his honey-brown eyes, passion melted her into his strong arms. A stuttered breath escaped her, nothing had ever felt this good before and Mila didn't know how to take it.

'Whatcha doin', Minx?' he asked. Rooster's muscular arms tightened around her waist and he pulled her even closer to his hard body. The swell of her breasts pressed against his chest and his hand cupped the small of her back. Mila's entire body was on fire with just a simple touch, not to mention she was desperately trying to regain her breathing.

'I'm not sure,' she whispered, finally aware that all eyes were on her now. Shit! What had she been fucking thinking? Oh right… she wasn't. She stupidly listened to her heart and groin, not her damned brain.

The growl that Rooster let out caused Mila's nipples to tighten in her bra and her muscles to tense. He bent down and threw her over his shoulder into a fireman's hold. She let out a surprised shriek of joy but was quickly silenced when his palm struck her ass.

As he spun on his heel, Mila caught a glimpse of the brothers of the

BAMC hanging around the parking lot. Many of them cheered and made crude hand gestures, she even spotted a few hearty hip thrusts and some very loud noises that should never be heard in public.

Mila giggled at their ridiculousness, enjoying how light-hearted they were. Her world righted as she was placed on her feet in front of Rooster's dark grey coloured Harley. The memories of the wind rushing through her hair, the fresh smell clinging to her clothes and the feeling of absolute freedom all came crashing back to her. The moment Rooster held out his hand and helped her on to the machine, Mila felt like she was home.

Rooster mounted the bike in front of her with a practiced grace that she never thought a man would be able to possess. All the warm and fuzzy feelings fluttered in her stomach, and this time she didn't tell them to go away. Maybe it was time to let this feeling for Rooster run its course. It was taking up too much energy to fight it.

Without instruction on where to place her feet, Mila enjoyed the shocked look on Rooster's handsome face when he turned around. She wrapped her arms around his waist and buried her face into the logo on the back of his cut, taking in a deep breath of the worn leather.

She felt her pulse in her throat when he throttled the engine. Mila scooted closer to him, her legs lining up against his perfectly. He took off without warning, and the world sped past them.

Warmth radiated through Mila's body and her heart was racing in her chest. This was way better than riding with Foghorn.

Mila couldn't tell where her body ended and Rooster's began. They were almost one person as they leaned together around the corners. She gripped his waist tighter as they continued through their peaceful town. While she hadn't been here long Bryson City had quickly become her home.

She closed her eyes and let the wind kiss her cheeks and the rumble of the bike flow through her muscles. She heard trees pass them in quick succession of each other, Rooster's palm left his handle for a moment and cupped her thigh.

She opened her eyes when she felt dirt bellow up around her legs. As they sped down the dirt driveway toward the clubhouse, Mila felt a little disappointed that the ride was almost over. She wondered if she would be able to convince Rooster to take her for another ride soon.

The gate was already open and she waved to the prospect on guard duty as Rooster pulled in a spot at the front of the clubhouse. One that was empty on purpose, clearly saved for the president of the club.

He didn't wait for her to climb off the Harley before he was up and holding his hand out for her to grab. As soon as her fingers slipped over his calloused palm, Mila was practically dragged through the clubhouse. She giggled at the cheers and the comments from more brothers as they climbed the stairs. She turned to see Gunner at the bar holding his drink to her, she grinned at him when her world turned upside down again as Rooster stopped abruptly and threw her over his shoulder again.

***

The wooden door to Rooster's private room came closer and closer with each hurried step, the weight of the woman over his shoulder had his cock swelling against the zipper of his jeans. He was about damn ready to explode. No woman, club whore or civilian had ever made him feel like this before.

Rooster dug the keys out of his pocket and unlocked the door enough for him to squeeze through, before he placed the woman currently digging her nails into his jean covered ass, on her feet.

But he didn't let her go, instead he had her up against the closed door, his lips taking hers in a savage kiss. The electricity that flew through him was intense, he had to lock his knees to keep himself upright. What the hell was it about this woman that made him even think like this?

Slowly he kissed down her lips, her jaw, her neck. Her needy response kept him going. She let out a groan that Rooster felt right down to his cock. Her skin tasted like sweet strawberries and fresh cream. He moved his hands from roaming up her back to go under her skimpy black top.

Fuck she was so fucking sexy.

He pulled at the fabric and ripped it over her head, Mila's blonde hair fell down around her face. He stopped for a moment and took in the sight before him, her eyes closed, lips apart waiting, wanting his next assault. God, she was fucking gorgeous. Rooster took a small step back and admired her in full, her stomach flat and toned, her tits barely held by the black strapless bra as she heaved in breaths.

He had no interest in wasting a second. He grabbed the top of the fabric and pulled down, exposing her pretty pink nipples. Rooster's groan was almost painful, she was so fucking beautiful against the door, her legs crossed slightly and her top half completely exposed. She rolled her tongue over her bottom lip, tasting his kiss. The look she gave him invited more.

His hands moulded to her full bust before he moved down and pulled the stiff peak into his mouth. Mila's hands ran through his hair, urging him closer without a word. Rooster was only too fucking happy to oblige, he hollowed out his mouth and heard the thump of the woman's head hitting the door. That wasn't even the best thing he heard, she moaned her need loudly and Rooster knew in that moment that he was in trouble.

He felt the pull at his scalp, her grip tightening every time his tongue lapped at her pebbled beads. Her body grew taunt against his, the smell of her arousal surrounded him.

Fuck, she was so ready for him. Rooster was sure that if he brushed against the seam of her tight jeans, his palm would be hot with her arousal. He refused to touch her any more to bring her over the edge.

Rooster's need for her had taken over his mind. He released her nipple with a pop and grabbed at her thighs, pulling her legs around his waist. He needed Mila on his fucking bed.

He pressed a small kiss to her lips before carrying her across the room. He tossed her on to the bed and marvelled at the girly giggle that escaped her mouth as she bounced, the joy on her face was something so different. She was just so fucking real. He growled at her again and stopped her mid bounce, his arm pushed down on her abdomen. The need to taste her burned inside him, it assaulted his senses, made him absolutely fucking crazy for her.

He made fast work of her belt and unzipped her jeans. His lips touched the waistband, the black fabric preventing him from seeing the rest of this woman. He breathed in the scent of her skin. His hands cupped her ass and hooked the belt band around his fingers, slowly removing them from her body. He pulled her lacy black panties down as well, leaving her completely naked in front of him apart from the bra around her waist.

He waited as Mila sat up slightly, unhooked her bra and threw it onto the ground. Fuck, he needed to get his mouth on her badly. His fingers brushed over her wet heat, slipping in and out so easily, she was so fucking hot and wet and her scent called to his body like no other had ever done. She turned him on so much that Rooster had no choice but to thrust his cock into the mattress.

God, it was so fucking painful against his zipper. Rooster was sure there would be an imprint.

Rooster breathed in her addictive scent, and finally spread her open. He licked her from asshole to clit. Her taste burst onto his tongue, the fucking sweetest honey. Mila bucked and let out a groan, her hands in his hair, holding his head in place. Rooster could tell that her clit was already fucking sensitive. His breathing increased, matching hers. No words were needed, he knew what she wanted.

He licked, sucked, nibbled and ate her out like she was the last thing he was ever going to consume. She tasted better than anything he'd ever had in his life. He knew if he died the next day, it would be with a big fucking smile on his face.

Mila squirmed beneath him, but he didn't want her to peak just yet. Rooster wanted to tease her, make her shake with anticipation. He pulled her body closer to his face, his hands cupping her ass again and adjusted her to an angle Rooster knew was going to drive her completely crazy.

The muscles in her legs tightened and even started to shake. He knew she was close, so fucking close. He pulled away and blew on her sensitive clit and started to ask her if she wanted her orgasm to rip through her, but he was too late.

Mila screamed and shuddered, her ass cheeks tightened in his hands, and she fell over the edge of bliss. With a growl if disapproval, Rooster lifted his head and stared at the woman laying out in front of him. Her breathing was laboured as her toes began loosening their curl around the bed spread. She had the most fucking gorgeous sex flush creeping over her face and down her neck.

Rooster moved up and kissed her cheek, revelling in the heat under his lips before he came in closer to her ear.

'You came before I allowed you to, you naughty Minx,' Rooster grumbled as he flipped Mila over and spanked her stunning, rounded ass. On instinct, he dipped his fingers between her lips, marvelling at how the fuck she was getting wetter.

The woman was nothing short of fucking perfection.

'Goddamnit, Rooster!' Mila groaned, earning herself another spank.

'Do you want my cock inside you, little Minx?' Rooster whispered into her ear. This time when he said those words Mila let out a sexy as fuck groan and thrust her pelvis toward his hand.

Rooster leaned back, trying to catch his breath. Mila reached out for him and the look of rejection on her face pinched his heart. He cupped her face, pushing her chin up with his thumb and kissed her briefly.

'Relax, Minx, I just need to take my cut off. Although I wouldn't mind it if my leathers smelt like your delicious pussy.' He winked. He enjoyed the way she sucked in a breath, Rooster fucking loved how much his words affected her. He shucked his cut and Mila watched as he hung it on the back of a chair. His tight, black shirt followed next before he dropped his jeans and reached for a condom in his bedside table.

Sheathing himself with it, he stalked toward Mila. She was laying on her back, as he leaned his knee on the mattress. She reached out for him and pulled him closer to her, lips attaching to his.

'Please, Rooster,' she whispered against his mouth. 'I need you. I need to feel you.'

Normally Rooster would flip the woman over and take her from behind. He couldn't afford any kind of complications or any woman getting the wrong idea about what they were doing, but with Mila he wanted to watch her come apart for him.

Mila's legs welcomed him as he positioned himself at her entrance. Slowly, oh so fucking slowly, he pushed inside her hot, tight, wet cunt. Rooster wanted her to take him completely, he wanted to savour each ripple of her walls against his cock. He wanted her to feel every inch of him, to feel he was bigger than most men.

Her walls tightened around him and Rooster pressed his head

into her shoulder to keep himself under control. There was no way he was going to blow his load like a fucking pre-teen but he also couldn't slam home like he wanted to. He wouldn't last a fucking second if he did that.

'Fuck me,' Mila cried out when he was finally fully inside her.

'I am, babe,' he teased back. Mila's legs locked around his waist, pulling him even closer. If that was even fucking possible. She wasn't holding anything back, not even her cries to God, as he picked up speed. Rooster could feel himself getting close, just as he could feel Mila's walls contract around him. 'Don't you fucking come yet, do you hear me, Minx? You only come when I say you can.'

Mila moaned, and Rooster grabbed her legs and held them over his shoulders. He flicked his thumb over her clit, matching every stroke inside her. He could feel the beginning of his orgasm creep up his spine.

'*Now,* Minx!'

She went off like a fucking firework, her walls gripped his cock oh so fucking beautifully. Rooster's body shuddered and brought him higher than ever before.

He fell on to his arms, careful not to crush the woman beneath him. He turned and lay on his side, took Mila in his arms and snuggled her close to him. Never in his life had he wanted to hold someone after they fucked, but his Minx was so different from any other woman in his past.

He wanted to feel close to her, her body against his, always, like this moment. With one hand in her hair and the other on the small of her back Rooster held the woman as she fell asleep.

CHAPTER 12

Mila's eyes didn't want to open the next morning. Panic set into her stomach when she wiggled her hip and realised her body was held down by something hot and heavy slung over her waist.

She cracked an eyelid and waited while she adjusted to the low lighting of the room, and the man lying next to her. She could feel his hard cock resting between her ass cheeks, she must have moved in the middle of the night, because she definably remembered falling asleep to the soft lull of Rooster's breathing.

Mila's stomach started to tense, as her mind ran rampant with the different possibilities when Rooster woke up. She was desperate for answers, but not enough to actually wake the man who was trapping her to his mattress.

The image of the way Rooster had his way with her body for most of the night assaulted her. It was like he couldn't get enough of her, and neither could she. Mila distinctly remembered reaching for him in the middle of the night.

She was exhausted, sore and oh so satisfied.

What the fuck had she done? Mila ran her hands over her face as she chastised herself. She had given in to her desires and landed herself in the bed of another biker. After her stint with Foghorn, she promised herself that she would never be with a biker again, they were nothing but trouble…

There went that promise. In spectacular fashion if she was completely honest with herself.

Mila honestly believed that if she fucked him and got it over with, then all would be fine. Except it wasn't fucking fine. She wanted him for another night, for another day, fuck she would settle for another shower. She just wanted more of him.

Mila attempted to sit up, hoping that in his slumber his arms would be loose and easy to escape. Instead, she yelped when he pushed more of his weight down on her.

'Where do you think you're going?' his morning voice gravelled. Mila tried to fight her shiver but the breath against her shoulder made it impossible.

'I need the bathroom,' she lied. Mila waited with bated breath until he finally loosened his arms from around her. She didn't waste any time and scampered over to the connecting bathroom.

She hadn't bothered to cover herself up, but as soon as the door closed behind her, she spotted one of his shirts in a pile in the corner. With a quick sniff test to make sure that it was wearable, she slipped the fabric over her head. Rooster's masculine smell surrounded her, causing her mind to go in to overdrive.

Mila gripped the sink and her muscles contracted. A reminder of what she and Rooster had done throughout the night swept through her. Fucking hell, the way he touched her, her body caught on fire with every swipe of his finger over her skin. It was something out of a fucking romance novel she sometimes indulged in.

Goddamnit! She needed to keep her wits about her.

Mila released the basin, ran the cold tap and splashed water on her face. It did nothing to help her raging mind. What Rooster had done to her, what she let him do. No man had ever made Mila feel the way the

BAMC president had. None of her previous partners had ever made her come as many times as the man on the other side of the door did.

God, she was so fucking screwed.

'Minx.' Rooster's voice penetrated her brain, causing her to jump slightly. His deep timbre held such a presence, it was no wonder he was president. She was so caught up in her worn thoughts that, when she didn't answer, a knock sounded through the door. 'Minx, you need to get your amazing ass out here now.'

Mila considered ignoring him, but this was also his room, his bathroom. He probably had a key for it and would be able to pop her privacy bubble.

She had completely forgotten that she was wearing his shirt and nothing else when she opened the door. Mila opened her mouth to speak but Rooster claimed her lips instead. His hand cupped the small of her back as he dipped her slightly. His chest was bare under her palms, his muscles rippling as she brushed her fingertips over his tattooed skin.

Rooster's hands wondered to her ass and pulled her close to his erection. With a nibble to her bottom lip, he raised his head. The gorgeous honey-brown eyes of his bore into her blue, like he was searching her very soul.

'I've got some club business to deal with, but I'm not fucking done with you yet, Minx.' He pressed his lips to hers again to stop any protest from coming out her mouth. 'Daisy, Ma, Angel and Mama Bear should be in the kitchen. Go down and grab some coffee and food. I'll be in my office or in church until later. I'll look for you, baby, whether you're here or somewhere else.'

Rooster gave her ass a cheeky tap before turning to his cupboard and pulling out a new, clean shirt. Mila just stood there watching him, stunned.

What had she gotten herself into.

***

Rooster's hands went to his hair and tugged. What he wouldn't fucking give to be back in his bed and have Minx wrapped around him. Even seeing her in his shirt this morning almost had him ignoring his VP when Gunner came knocking at his bedroom door. Instead, he was in his office with his best friend giving him the latest bad news.

'Who?'

'Naomi,' Gunner replied. 'She asked to go visit her mom, apparently her brother called and told her that the old woman didn't have long left.'

Rooster paced around the room, there was no way he was going to be able to sit back at his desk. What the fuck was going on?

'Where was she found?'

'Just outside the compound. Her cheek had been cut, and she didn't have any underwear on.'

'The fucker had taken her underwear?' Rooster asked. Gunner just scratched his close-cut beard, they both knew what had happened to their best sweetbutt. Naomi wasn't just a slut who could suck cock better than any whore they had, but she was also a decent person. She kept to herself, didn't cause any drama with the ol' ladies and the brothers. She knew how good she had it with the brotherhood.

She didn't fucking deserve to die the way she did.

Rooster kept pacing, his mind running a million miles an hour. He had to do something.

'Who else knows?'

'Stone found her while he was doing his patrol around the gate. Apart from that, only you, me and Diablo.' Gunner's voice deepened. Rooster knew that his VP wanted to kill the motherfucker who hurt a girl under the club's protection.

They both had two younger sisters, around the same age as the girls who had already been killed. Rooster was becoming more irritable and could barely hear his friend over the buzzing in his ears.

'Okay, good. See if you can get Stitches to look at her, if not call the badges on our pay roll. We need people we trust on this.' Rooster needed to keep his head. He couldn't afford to have anyone link this last murder back to the club. Fuck, this was turning into a complete shit show. Rooster slumped down in his seat behind his desk and opened up his computer.

Even though Black Alchemy was an outlaw motorcycle club, they had an agreement with the police department.

The BAMC never dealt in hard drugs to the skin trade, even when they first founded the club. In fact, the originals fought to keep it out of their county. The badges let them do their gun runs, turning a blind eye, so long as Black Alchemy kept the hard shit out of Bryson City.

But even Rooster had to admit that he had been second guessing his club's involvement in guns.

'There were two more things,' Gunner interrupted Rooster's thoughts.

Goddamnit, he wasn't going to get a fucking break any time soon.

'What?' Rooster groaned and looked up at his VP. He was so sick of all the bullshit. 'What now?'

For a moment doubt trickled into Rooster's mind. Maybe he wasn't as cut out to be president as everyone thought he was. Gunner didn't say a thing, instead he picked up something and threw it on to the desk. It was Naomi's sweetbutt rag, it was supposed to give her protection. Instead, it was slashed into pieces, the club's insignia destroyed with cuts and dirt rubbed into the white thread.

Fury ran through Rooster.

This called for revenge.

'What's the other fucking thing?' Rooster asked, not able to tear his gaze away from the leather in his hands.

'Rag's mother was killed last night too.'

Fuck!

Rooster hung his head in his hands. Everyone knew the woman; she was once a beautiful sweetbutt that pre-teen boys fantasised about. When the drugs became her life she was kicked out of the club and left to fend for herself. Even though she was estranged from the club, anyone could make that connection, and the blame would be hard to shake off.

'You think it was the same guy?'

'Yeah... he's taking bigger risks. Two girls in one night.' Gunner rested his hands on his hips, hung his head and shook it. Rooster couldn't stop looking at Naomi's ruined leathers.

'I'm calling a church,' Rooster said and stood behind his desk. 'Get all the brothers in the chapel. Now. Make sure that the only badges that look at Naomi are the ones we have in our fucking pockets. You pull Rags aside, tell him about his good-for-nothing mother and how she died. We don't need him learning about this during church.' Rooster slammed his fist into the desk, leaving a slight dent in the wood, blood already pooled at the knuckles.

Gunner left the office and Rooster followed behind. The chapel was empty, and he was still hesitant as he took his father's seat at the head of the table. It had been a long time since they called a full club church, but the brotherhood needed to know what the fuck they were up against.

Brothers spoke over one another as they filled into the room, oblivious to what Rooster had to say. Obviously, Gunner hadn't given anything away about the dead sweetbutt, but as soon as Rags trudged in Rooster gave his brother a nod, to acknowledge his loss.

Rags returned the gesture but Rooster could see that his brother was struggling with the information.

The rest of the members didn't pay attention to anything, they were all talking about the latest custom jobs or the latest hook ups. Typical biker discussions.

Rooster crashed the gravel on the table as the last brother squeezed into the small room. He was still impressed that the entire room silenced with just a crack of the gavel against the wood. Rooster looked around the room, he wanted to make sure that all eyes were on him.

'Brothers, there have been another two women killed by the Bryson City Slasher. One of them was Rag's mom, the other… the other was Naomi.'

The outrage was deafening. Cursing and slamming of fists rang through chapel. Pounding the gavel to the table again, he gained control again.

'That's not all,' Gunner said. 'We have received a message from this asshole.'

His VP held up the dead sweetbutt's ruined leather, the room erupted and more abuse came flying.

'Kill him!' Ghoul shouted, his hands clenched and flew in the air with a few more of his brothers. 'This is a fucking message for war!'

'Where the fuck is this asshole?' Diablo grumbled, fury tinged his normally even voice.

'We don't know where he is.' Rooster brought the room to silence again. 'The total of this guy's victims is now six. The first three were just random hook ups from The Blind Hog, then Amanda, now we've not only lost a former sweetbutt, but a current one. Brothers, we can't just worry about Jokers Ace anymore. We've got a serial killer and he's hunting our women. We need to find him before he hurts another one under our protection.'

Rooster's brothers all nodded their heads, and one of them started to thump on the table with his fist. Soon all the men were hitting the table in unison, a sign of the men being on board with the president's commands.

'Black Alchemy forever!' Rooster shouted.

His brothers chorused back. 'Forever Black Alchemy!'

CHAPTER 13

Mila peaked her head out of Rooster's room hoping that she didn't encounter any of his brothers. She cringed at the thought of running into any of them and being the butt of their jokes.

She knew that she shouldn't have given into Rooster, but that man was an enigma. There was just something about him that she couldn't stay away from, almost like there was an elastic band connecting them and every time she tried to pull away Mila was snapped back to his side.

Mila continued to creep through the surprisingly empty hallways when a loud roar from the room she knew never to enter halted her for a moment. When no one came rushing out in a panic she continued the familiar exit route. She could see the front door from the second-floor landing. This might be her chance to escape, despite Rooster's warning of finding her if she was at the clubhouse or not.

Mila slowly stepped down the staircase Rooster had carried her up the night before. The three-story schoolhouse's first floor had been gutted out, making a large room. It was complete with pool tables, dart boards, flatscreen TVs and black leather couches. The bar that she sat at a few months ago near the entrance was being wiped down by one of the prospects. Mila smiled against her will, as she replayed the night she met Rooster at that very bar.

Tank popped up from behind the bar with a rag in his hands as he joined his fellow prospect wiping down the wood and glasses. The other young man with the prospect patch on his leather cut flicked his wet rag toward Tank who almost dropped the glass he was holding. Mila watched in amusement as the boys started to play wrestle with each other.

Mila reached the bottom of the stairs and looked around. Her curiosity was getting the better of her, so she stepped to the side to explore the rest of the common room – as she had dubbed it – when the prospects looked up from their match and nodded behind her.

'Prez said to tell you that the ol' ladies are in the kitchen,' Tank said and pointed to the door beneath the stairs before turning back to his task, playfully shoving the shaggy haired prospect. She was sure that she had taught both the boys at one point earlier in the school year.

Mila turned to where he pointed, and the sound of loud feminine laughter erupted from behind the door beneath the staircase. Immediately, Mila was reminded of *Harry Potter*, and being the boy under the staircase. She wondered how so many people could fit in such a small space.

Nervously, she opened it and came face to face with Angel. The smile on the woman's face was toothy and should have looked fake but it had a genuine feeling to it that Mila found contagious.

'Hey, Mila!' Angel greeted with a hug. She was wearing a black apron with large angel wings on the front, and she had a smirk on her face so similar to her brothers as she pulled away that told Mila it didn't go unnoticed what she was wearing. Especially since her face was bare of makeup and her hair was in a messy ponytail.

Mila tried not to let her jaw drop to the ground when she took in the room in front of her.

It was huge like a commercial kitchen but had a large dining table off to the side with mismatched chairs. The tiling was a little outdated and so was the wooden slab on the kitchen counter.

A rectangle window looked out over a large backyard. A large sink and more counter space sat below the window, with a stainless-steel stove and oven tucked into the corner. A hanging rack with pots and pans dangled above it. To the left of the counter space was a white door that Mila guessed led to the back yard.

Mila was still gawking at the large space when Daisy came walking in through the swinging door separating the kitchen from the rest of the clubhouse. She didn't know how to deal with these feelings that were bubbling up inside her. There was a warmth in this building, and the kitchen felt like the heart of the compound.

'What are you doing here, Miss Rice?' Daisy asked. Angel's smirk deepened, and the shade of red on Mila's cheeks grew brighter.

'Angel, Daisy. You leave the poor girl alone,' an older woman scolded while buttering some bread. She was a short, stout woman dressed in leather and jeans. Her top was modest, but low enough for a tattoo of a crown around the same insignia that was on the back of Rooster's cut to be seen over her heart.

Her hair was a similar shade of brown as Rooster's and the other two girls, but her eyes were blue. Mila surmised that Rooster got his mesmerising eye colour from his father. She wondered what Patriot looked like. She had seen a few photographs hanging around the clubhouse, but she hadn't had a chance to study them properly.

Mila made a mental note to rectify that as soon as she was given the chance.

'You must be Mila,' the woman said as the two girls went back to what looked like a production line of sandwiches. Leaving Mila to the mercy of the ol' lady. 'How are you, dear?'

Mila was taken aback by the smile on her face, it was similar in kindness to Angel's but there was a sadness in her eyes. A few wrinkles around her eyes and mouth, Mila wondered how her own mother looked now. If she would recognise the woman who birthed her if she passed her on the street. The woman reached Mila and pulled her into a large hug, and for a moment she was stunned. She went completely still as the warmth from Rooster's mother's hug spread through her body. She hadn't had a mother's hug since she was a freshman in college and Mila had no idea why she wanted to burst into tears.

Mila glanced back at her student and Angel, neither of them were looking her way. Although they were stifling giggles, Mila imagined that was just how siblings interacted with each other.

She liked it.

The woman kept staring at her like she was expecting a response. It was only then that Mila remembered she *was* asked a question.

'I'm so sorry. Everything here is so overwhelming.' Mila grinned, allowing her blush to grow further down her neck. 'I'm good though, thank you but, umm. I didn't catch your name.'

'Oh, how silly of me. I'm Queenie.' The woman smiled, it explained the crown tattoo, but Mila still couldn't place where she might have met this woman before. She just felt so familiar. 'I'm Daisy, Angel and Rooster's mother.'

'The matriarch, right?'

'Former, now that Rooster is the president. I'm the former matriarch of my Finnigan's club. Patriot… Patriot's club.' Queenie turned her head downwards and Mila noticed the woman's shaky hands, how her lips would tremble when she pressed them together.

'I am so fucking sorry for your loss, Queenie,' Mila said, wishing like hell she could take Rooster's mother in her arms and comfort her. She didn't even realise that she had sworn until Daisy let out a loud giggle. She should have been embarrassed, but Mila couldn't bring herself to care, especially with the way that Queenie and Angel were fighting smiles of their own.

Queenie picked up Mila's hand and patted it. 'Thank you, dear. That means a lot. Why don't you take a seat, I'm not sure how long these boys will be and it would be nice to have a fresh face around here.'

'For a change,' Daisy muttered to herself. Queenie threw her daughter a scathing looking, but Daisy didn't flinch. Something that Mila found very entertaining.

She spent most of the morning talking with Queenie and the Bates sisters about everything to do with the club. Mila was entranced by how they all seemed to respect the club and how the club respected their women in return.

Mama Bear joined their little kitchen meeting closer to lunch time while Angel was making cookies for the brothers. Mila had never seen a batch of cookie dough so big before, but she had to admit that she snuck a taste or two while Angel wasn't looking.

She enjoyed that her personality was able to be free here, there was no need to pretend to be anyone else but herself. It was refreshing and almost enlightening.

Mama Bear didn't spare Mila a glance, until Queenie sat a mug of steaming coffee in front of her and the old woman squinted her dark eyes. 'We feeding the sweetbutts now, Queenie?'

'She's not a sweetbutt, Mama, she's Rooster's new girl, and she's Daisy's teacher,' Angel said, glancing over at Mila over her shoulder.

'She's a civi?' Mama Bear was shorter than Queenie but looked fit beneath her leather and denim uniform. Her hair was short, but still feminine and Mila instantly felt like she was the grandmother that she never had. The older woman continued to scrutinise Mila, to the point where she was squirming in her seat. Finally, after what felt like minutes, Mama Bear smiled and nodded her head. 'She has much to learn, but she will be good for him.'

Mila's jaw went slack and she looked around the kitchen. The younger girls were giggling to each other, while Queenie just stood there with her arms crossed and grinned. Mila went to defend her non-existent relationship with Rooster when the man in question came swaggering through the swinging door.

'Ladies.' He grinned before placing a kiss to his mother's cheek. 'Hope I'm not interrupting anything important, but would it be alright if I steal Minx away for a little bit?'

Rooster gripped Mila's hand and brought it up to his mouth for a chaste kiss. Her heart sputtered in her chest at the sweet gesture in front of his family. Mila honestly didn't know how to act around the women anymore. When no one said anything, Rooster threw her a wink and his handsome smirk before he pulled Mila to her feet, dragging her out into the common room.

'Don't fuck this up, Rooster!' Mila heard Mama Bear shout. 'We like this one and want her to stick around.'

Mila immediately put on the brakes. Her heart was in her throat and she was getting the sweats. They had only spent one night together, there was no relationship, there wasn't any reason for her to be spending so much time with these people.

She glanced up at Rooster who was pinching the bridge of his nose. He let out a patient sigh in response. Mila opened her mouth to tell him that it was about time she headed home when Angel came out of the swinging door with a mountain of cookies on a plate.

'Pay no mind to Mama Bear, she's old and never really learnt – or cared for that matter – about social norms.' Angel gifted them with her megawatt smile as a man with long brown hair pulled back slightly in a man bun and a strong jawline covered in a tidy goatee approached them.

He leaned down and pressed a kiss to Angel's hairline as he stole a cookie from the huge pile. Mila watched the interaction and was fascinated when the man tucked Rooster's sister into his side.

'Hey,' he finally greeted Mila. 'I'm Rubble.'

'Mila,' she replied, still shell-shocked by everything that had happened this morning. She knew that getting involved with a biker again was bad news and yet she didn't fucking listen to herself and now she was dealing with the fucking consequences.

'Hey, Angel!' a voice yelled from the other end of the common room. 'Throw us a cookie! Betcha can't make it into the coffee again.'

Mila turned to see a blonde-haired biker with a large grin on his face. He held up a black coffee mug and had a twinkle in his eye that just screamed mischief.

'Last time I did that you spilled hot coffee all over your hand and had burns,' Angel yelled back with a roll of her blue eyes.

'Nah! Nah! I let it cool this time, c'mon, Angel. Give us your best shot.'

'Just remember you fucking asked for this Ghoul,' Rubble mumbled around his own cookie as Angel reared back her throwing arm and lobbed a cookie toward the teasing biker. Rooster took this moment to tug Mila up the stairs again.

The last thing she heard when she got to his room was Ghoul yelling that his coffee spilled all over his hand and Angel loudly claiming, 'You didn't leave your coffee long enough!'

Mila smiled to herself at the family dynamic of the entire clubhouse. It was nice, but she had to remind herself that this wasn't permanent. She and Rooster had a fun night, but that was it. She had to try and get back to her everyday life. When she glanced at the persistent president Mila's heart sunk to her stomach, nothing about the way that he was looking at her screamed temporary.

Yep, she was fucked.

CHAPTER 14

A soft knock on his office door caused Rooster to look up from this computer. His scowl followed through in his words of entry, but that quickly went away when Minx's long blonde hair came into view. She carried a small smile on her face and even looked a little nervous. Rooster's heart pounded in his chest when he realised that she had ventured out to the clubhouse on her own, probably to see him.

'Your mom said that you've been in here all day.' Her sweet voice danced through the silent room.

Rooster pushed back his chair and threw a smirk Minx's way. He chuckled when she rolled her eyes but that blush crept up her cheeks. He watched as her hips rolled and swayed in that tight skirt she insisted on wearing to work. Fuck, Rooster loved how she moved.

He adjusted the growing erection in his jeans. He ached for her weight against his thighs, so he crooked his finger toward her and patted his lap with his other hand.

Minx's blue eyes darkened as she slid onto his lap gracefully. She swung her legs over the arm rest and her arms went around his neck. Her nose rubbed against the skin near his Adam's apple. Rooster's cock swelled again, he loved that this woman had a fixation with his neck. She was still in her teacher get up, her tight pencil skirt didn't allow her to straddle him like he would have liked.

'Whatcha doin' here, Minx?' His hands splayed out on her ass to keep her close to him.

'I thought you could use a break,' she whispered, her hot breath against his throat. It wasn't the answer that Rooster was after, he wanted her to admit that she wanted to see him. That she drove out to the clubhouse because she wanted to see him. One of her hands moved down, her fingernails lightly grazing his chest and his stomach as it ventured down, effectively erasing all thought from his mind.

'You're playing with fire, Minx,' Rooster growled, as Minx ran her tongue up his throat. The tightening in his pants got worse. He growled again and claimed her lips. Without breaking the contact, he had her up on his desk. Minx wiggled as he pushed her skirt up her thighs, spreading her legs.

A hot rush of blood stirred his cock to attention. 'No panties, Minx?'

'I took them off in the car.' She moaned as he teased her pussy lips with the tip of his finger. Rooster lost all sense of control, he was fucking beside himself with lust.

He went down on her glistening lips, flicking his tongue over her pulsing clit. Minx's hands slammed on the paper covered desk and her head threw back, exposing her delicate throat.

Rooster noticed that she had taken her hair out and it was down around her waist, touching the wood. Fuck, he loved it when he could tangle his fingers in the strands.

He glanced up and watched as her breasts rose and fell at a fast pace. Her face was the image of pure ecstasy. Fuck, he loved how responsive she was.

Rooster's hard cock strained against his zipper, but the picture *of Minx splayed out on his desk, letting him pleasure her, was a freaking wet dream. One that would not be leaving his spank bank anytime soon.*

The words on the computer screen in front of Rooster blended together into one big fucking mess. He needed to get his head back in the game, he needed to find out who was killing the women associated with the club, but he couldn't get his mind off Minx.

God, she was just so perfect.

It had been a week since Rooster first had Mila in his bed and then taken her again the next day on his desk. He couldn't get enough of her. When he told her as such, Minx took him into the shower with her and impressed him with her skills on her knees.

The woman had continued to come to the clubhouse almost every night to satisfy the both of them. Rooster still hadn't gotten her to admit why she kept coming back, but he would eventually.

Now, he was back behind his desk. He blinked at the screen, adjusting in his seat, trying to tame his cock's reaction to the memory. He had to get the numbers to stop blurring and start making some fucking sense. There was so much to do but all he could think of was sinking himself into Minx's hot, wet, pussy again. The thought of her naked and beneath him, had him grabbing his regular cell phone.

Rooster: Dinner tonight. I'll pick you up at 7

Rooster smiled to himself, he had no idea why he wanted to take this woman out for dinner first. He was sure that Minx would come to the clubhouse after she finished her work day, and would surely get some without having to feed her first, but he wanted to get to know Mila better.

Minx: Sure! I'd love to go to dinner, thank you for asking :)

He shook his head, goddamn snarky mouth of hers. This woman

was fucking trouble, in the best kind of way. He was looking forward to the fun.

Needing to get away from the screen, Rooster sat on the leather couch wedged into a corner of the office. The day's newspaper was sitting next to him on the cushion and he was met with the face of Naomi. The blank stare of the printed photo lifted the hair off the back of his neck and sent a quiver through his stomach. They hadn't been successful with keeping her murder quiet. Rooster wanted to know who leaked the information, but that was a problem for another day.

So many problems, so little time to actually face them all.

Why the fuck was his club being targeted? This sick monster was obviously too much of a pussy to come after one of them, so they were going after the women… but why?

There were too many questions, why did he start with the hang arounds and the one-night stands? Was he working himself up to something, or someone in particular? Could this have anything to do with the ongoing war with the Jokers?

Rooster ran his hands through his hair and gave a slight tug, trying to loosen the strain on his brain.

The club was now down a sweetbutt. Normally that wouldn't be too big of a problem, but since Rooster didn't want any more civilians targeted, he had shut down the parties. He knew his brothers were becoming restless, they would need something to do or at least would need to find someone who was as good as Naomi. They needed to bring the club back to business as usual and do it fucking fast.

Rooster was tempted to call an entire club lockdown, families included, but he didn't think it was the right move just yet. He knew who was protected by his club and, since the brothers had been informed about the maniac targeting their families, most of the men had taken their own precautions to protect those they loved the most.

Rooster would just have to hold off on the lockdown, even though his gut was screaming at him not to ignore the pit in his stomach.

Rooster hadn't felt like this before seeing a woman, since his first time. He felt like he was fourteen again. He raised his fist to knock when the door swung open and there stood his Minx. Looking fucking beautiful. Rooster forgot how to speak for a moment and stammered out a gruff, 'Hello.'

He had never seen her look like this before, and while he liked her in her teacher and weekend clothes – in fact, they turned him the fuck on – Minx dressed like a biker chick made his cock strain uncomfortably against his zipper at lightning speed.

Fuck, this was either going to be the worst or the fucking best night of his life.

Minx's long blonde hair was pulled back in her signature ponytail, only this one was loose at the bottom of her skull, with cute fly aways framing her face. Her makeup was a bit heavier than usual, her berry-coloured lipstick standing out against her light skin. Rooster appreciated the way her jacket was tight across her breasts, the black skinny jeans that she matched it with moulded to her legs. Paired with studded boots and her outfit was complete.

It almost had him panting at her feet.

'Fuck me,' Rooster groaned. His tongue was practically hanging out of his mouth, but he didn't give two flying fucks. He wanted inside his woman, and he wanted it really fucking badly.

'Not right now.' Mila smirked and patted his face, her soft hands a contrast to his slight stubble. 'But later tonight might work.' She winked at him.

She turned her back to him to make sure that her cottage was secure and the image of his name on the back of her jacket sprung into his mind. Rooster didn't know where that thought had come from, but he had to admit, it didn't give him the sweats like it would have done with another woman.

Rooster waited until she locked her door and turned to face him, He lowered his head and claimed her lips with his own. He tried to fist his hands into her hair and growled when he couldn't feel her silken strands through his fingers. He yanked out the hair tie, setting her blonde waves free.

He swallowed her moan of displeasure and tilted her head to the perfect angle. Minx's lips moulded to his in a way that completely fucked with his head. She moaned, snaked her arms under his cut to hold on to his waist and melted into his kiss. Rooster almost said *fuck it* when it came to dinner, she had tempted him beyond reason. He was so fucking close to kicking down her front door and taking her against the entry way, but his girl deserved more.

He wanted to give her more.

Rooster pulled away and groaned at the loss of her against him. 'You look fucking amazing,' he said as he cupped her cheek and leaned in for one more chaste kiss. Mila's hand ran up his forearm and held his hand on hers. Rooster pulled their now joined palms and led her toward his bike.

CHAPTER 15

Arrogant man, Mila thought as a smile played on her lips. She wanted to retort, even opened her mouth to do so, but it was drowned out by the bike's powerful purring engine. Dust flew up around them, leaving a cloud in her driveway as he took off into the night.

Mila let the wind sweep over her face and tangle her hair. She tightened her arms around Rooster as they took sharp corners and when he would break the speed limit.

They rode down the highway for about ten minutes before he pulled off down the exit and to the main road of the neighbouring town. Rooster slowed down as they pulled up in front of a lovely little Mexican restaurant. Mila honestly would have missed the small hole in the wall place if she hadn't been invited by Rooster.

The man didn't even wait for her to get off the bike. He swung off the seat, helped her off the machine and into his arms. Rooster pressed his lips against hers, and the rest of the world just disappeared.

His lips were searching but soft, and she wanted them all over her body. Mila wanted more, but she was also very aware that they were in a public place. Resting her hands on his chest, she pushed just slightly. A groan came from his throat, but he moved far away enough for her to attempt to think clearly.

'So where are we?' Mila asked breathlessly, trying to create more space between them, but Rooster was having none of that. Draping his arm over her shoulders, he steered her toward the entrance.

'*Restaurante la Familia*,' Rooster said with a perfect Spanish accent. Mila turned to the man and tried to suppress the shocked look that spread across her face. 'Rubble's grandmother owns this place. He's a member of the club and claimed my sister Angel. The old woman had always wanted to open her own restaurant with genuine Mexican food. So, this is it. Abuela literally beat it into all the brothers on how to pronounce the name properly. I'm sure I've still got some scars from that lady's wooden spoon.'

Mila barked out a laugh but quickly covered her mouth with her hand. The image of a younger Rooster getting swatted with a wooden spoon, by a little old lady at that, was downright hilarious.

Rooster quirked an eyebrow but grinned at her. He shook his head with a chuckle as he opened the door for her like a gentleman. As soon as they were both inside Rooster placed his hand on the small of her back and led her through the restaurant. The girl behind the hostess stand smiled at the both of them and guided them over toward a booth at the back of the room. A bottle of beer and a margarita were already waiting for the two of them.

'Come here often?' she asked raising her eyebrow.

'Not as much as I would like.' Rooster smiled at her scepticism. It seemed like nothing fazed this man, and Mila didn't know if she liked that or not. He must have sensed her shutting down on him, because he continued, 'Don't go looking at me like that. I don't bring anyone – except for my sisters and my mom on occasion. Angel is always on about the margaritas. So I had the hostess have it ready for when we got here.'

Rooster pushed hair from her shoulder and pressed a kiss to her cheek. Mila didn't know what to say, she was stunned by his tenderness but also by how much power he had. Even outside Black Alchemy, it honestly scared her.

Continuing with the gentleman act, Rooster pulled her chair out and tucked her into the table. They talked for hours, and Mila was highly entertained by his stories about the people he had grown up with, and the adventures his father took him on when he was a boy. He talked about the mischief that he and the brothers around his age got into when they were teens and the life that he had grown up in and wanted to improve as an adult.

Hearing those stories, Mila longed to have someone in her life she was close to, to have stories to tell and laugh about. Unfortunately, she didn't. Even as sad thoughts tried to permeate her mind, the way he smiled was enough to fill that void for the moment. She felt a closeness to the Black Alchemy president. A man she had never felt this way about before.

They were still waiting on their dinner order when Rooster's phone started ringing. When he threw her an apologetic look, Mila's heart fell.

'What?' he barked, and she watched as Rooster's easy-going nature changed before her very eyes. He turned into the BAMC president she had heard so much about.

'Is anyone hurt?'

That question made her skin prickle. She perked up from behind her margarita glass, her mind going to the newspaper articles that had been going around. Of course she had heard the rumours of the Bryson City Slasher going after the woman associated with the motorcycle club. There had even been speculation that Black Alchemy were helping the murderer. Mila would be lying if she said that the coincidences between the club and the murdered girls hadn't sparked her interest, but her worries were immediately quashed when she saw the pained expression on Rooster's face.

'Seriously? No, I meant how badly are your guys hurt?' Rooster growled before he threw some money on the table, it was definitely enough to cover the bill and then some. At least the man tipped well.

That was a green flag.

He grasped Mila's hand, and practically dragged her out of the restaurant. Throwing her an apologetic look as he went, his phone still firmly planted on his ear. 'Fuck! Okay. I've got to get back to my clubhouse. I'll be there in thirty with some of my boys.'

And with that Rooster hung up.

He didn't say anything to her, he just hauled her through the parking lot and lifted her on to the Harley. She had no idea what the fuck was going on, Rooster didn't stop to explain anything all the way back to the Black Alchemy clubhouse. Mila had been so lost in her own thoughts, she wasn't sure what questions to ask, numb to their march up to the schoolhouse.

'I'm taking you up to my room. Stay here tonight, okay? Don't open the door to anything. Only I have a key, so you'll be safe,' Rooster said as he escorted her across the yard. Mila wasn't having any of this bullshit. This was the first time he had spoken to her since he got that call and all he was doing was commanding her?

'So what? You're just going to lock me up like a caged animal?' Mila wrenched her hand from his hold and crossed her arms under her breasts. Shit, she should have worn something more supportive than a tank top under a fake leather jacket.

'Minx, please. There is some shit going down with another club starting up outside of Blowing Rick. I'm going to be taking most of my officers with me and, since you don't have a patch on your back, the other brothers might think you're fair game. Having you in my room is more for my peace of mind than anything else.' Rooster came closer to her and brushed a piece of her blonde hair away from her face.

'Why don't you just take me home then? I won't be in the way and you won't have to worry about me,' Mila said, breathing in his leather and wind scent. God, it wasn't fair for him to smell this good when she was trying to make a point.

'Because I would worry about you more if you weren't under the clubhouse roof. I know you're safe if you're in my room. I know that no one can harm you if you're here, Minx. I can't be worrying about you while I'm trying to fix whatever fuckery is happening with the Dark Angels.' Rooster pressed a kiss to her hair to finish his speech.

Mila didn't know how to handle anything that was happening, so she nodded. She was still unhappy about being locked in his room, but she would be lying if she said that his speech hadn't moved her.

They ascended the stairs quickly and he threw her one of his cocky smirks before he darted out the door. She heard the click of the lock before Rooster's very loud call for his officers broke through the surprisingly quiet clubhouse.

CHAPTER 16

Mila only rested her head when she got tired of pacing around the room. She dressed in one of Rooster's clean shirts to wrap his masculine scent around her.

Her fears licked at her ankles as she scrambled into the large bed. She had to lull herself to sleep by remembering the stories Rooster told her. Mila imagined him young and happy, horsing around with his brothers and getting up to all sorts of trouble. She imagined him with Angel, Daisy and Queenie, and all the warmth of a family they shared throughout the clubhouse. She inserted herself in there too, making up her own little scenes where everything was bright and unburdened and... whole.

She imagined him as a high school student throwing girls his panty melting smile. In one moment she saw her own younger self walking the halls of Bryson City High, blushing when the cute biker boy winked her way. Mila could see her walking with Angel and her friend rolling her eyes at the fact that her brother was hitting on her best friend.

Maybe it was a selfish invasion into his life, maybe a hopeless, unattainable dream, but at least in them, he was safe. At least in them, she was with him. With these false memories, she sunk into a deep, deep sleep.

But she couldn't fight off her subconscious. The deeper she fell, the more her sweet visions morphed back into the reality that was stalking around town. Rooster could get a call and leave the family dinners, he would mount his beast and ride off, and she would be left alone again. Shadows would creep in through the windows, chase her down. Her wrists would sting with the burn of a tight rope, her heart would hammer in her chest, and someone else, someone out there, would take his place whether she liked it or not.

A figure slipped into the king-sized bed behind her. Her whole body jerked awake. She had trusted Rooster when he told her that no one was going to be able to come into the room.

A thousand thoughts ran through her mind. What if he had been hurt? Did someone know she was staying with him? What if the Bryson City Slasher had broken into the clubhouse? Mila thought back to those women in the papers and on the local news. The last three *had* been identified as having been associated with the BAMC.

'Relax, Minx. It's me baby.' Rooster's gravelled voice in her ear made her panicked heart ease some. His arms came around her middle and pulled her closer to his half naked body. She let out an audible sigh of relief when he snuggled his face into her hair.

Mila knew that she shouldn't be getting this comfortable with him, that this could end very badly with her heart not just broken but destroyed. Yet, she couldn't make herself get out of the bed.

She lifted her head to turn over in his arms, laying her head in the crook of his arm. Her hand between them came up to trace the tattoos on his muscles, a large skull with a BAMC bandana covering the bony mouth faced back at her covering the left side of his chest. The skin beneath her fingers rippled for a moment before she slung her arm over his taut stomach. Rooster's own hand threaded through her hair and he pressed a kiss to her forehead.

He held on to her tight, she wasn't going anywhere. Not that she wanted to escape, being in his arms was a better feeling than anything she had experienced. Rooster tangled their legs together and for the first time Mila noticed that, not only were his thighs insanely muscular, they were also tattooed. She couldn't make out what they were but the black and white markings across his slightly tanned skin was an impressive sight.

A girl could definitely get used to this.

She knew that was impossible. One day soon Rooster was going to get sick of her and she was going to be left to pick up the pieces of her reckless heart.

They both woke later that next morning, reaching for each other. Rooster whispered dirty words of praise in her ears, as he stretched his fingers over her stomach. Mila made a mental note, as he played her body like an instrument, to wear his large t-shirts more often.

It was closer to mid-morning by the time Rooster and Mila emerged from his room. He had convinced her to call in sick to school, or rather she lied and told them that she had car troubles. She wasn't going to make her first couple of classes, however, Mila did insist on going in for the afternoon periods.

She was still waiting for a proper response to her question about what happened the previous night, but all Rooster gave in return was, 'Club business, Minx.'

To say that Mila was thoroughly unimpressed by that answer would be a fucking understatement. Then the man had the fucking audacity to tell her to go to the kitchen with the other ol' ladies while he went to church. That sparked an argument with her. How fucking dare he tell her to go to the kitchen like some little woman?

'It's like women's rights never existed!' She fumed as Rooster pushed her back into his room.

'I didn't mean it like that, Minx.'

'Then pleeeease, oh mighty president. Tell me exactly what the fuck you meant.' Mila exacerbated and stuck out her hip, her hands landing on them with attitude. She noticed Rooster's eyes flare with heat at her sassy response. Mila had to admit that she liked it... a lot, but she couldn't get distracted from her argument.

'For fuck's sake, Minx. The ol' ladies are spending time in the kitchen. I don't know why they do, I just thought you would like to spend time with someone with some brains, that aren't looking for their next fuck. I'm going to be in meetings for the rest of the morning, and I'm not ready to say goodbye to you yet.' Rooster shook his head and hung it low as his hands mimicked hers on his hips.

Mila was almost ashamed to admit that she was touched by his little speech. In all honesty, she wasn't ready to say goodbye to him either. She wasn't ready to admit why that was just yet, just like she wasn't ready to admit why she had been spending so much time at the clubhouse instead of keeping her distance from this man.

'This is all new to me, Rooster. Sometimes I'm going to need a little less mansplaining and a little more patience from you,' Mila said after she slinked her arms around his waist, and gently moulded her lips to his. Rooster sighed into her kiss and rested his forehead against hers when she pulled away. For a moment it was just the two of them, no club business in between them.

'This is new to me too, Minx. I don't normally get involved with citizens.' Rooster brushed her lips against hers again.

'I'll go and see your mom and sisters. You have a meeting to get to.'

'Thank you, Minx.' He left her with one last kiss and walked her down the stairs toward the kitchen. Mila noticed just how empty the common room was. Normally there would be women and bikers all around the big room, sometimes in various stages of undress or drunkenness, but today the men were missing, and the women were separated into groups.

One girl grabbed Mila's attention. This woman walked around in a leather skirt that was so tight and short that the bottom of her ass was almost hanging out. Her top was a simple tank top that enhanced her small breasts. Long silky black hair hung halfway down her back, the ends had been dipped in hot pink paint.

She had a sass about her that Mila admired.

She smiled at the girl and was shocked when she received one back. She didn't even realise Rooster had let go of her hand until she chuckled above her.

'I'll see you later, Minx,' he called out and rushed up the staircase.

Mila huffed before turning back to the woman with the black and pink hair. She was a tiny thing, barely five foot three. She walked by Mila with a tip of her head and opened the door to the kitchen, holding it wide for Mila to step through.

'In 'ere mate!' Mila was taken aback again, she couldn't place the strange accent.

'Mila dear!' Queenie called out and embraced Mila in a motherly hug that made her smile but miss the times with her own mother. 'Thank god you're here. We have someone to introduce you to. This is Lyric.'

'G'day.' Lyric smiled at Mila.

'Ahh... hi there,' she greeted in return. Mila turned to Queenie just as a cup of coffee appeared in front of her along with a plate full of food. Breathing in the amazing aroma, Mila took her first sip.

'So, you're the prez's woman?' The accent was broad and, as she spoke more, Mila finally picked it as Australian. It still made her almost choke on that first heavenly sip.

'What?' Mila hacked. 'No, I'm just...'

She had no idea how to answer the question. She and Rooster had been with each other almost every night for a week and a day, but neither of them had talked about being exclusive, and why would they? They were just having fun... right? It was just a week of fun...

'We're just friends,' she finally said, but as soon as the words left her mouth she flinched.

'Well, you guys must be *hella* good friends.' Lyric winked causing Mila to blush and Queenie to laugh. Both the women looked at the matriarch as she laughed. The sound was nice to hear. Something she had noticed was that the former matriarch didn't so much as crack a smile let alone laugh.

Soon Angel joined the women in the kitchen. Her own mug of steaming coffee cradled in her hands, her brown hair looked to have been recently mussed up and a satisfied, dazed look was in her eye. Lyric saw the tussled looking Angel and immediately started to razz on her.

Mila was so immersed in the conversation and the feeling of sisterhood that when her eyes caught sight of the time above the oven, she nearly dropped her now empty mug.

'Oh shit! I've gotta get to school!' She scrambled to her feet and was about to run out to her car when she realised that she didn't have a vehicle. God, how did she lose track of time like that? She was sure that she had set an alarm on her phone.

Her phone.

Which was still in Rooster's room.

On the second floor of the clubhouse.

No wonder Mila didn't hear any annoying twinkling sound during her time with the women. She heard some of the men outside in the common room and thought she would be safe to ask Rooster for a ride to the high school.

'Shit,' she said as she took in the common room. It was completely filled with the brothers moving around with a sense of purpose, the sweetbutts were noticeably absent from the large space. She glanced around the room, looking for the president. When she spotted him, he was leaving the clubhouse with Gunner striding next to him.

'Rooster!' she called out and pushed her way through the crowd. She reached out and touched the soft leather of his cut, stopping him in his tracks. 'Where are you going?'

'Club business, Minx, I can't say much more than that.'

'Well, do you think you could at least drop me off at the high school? I have to teach.'

'Minx…' Rooster gave her a warning look. His lack of interest in what she needed and was saying was really pissing her off.

'It was your idea to go out last night, you even insisted on driving, and now I don't have any mode of transportation.' Mila cocked her hip to the side and dared the man in front of her to leave without saying anything.

Rooster scowled at her, and for a moment Mila was worried. She knew that if she wanted to be taken seriously by him, she had to stand up for herself, but she also knew that she couldn't make him lose face in front of his men. Mila opened her mouth to apologise when Rooster shouted for Lyric.

The black-haired woman stopped picking up trash and walked over to them.

'You've got your cage, yeah?' Rooster grumbled.

'What the fuck is a cage! Are you going to lock me up! What the actual fuck, Rooster!' Mila's voice trilled, on the verge of stomping her foot, all thoughts of apologising leaving her mind with rage.

'Hahaha! Ah Mila, a cage is what these guys call a car,' Lyric said, coming over and standing next to Mila. A fierce red blush swamped over her face. She had just embarrassed herself in front of the whole club. She could feel the eyes of all the men who were trying hard not to watch the spectacle she had created.

'Oh… okay,' she mumbled, not able to look Rooster in the eye.

'It's alright, Minx.' Rooster's fingers tipped her chin so that their eyes caught, giving her a quick kiss that had her heart melting. The kiss ended too quickly for Mila. His big hands cupped her face so that she continued to look in his honey gaze. 'We're going to need to talk about your temper later, but I have to go. If I'm not there to pick you up when school ends, Lyric will be.' Rooster offered her a small smile before shutting the door behind him. Most of the brothers were already outside.

The roar of about twenty bikes was deafening, and even with the walls of the clubhouse between them, it was enough to make Mila cover her ears.

'Come on, Mila,' Lyric said, waving Mila to follow her. She led her outside to an amazing black muscle car. Lyric started the car with a few hearty revs, spun the wheels on the gravel kicking up rocks and dirt, before she threw it into gear and sped out of the gates. This tiny dark-haired biker babe knew how to handle the power of the pony.

Mila clung tight to the 'holy shit' handle. Lyric didn't waste any time, speeding out of the gates.

'So, do you know much about the club life?' Lyric said, causally looking over at her passenger while driving at speeds Mila was still getting used to.

When Mila shook her head, Lyric took it upon herself to educate her. 'Well for one thing, if a brother tells you that something is "club business" he can't tell you anything about what he is doing because he is trying to protect you.'

'So, even if I'm in trouble and Rooster fixes the problem, I can't know he did it?' As the words left Mila's mouth, she had a hard time processing the information. What kind of thing was Rooster getting up to for her to be in danger?

Lyric continued to talk. Every word was something new for Mila to comprehend. Before she knew it, Mila was at the high school, shaken by the speed lesson in biker life and mentally trying to switch to face her students and the staff members.

Nothing would be the same again. Mila wanted to remove herself from Rooster and the rest of that world she had entered into. But as she thought more about it, she didn't want to…

She was in deep.

CHAPTER 17

Rooster slammed his shot glass down on the bar. The asshole had gotten away from them. He wasn't sure how he managed to do it, but the Bryson City Slasher got away.

Diablo, his enforcer, had gotten a tip from one of the homeless bums who were desperate for a bit of cash. Rooster rested his head in his hands propped up on the bar. Maybe the intel was bullshit because it was a junkie looking for his next fix.

He and his boys had wasted a trip to a rundown, barely functioning cabin on the outskirts of town. When they got there, the place had been scorched, there was no way of telling if anyone had been there, past or present.

Rooster slapped the bar twice and another round of whiskey hit his palm. He groaned when the smoky taste ran down his throat. He could be spending the afternoon in bed with Minx, but she had to get to work.

God, he couldn't stop thinking about the woman. Rooster had no idea if it was the way she writhed against him when he first entered her, or if it was the sounds she made when he was about to become undone. Hell, even her sassy, feminist mouth was a fucking turn on. Everything about her made him crazy. He had never felt this way about a woman before, let alone a fucking citizen. That fact should have turned him off, but she was taking to the club life like she was born into it. Fuck, he should have explained to her what they were doing, then again there wasn't much he could say.

There was a reason the men of the BAMC didn't tell their women anything. They had to keep them safe, especially if the badges came knocking. Plausible deniability was the best option in case something did happen and the badges got involved.

He sat with his brothers at The Blind Hog, the club's roadhouse. The regular crowd was a nice background noise while his brain ran through all the scenarios. Rooster downed another drink and nodded to the offer of another whiskey. He needed the strong burn to help clear his thoughts.

It didn't help.

'Rooster.' A voice he never thought he'd hear again sounded out through the roadhouse. He turned and shook his head at the fucking audacity of some people. His grandfather on his mother's side was a long-time member of the Jokers Ace, who had never been able to amount to anything other than being VP to a founding member's bloodline.

Bulldog looked exactly as his road name suggested. His round face and squinty eyes made Rooster thankful that he took after his father. His older brother Steven hadn't been as lucky.

The entire room froze as more men from Jokers Ace walked into the bar. Rooster tried not to smirk, it really sounded like a bad joke. After some posturing from a few members that Rooster didn't recognise, Decay came and stood right in front of him.

'If it isn't the biggest fucking chicken president in Black Alchemy history,' the man breathed out, hitting Rooster with the scent of rotting teeth. The president of Jokers Ace was well known for his fascination with the decomposition of dead bodies, but that wasn't why he got his road name. The man was rotting from the inside out, personal hygiene was not at the top of this man's list.

'What the fuck do you want?' Rooster asked. He didn't move from his stool but he did pull back so that he wasn't dealing with the rotting smell. The asshole had some fucking big balls to walk into The Blind Hog like he owned it. Hell, like he and his fucking club was even welcome.

'We're just here to talk. We hear you have an affiliate club starting up in Joker territory.' Decay sneered and Rooster tried to reign in his rage. He'd watched this man kill his father, but there wasn't much he could do in the crowded bar. The Blind Hog might be BAMC owned, but it was welcome to anyone who wasn't a fucking Joker.

There was a time and place for revenge. This was not it.

'There isn't much to talk about because it isn't on Joker territory. Do you need to see the map again, dick-cay?' Rooster taunted and stood tall. He wasn't going to lose face in front of his men. 'Maybe you should have a look at the treaty while you're at it...'

He watched out of the corner of his eye as his brothers stood beside him, some reaching for blades while others had their guns at their sides. Some prospect Jokers whispered to each other and mirrored their stances. Rooster waved his hand at his brothers to stand down. If he didn't defuse the situation soon, it was going to get ugly, and fucking fast.

'I'm sure the Dark Angels are fine setting up where they are, outside of Blowing Rock. I think you should all turn around and go back to your clubhouse.' Rooster crossed his arms, fighting an exhausted sigh. He was so over this bullshit.

There was silence for a good minute and Rooster thought that Decay was actually going to leave quietly. As if in slow motion, Rooster watched one of the Jokers raise his own gun and shoot toward Black Alchemy.

Rooster watched as the bullet hit the top of the wooden frame around the bar, almost like a bell sounded, and an all-out brawl started between the two clubs.

Brothers were using blades and brass knuckles to defend and attack. Rooster had his own blade in his hands. The small knife had been his father's and grandfather's before it was his to wield.

He watched as one of the new bartenders went down with a Joker, the kid had no chance. Rooster fought his way over to help him, distracted enough to feel an ice-cold blade pierce his skin. Looking behind him, he smelt the rotting smile before he saw it. Decay had stabbed him.

Rooster winced as the asshole twisted the knife, pain seared, the noise in the room slurred as his cheek hit the floor. The pressure of the man's dagger was still in his shoulder.

The fucker stood over him and laughed a like a mad man.

'Shame what's happening with those girls from your club, chicken shit. It's a damn pity that you missed out on finding the guy killing 'em today, isn't it? You have to wonder if the total is going to pass – what is it – six? What're you gonna do when more turn up dead?' The searing pain in Rooster's shoulder didn't distract him from the rancid smell of Decay's breath.

But one question was playing on his mind more than how often this guy brushed his teeth.

How could this asshole know about those girls? The first three had only been hood-rats, hang arounds of the club that were looking for a good time, and civilians looking for a one-night stand to fire up their boring everyday life.

It was only the last three who were connected with the club.

'What do you know about the fucker committing these murders?' Rooster somehow managed to get out. He could feel the pressure of the blade in his shoulder, the fucker behind him was trying to put him on the floor.

'Only that it was a good thing we got to him before you did.' With that Rooster was shoved completely on the ground and hit with a pair of brass knuckles.

***

Lyric had picked Mila up from the high school right on time. While she was glad to have finally made a friend outside of work, she was also disappointed that Rooster hadn't finished his club business.

Mila sat at the bar to wait with Stone slinging drinks in front of her. The young prospect was relaying a story of when he told his father he was moving to North Carolina and joining a motorcycle club. The young man was getting more animated with every word and hand gesture.

'So then Pops says, *"You'll come crawling back when you fail. Mark my words boy"*.' Stone chuckled at his own impression of his father, before he picked up a rag and cleaned some glasses as he shook his head.

Mila halted at the sound of motorcycles roaring into the lot. She stood in the doorway, but something felt off.

The brothers rushed in like a bomb went off. Some were limping while some were helping other members over the threshold.

'What the fuck?' Stone cried out, and jumped the bar before he dashed over to one of the brothers who was struggling to breathe. Mila scanned the room for Rooster. He was nowhere amidst the chaos. She tried to make sense of what was happening around her, but in the tumult of noise it was virtually impossible.

'Where the fuck is Stitches?!' Gunner's voice rose clear above the noise. It was so loud Mila jumped, her hand clasped at her thumping chest. Her heart peaked when she saw Rooster slung over his friend's shoulder, unconscious. His face was splattered in blood, the rest of his body was covered in guts and gore, like something from a slasher film.

Only one person – an older man – moved about the room with any purpose. He pushed Mila out of his way and instructed Gunner to take Rooster upstairs. Mila followed on autopilot through the door to Rooster's room and hurried into the adjoining bathroom in search of a wet cloth. Anything that might help.

She rested her hands on the cold, yellowing sink. Catching sight of her own reflection she noted the look of fear in her eyes. Her work clothes were askew, and her hair was falling out of its usual ponytail. Mila ripped the hair tie from her head and pulled it back into a messy bun.

She emerged, ready to help and trying to look braver than she felt. Rooster was lying on his stomach and the old man was stitching up his back. Holding the wet fabric in her hands Mila stood watching, terrified.

'Girl, come here,' the man said, not taking his eyes off his task. With tentative steps she moved. As she reached the man, she was surprised when he grabbed her hand and led her to dab the blood off Rooster's body. She was careful not to hurt him. Mila was almost thankful that he was still passed out.

The man nodded his head and finished up. Gunner pulled the old man into a brief bear hug. Mila heard him utter the words, 'Thanks, Doc.'

'All in a day's work.' With a slap on Gunner's back, he left.

Mila flopped into the seat the doctor had vacated, allowing the cloth, now soaked red, to slop onto the nearest surface. Gunner stood by the window, arms crossed over his body, making him seem bigger than he already was.

'Is he going to be okay?' she asked, looking from the giant before her and to the man lying on the bed. Rooster's hair had fallen over his gorgeous face, and Mila wished to see that dangerous glint in his honey irises. He made her insides turn upside down. She wanted to see those eyes, the life they bred. She brushed his stray locks aside.

'He'll be fine.'

She looked at Gunner's steely expression.

'What happened?' Her eyes pulled back to Rooster. She continued to touch him and make sure he was still warm.

Gunner shrugged and shook his head.

'What the hell? Your president is lying here unconscious, and no one can tell me a damn thing. Even pig grunt, Gunner, shaking your head isn't telling me a single damn motherfucking thing.' Mila stood as tall as a five-foot-eight woman could, ready to tell the six-foot-seven vice president what she thought about him and his code of silence. But Rooster's hand grasped hers, pulling her back down.

'It's club business,' he groaned. 'I don't want you knowing anything that will get you in trouble. I don't want the badges to start asking questions.' Rooster's voice sounded like gravel.

Even seriously injured, the man was still barking orders. Mila wanted to argue.

'I was scared,' she blurted out.

Rooster shook his head slowly. 'You don't ever have to worry about your safety around us, Minx.'

'I wasn't scared about me, Rooster. I was scared I would fucking lose you.' Mila brushed his hair out of his eyes again, wanting to see all of him. She had just admitted what she had been avoiding since she met him. It should have scared her more, but really, it was a relief that everything was out in the open.

'This is no tea party life, it's dangerous, Minx. What happened at the bar is a normal part of it. Babe, I don't know if this is the life for you.' With a grunt, Rooster managed to get himself up on his elbows.

'You shouldn't be moving.' Gunner's gruff voice pierced the room.

'I'm good.' Rooster puffed as he sat up, craning his head. 'Now, get out. Mila and I have some things to discuss.'

The sound of her law-given name from Rooster's lips caused her heart to beat out of her chest and she could feel the warm wetness trickling down her cheeks. What if he didn't return her affections? Then they really were just wasting time together and she had gotten too invested.

Rooster's blazing stare distracted her from watching Gunner leave the room. He swiped a stray tear from her cheek. 'Baby, what's wrong?'

'You called me Mila. That's not my name… not anymore. It's Minx.' Mila swallowed a hiccup and snuggled into Rooster's palm. His warm hand was resting on her cheek. He pulled her closer to him, resting their foreheads together.

'You think you can handle a world like this?'

'I can handle anything as long as I have you by my side.'

CHAPTER 18

A dinner at his mother's house was the last thing Rooster had time for, nor did he particularly have the patience for his sisters. With the new information that the fucking Jokers Ace was helping the Bryson City Slasher now brought about a new danger to the families of Black Alchemy.

Rooster had seriously considered having a lockdown, but he didn't want to alert anyone who might be watching his family. Especially the goody two shoes cops wanting to make a name for themselves. He couldn't afford to have anyone looking deeper.

Rooster needed to catch this bastard soon, too many women were getting hurt.

Not to mention his shoulder still ached like a son of a bitch.

Rooster shook out his arm as he pulled up to a stop next to Angel's SUV, the one that Rubble insisted on her driving. His sister always claimed that it was a mom car and she was still young. She should be driving something sporty, but she always lost the argument because her man wanted her to be safe.

Rooster shook his head, with a smile playing on his lips and walked up the familiar path up the front porch.

His mother's small frame was waiting at the front door. He could feel her sad smile before he saw it, his father's death was something that his whole family was working through. Rooster didn't know how his mother was able to smile but he was glad to see it.

'Hey, Ma.' He jogged up the front steps and grabbed her into a tight hug. Rooster tried to hide his wince from the pull of his stitches, but he knew that he couldn't hide anything from his mother. He kissed her cheek and walked into his childhood home.

'How are you, sweetheart?' she asked softly as she followed him inside. He turned back to her, and her eyes told a different story than her question. She was curious about his Minx.

'Ma…' Rooster mocked a warning. She knew to butt out of his love life. His mother knew not to discuss club business so it had to be about the girl. Ever since he had brought Mila to the clubhouse, and she kept on coming back, Rooster knew this conversation was inevitable. He still planned to avoid it all the same.

Things had changed between him and Mila since she sat by his bed after the club doc had cleaned up his back. She was a staple in his life that Rooster wasn't sure he could live without anymore. That thought alone scared the shit out of him, but he was ready to jump headfirst into whatever this thing turned out to be.

Rooster knew that his mom would have more questions, but he was already prepared with subject changes.

'Smells fucking amazing, Ma,' he said as he approached the fully set dinner table. It was overflowing with food, so much fucking food for just four people. 'Did you invite the whole brotherhood?'

'No! I just wanted to have the family together tonight. You know what today is, don't you, Rooster?'

He did.

It was the day many, many years ago at Sturgis that Patriot 'kidnapped' Queenie and brought her back to the Black Alchemy clubhouse. They had been exchanging letters back and forth for months before, they met at a different biker rally but neither of them knew who each other was. After a run in with the Jokers, Patriot took one look at Queenie and asked her if she wanted to be with him. She said yes, and the rest was a messy history but it was their history all the same.

Rooster knew the story by heart.

They all did.

He grabbed his mother again and hugged her tightly. He hated seeing his strong and fierce mother so broken. He had been so sure Patriot was going to live on for many more years. Many more years for his mother and father to spend time together.

'I know you miss him, Ma. We all do.' Rooster kissed his mother's cheek again, before moving further into the house. His sisters were watching some bullshit, girly reality TV show. He snatched the remote from behind Daisy's head and switched it over to the Sturgis live stream.

'Rooster!' Daisy screamed. Angel groaned beside her and slid down the chair that she had planted herself into.

'Why are you so annoying!' Angel whined, making Rooster chuckle.

'Because that's my job as your older brother.' He smirked and ruffled both his sister's heads, earning him some shrieks, hand swatting and more complaining. He couldn't stop the laugh as he helped himself to one of the beers in the fridge.

'I don't know why we're surprised,' Angel remarked.

'I know! He does it every time!'

'And you love me for it!' he called back, chuckling when his sisters started laughing. It was a good feeling to hear their girlish giggles.

'Where's your man, Angel?' he asked as he plopped into his favourite chair before he took a large sip of the cold beer.

'He's at the clubhouse. Apparently, he needs to get the route for this weekend's club run done before he can have any kind of fucking fun.' Angel's glare had Rooster rolling his eyes, he was used to his sister's antics by now. He *had* told Rubble to get the run finished, he just didn't realise how serious his future brother-in-law would take it.

Rooster guessed he should give the man a call and invite him over for the family dinner. He knew it would make his sister happy, and his ma would be over the moon to have another biker in the house who could eat as much as she cooked.

Rooster: stop with the route and get over to the family home. Ma's been cooking a fuck ton.

Rooster didn't wait for a reply, he wasn't able to wait because his mother called the three of them for dinner and her rule since smart phones had been invented was still the same: no phones at the dinner table. They were to eat as a family and converse as one too.

Rooster went to take his seat next to Angel. His father's seat sat empty. He glanced at his father's chair. He could still see his father grinning at his daughters as they bickered over something trivial. Patriot would be holding Queenie's hand, sometimes bringing her palm up to press a kiss of affection. When Rooster had become older, he and Patriot would discuss a few things around the clubhouse. Looking back now, Rooster saw that the questions his father was asking him over dinners would prepare him for his own take over.

'Oh no, Rooster,' Queenie said, as she sat at the other end of the table. 'Rubble can take your chair, you sit at the head of the table.'

Silence descended over the dinner table, and Rooster glanced at his sisters. Daisy sat in her unofficially assigned seat with her mouth wide open. Queenie just took her seat and stared at Rooster, waiting for his response.

He hated the idea, but Rooster sat at the head of the table. He was more uncomfortable in this seat than the one at church.

The spread in front of him could easily rival some of the Thanksgiving dinners hosted at the clubhouse. He was still waiting for Rubble to erupt through the front doors, while his sisters and mother were talking. He had no idea what about. They had gone through at least three different topics in the past thirty minutes, but his mind wasn't on the ladies in his family.

It was on the beautiful Miss Mila Rice.

God what was it about this woman that had him thinking about her as his woman? Even just the thought of her blonde hair and how it spilled out on his chest as she slept was enough to keep him distracted. How her eyes would flutter just moments before she awoke, and he got to see those ocean-blue eyes of hers.

Fuck, she was the most enticing woman Rooster had encountered in a long fucking time.

'Dylan?' Rooster's gaze moved from his plate to the only woman who would ever get away with calling him by his law-given name. His mother's blue eyes stared at him, a bowl of salad in her hands. Two other sets of blue eyes, practically identical to each other landed on him as well.

Shit, he had been so lost in his own thoughts, Rooster hadn't been paying attention.

'What?'

'I asked you if you know anything about the monster killing the women affiliated with the club?' Angel asked, as she dished some mashed potatoes onto her plate. Her giant engagement ring flashed in the overhead lighting.

'Wait... were they affiliated with the club? I thought they were all just hood rats?' Daisy commented, plucking up a string bean and biting into it.

'You know I can't say anything,' Rooster said, taking the bowl that was passed to him.

'Since when did the Bryson City Slasher become club business?' His youngest sister ignored Rooster's unspoken command to stop asking questions.

'Since he started going after club-protected women,' Rooster let slip, wincing when silence filled the room again. Fuck, this was an awkward as shit dinner.

'Club business?' Queenie joined his sisters in their questioning. 'You mean like an ol' lady?'

'No,' Angel said immediately, not giving Rooster a chance to answer. 'We would have heard something. Plus, we were all accounted for in the kitchen this morning... Come to think of it though, I haven't seen Naomi around lately. She hasn't helped out for breakfast in a while.' Angel pointed a look toward Rooster. 'And I know she hasn't been cast out, she doesn't cause drama and the brothers like her too much.'

It was no secret that Angel and Naomi weren't the best of friends. Naomi had been Rubble's favourite fuck before he claimed Angel.

'Naomi's dead.' Rooster shifted uncomfortably in his chair. 'The Slasher got to her.' He sighed, there was no way he could hide it from his family any longer. The silence around the table was palpable, none of the women knew what to say. Rooster had shocked them all.

Daisy was about to open her mouth to speak when the doorbell rang. Rooster watched his teenage sister jump out of her seat.

'I'll get it!' she yelled over her shoulder.

Was she expecting someone?

Rooster was on the fucking edge... until he remembered it was probably just Rubble.

But then his sister's scream reached his ears. Rooster was up and out of his seat, the gun that he had tucked into the waist band of his jeans, out and ready. As soon as he rounded the dining room corner, he froze.

'What the fuck?' The words fell from his mouth, loud enough for Steven and Daisy to hear.

'Really, little brother? Surely you would have learned some manners by now?' Steven smirked, and sauntered into the place like he owned it, making Rooster's blood boil.

'What the fuck are you doing here?'

'Rooster? Who is it?' Angel and Queenie followed behind them, both of them seeing Steven at the same time. A sudden joyful sound came out of Rooster's mother as she joined her eldest and her youngest in a hug. 'Steven, what are you doing here?'

'I couldn't get time off until now,' his brother said, awkwardly returning his mother's hug. 'I'm sorry I couldn't get to Dad's funeral.'

'You didn't even fucking call,' Rooster said, rooted to his spot, gun hanging limply from his hand as he stared at the commotion happening. He hated that his brother was being welcomed back with open arms. Patriot had been dead for over four months now, how could his biological brother not even call? Club brothers from the other chapters around the states had taken time out of their busy schedules to come and pay their respects.

Rooster had needed the help with his mothers and sisters, god knows he has way too much on his plate with his new role in the club.

Where the fuck had Steven been... what had he been fucking doing?

'I couldn't,' Steven said as he pulled away from his mother and sister. Rooster took in his older brother. Steven's brown suit looked old, his arms were crossed over his lanky chest and his foot had started to tap.

'You couldn't call your family when your own father was killed?!' Rooster's fury was reaching a whole new level. He wanted so desperately to punch his brother in the face.

'That's enough, Dylan…' Queenie scolded.

'Mom told me how he died, it was his fault for putting his stupid club before his family.'

An audible gasp came from the women and Rooster's rage seeped through his skin.

It was the last fucking straw.

A growl came from his throat as Rooster charged forward, rearing his arm back and slamming it right into his brother's stupid, dog looking face. Unable to stop, he shoved his poor excuse for a brother out the front door.

'How fucking dare you!' He raged and landed another punch, putting Steven on his ass on the front porch. 'You have no idea what your father did for the club. Let alone what he did for his family. You fucking left! You have no fucking right to talk about Pops like that.'

'I didn't have a choice but to leave,' Steven declared and spat blood on the stoop. 'Dad wasn't going to let me live my own life, he just wanted me to be a brother and fuck his whores. What kind of legacy is that? Are you proud of yourself, little brother?'

Rooster lunged and tackled his brother, continuing to pound him into the ground.

'Dylan!' Queenie shrieked, her horror rang in Rooster's ears.

'Prez!' another gruff drawl came from the driveway. Rubble made his was over to support his brother.

Seeing the fear in his mother's and sister's faces, Rooster pushed off Steven and got to his feet, dusting off his cut.

Fuck, this was too public and the club couldn't afford to have the president locked up.

Steven staggered to his feet and drew his sleeve across his nose, wiping blood and snot across his cheek. Steven caught sight of his sister cowering in the arms of her biker fiancée. 'Are you going to allow this, Mom?' He gestured to Angel. 'Is this who Dad was going to allow her to marry?'

'You gave up any kind of right to say a fucking thing about how Angel *or* Daisy decided to live their lives when you fucked off at eighteen for California. You left!' Rooster shook his head. He held his composure, though triggered by his brother's entitlement. He glanced over at Queenie.

'Sorry about dinner, Ma.' He walked toward his bike. He heard his mother and sisters calling out to him, but Rooster was done. He didn't have control over his anger toward Steven, and he was afraid he'd show his hurt.

He needed one thing right then and there.

He needed his Minx.

CHAPTER 19

Mila's eyes strained against the pile of white papers in front of her, she really hated grading. It was the only part of her job that she could easily live without. She stretched her crossed legs and body with a moan, before she finally moved from her comfortable spot on the couch and headed for her kitchen in search of more wine.

She was pouring the rest of her bottle into the glass when a loud thumping at her door had Mila jumping and letting out a small shriek. Who in the world was trying to get her attention at this time of night?

Mila peered through the window in her lounge room. She jerked her head back and her mouth fell open at the sight before her. She almost spilled her wine all over her front. Rooster stood on her porch, his eyes were hard, and it looked like he wanted to punch something… or someone.

She scrambled off the window ledge and opened the door, slowly, unsure what to expect. She wanted to greet him with a hug, but something made her stop. Something wasn't right.

'What are you doing here?' Mila asked, cautiously. Rooster didn't say anything, he just stood at the threshold of her house as if he was waiting for permission to enter like some old-school vampire.

Mila offered him a sip of her wine, but he just shook his head. She grabbed his hand and dragged him into the warmth of her entry way. She closed the door and pulled his head down to meet her lips. She felt him give into her kiss. His groan reverberated against her lips, and she opened up for him even more. Rooster ran his tongue over her bottom lip. He was hungry. She could feel his need. Words be damned.

Mila pulled and led him through her house, up the stairs and into her bedroom, careful, tender and slow. She walked him backward, her hand on his chest and kissing him as she gently pushed on his hard chest. Rooster leaned on his back, his arms outstretched beckoning for her.

She climbed on top of him and settled herself against his hard cock. His jeans hid nothing, and the thin pink satin of her pyjama pants was a thin barrier against it. She drew her body up slowly, along the length of his tight jeans, and breathed out the pleasure of it.

Rooster's hands gripped her hips and held her firm against him, guiding her to move over him in slow, glorious motion. Mila leaned her head back and let out a sigh.

God, she needed the barrier of material gone. She wanted flesh on flesh and from the look in Rooster's eyes, he was right with her.

Fuck, if she didn't enjoy every single moment of it.

Rooster fisted her long blonde hair in his hand and, with a slight pull, he had her flush against his chest, his mouth claiming hers. Mila's hands gripped in his shirt. Goddamn, she could do this all night with this man. She whispered as much between his kisses.

'What, dry fuck? That's not all that's gonna happen tonight, Minx,' he growled, making her giggle.

Rooster's hand went back to her hips, helping her move over his groin. She groaned when the tip grazed her already sensitive clit.

Suddenly Mila was under Rooster, and he was pulling at her hair, tilting her head so that he could take her mouth in a way that he wanted. God, Mila had never felt this way with a man before. She didn't want to admit to herself just how deep her feelings went for him.

Rooster's hunger intensified, his rough hands grazing against her waist. Pushing up her tank top, his fingers brushed over a ticklish spot, making Mila squeak and pull away, which only made the smile on Rooster's mouth turn more devious.

'You got yourself a bit of a weak spot, huh, baby?' Rooster said against the skin between her neck and her chest. He started to suck and lick his way down her body as she wiggled out of her top.

'You're my weak spot, Rooster,' she purred.

'You're in trouble then, Minx.'

He stopped the moment her breasts sprung free. Admiring her body, he pressed his palm, warm and firm, over her stomach, spreading his fingers as he felt his way up her torso, leaving trails of fire in their wake until his palms spread across her skin and brushed over her stiff peaks. He pinched at her nipples and Mila arched into his hands, needing the branding heat, while his hot wet tongue traversed the curve of her neck.

He pulled back from her, leaving her needing his next kiss. He chuckled at her needy groan of disappointment and moved like a predator over its prey, sniffing and nibbling at her stomach, leaving his mark on her pale skin.

Mila's hands tangled in his hair, anticipating his goal. Pre-empting with greedy need, she pushed his head further down her body as she lifted her hips. She felt his breathy smirk at the waistband of her pyjamas. He made quick work of removing them but slowed at the lace edge of her tiny panties. He leaned down and kissed her lace covered mound.

'Rooster, don't tease,' she whimpered. He leaned in and dragged his teeth over the lace this time. Frustrated and pleasured by his torment, Mila lifted her hips to meet his mouth and he pulled the lace down exposing her wet pussy. He wasted no time and Mila's pleasure grew as his tongue moved up through her slit and circled her pulsing clit. She closed her eyes and gripped handfuls of his hair, Rooster wasn't going anywhere until she got her fill.

He didn't disappoint, lapping at her, suckling at her clit, fingers inside her, sensations she'd never known before and she could feel it coming, it was coming. Breathtaking pleasure, it was coming.

Her legs fell apart, she pulled at his hair and cried a long, loud moan. Her body shuddered and buckled as she came, breathing out his name over and over.

Rooster moved his muscled frame up her body, a proud boyish grin graced his face, and he didn't give her leave to speak. He lowered his entire weight on her and slid his hot erect cock along her engorged folds.

Breathless she begged him. 'I need you inside me!'

Rooster's molten honey gaze burned into her blue. She saw the urge, his primal urge. It matched hers. He held her gaze, she opened her legs offering him entry and he obliged, slowly slipping deep inside her.

He pulled back and relished in a second slow thrust. Slowly he pulled out of her inch by painful inch and just as deliberately thrust into her. Mila was wet and ready for him. Hot and willing.

She grabbed his ass and dug her nails into the skin. He couldn't contain himself any longer and buried himself deep inside her. Lost in his lust, he pounded into Mila. She watched his desire.

Rooster grabbed her wrists, pinned them over her head and entwined their fingers together. He had created such an intimate moment that Mila came so close to blurting out something she knew she would instantly regret.

She felt his pulsing orgasm just as another blissful climax took her over the edge along with him. With their eyes locked on another, Mila's lasting moan was captured by Rooster's mouth. She caught his groan into her as his seed filled the condom and a whimper came from her throat.

***

Mila lay there trying to catch her breath, Rooster's body heavy on hers. His chest matched her rhythm. Slowly he came back and rolled over, taking her with him.

Rooster held Minx close, her warmth and her softness were exactly what he needed to calm himself down after the shit show at his childhood home. Filled with endorphins, Rooster could finally relax as his woman spread her nimble fingers across his chest and caressed his skin. The electricity he felt that first day he met her was zipping through his body and warming it better than any shot of whiskey he'd ever had.

'Your name isn't really Rooster, is it?' Minx's voice was like velvet, breaking the comfortable silence.

'It's just a road name,' he grunted. He didn't know how to explain to her that he wasn't Dylan Bates anymore, if he was ever really Dylan Bates.

He was Rooster, just Rooster.

'What is your real name?' Mila asked, looking up at him with her sea blue eyes. Her piercing gaze fluttered through her long lashes, making them seem huge, but he knew what she was doing.

He did have two younger sisters after all.

'Not gonna tell you,' Rooster said, feeling the sweetness of the after-sex glow subsiding. He didn't want to talk and braced for the bitching to start, like it always did when a woman asked him that question.

But it didn't, she stayed silent.

Instead, her hand went to his tattooed chest. Her finger started to trace the skull with the BAMC bandana tied around the mouth. Rooster closed his eyes, enjoying the way she touched. He liked that about Mila, she touched him so freely and he fucking enjoyed the electricity that buzzed over his skin.

'Do you want to talk about it? What got you so shook up tonight?'

He looked down at the woman in his arms. Rooster wondered how she read him so well. What scared him the most was that he wanted to tell her everything. Not only that, but he was ready to admit feelings he never thought it possible to feel. He needed to touch Minx more, so he buried his fingers into the soft, silky, blonde strands on her head. Rooster buried his nose in her hair and took in a breath of her creamy, berry scent.

'Forget it,' Minx whispered when he didn't answer. Instead, she snuggled in closer to his chest. Her lashes fluttered over his chest and a sigh escaped her mouth. 'You'll tell me when you're ready.'

'No...' He stopped her, hooking his forefinger under Minx's chin and forced her to look at him. 'I want to tell you what's going on baby.'

Rooster moved himself up and rested on the headboard. She moved with him, her arms coming around his middle. Just having her in his arms gave him the courage and strength to tell her about his brother and his father.

'I have a brother, Steven. When I was fourteen, Steven had just turned eighteen. He and my pop were becoming more and more estranged each day and there was some serious tension. When I was a kid, I loved going with my pop to the clubhouse, but Steven... he hated it. He hated everything that the clubhouse represented, but Pop used to take him in the hopes he would get his eldest to prospect. Steven straight up refused, even going as far as calling it a place of sin where men disrespected women and got commended for it. I think he called Pop the sweetbutt's pimp and accused him of cheating on Ma.'

Rooster shook his head. Steven knew as much as he did that Patriot would never cheat on the woman he risked everything for. When the Jokers accused the BAMC of stealing their princess, the war became more tense. Patriot wouldn't have risked his family for just some woman he was going to cheat on years down the road. Queenie and Patriot were endgame.

He glanced down at Minx to gauge her reaction. She looked interested and concerned for him, but kept up her light petting, encouraging him to continue.

'Pop tried to argue with him that Steven knew what he was saying was complete bullshit, my brother just stormed up the stairs and told the family he was leaving for California for college. Ma cried for days when she found out, she hated having a gap like that in the family and hoped that if she just spoke to Steven, get him to change his mind, he would stay. Soon as he graduated, he moved to LA. We haven't seen him since, and then he had the fuckin' nerve to show up out of the blue. Right after Pop's death and expected to be treated like a fucking hero. Fucking selfish prick.' Rooster's breathing increased.

His family was so important to him, and yet when it came to his older brother he felt nothing toward the man. The two of them never really had a great relationship to begin with. Rooster wasn't even sure why, when he was a kid, he looked up to Steven. He'd thought he was the best, but his older brother wanted nothing to do with him. And now, the feeling was fucking mutual.

When Minx tightened her arms around his stomach, Rooster felt his heart rate slow from rage to a simmering anger. He didn't want this woman to see the temper that could sometimes explode, not that he would ever hit a woman.

He just didn't want to scare her.

Rooster's surprise grew when Minx threw her leg over and straddled him. Her hands cupped his cheeks, forcing him to look into her deep-sea eyes.

'You don't know what to do, do you?'

Rooster shook his head. He couldn't lie to this woman, even if he wanted to, but she was making him see the truth he was trying to hide. Even from himself. He was the fucking president of the national charter of Black Alchemy. He should have at least some kind of idea as to what to do, with the Bryson City Slasher, with his blood brother… hell, even with the woman who was sitting on his very satisfied cock.

But he had no idea.

Minx, like she could sense his internal mind fuck, kissed him. As her tongue entered his mouth, Rooster actually felt his worries wash away. Even if it was just for a moment.

Fuck.

'You don't need to know right now… okay?' The smile that his Minx gave him caused Rooster's stomach to drop. He'd witnessed many of her smiles before, but this one changed everything inside him.

Rooster wanted forever with this woman…

CHAPTER 20

Mila woke to feel Rooster moving around behind her. The heavy weight of his arms left her body and took the heat of his chest with him. She turned, catching his hand as a whimper escaped from her throat.

'Hey.' Rooster knelt on her mattress, his eyes were full of worry and his hands went to her forehead. He pushed some of her blonde hair away from her face. 'You okay, Minx?'

'Where are you going?' she asked before she could stop herself. She didn't want to seem like another desperate woman trying to keep him around. She wasn't like that at all, but there was something about him that made Mila throw all caution to the wind.

Rooster's honey gaze burned into her, making her shiver and a small smile slipped over her lips. Her heart was beating faster and faster in her chest. That dangerous, four-letter word danced on her tongue.

'I have to go to church, but I'm coming back for you in a few hours. What time do you finish work today?'

Mila's heart skipped a beat. After last night, after learning so much about Rooster, she had hoped that he didn't think it had been a mistake. The possibility of Rooster picking her up from work, it gave her hope.

'I'm there until four-thirty today. I've got to cast the students for the new musical.' Mila sat the rest of the way up, tucking the sheet around her and making sure her bare breasts were covered.

'I'll be there at four-thirty-five sharp. Don't make me wait Minx.' Rooster winked before descending on her and kissing the absolute crap out of her, proving he found it just as hard to leave her. He scraped his teeth over her bottom lip, as his hand snuck a squeeze of her boob.

Mila squeaked and swatted him away. She watched the way her man's jeans shaped to his ass perfectly as he walked out of her room.

'See you later, Minx!' he called out, before her front door shut and she heard her lock engage.

Scrambling to her feet, Mila watched as one of the prospects pulled up just as Rooster mounted his bike. He tossed her a wave before the sound of his straight pipes took over the chirping birds by the window.

'See you later, Rooster.'

***

By the time Rooster slammed the gavel on the wooden table in front of him for what felt like the hundredth time this church, he was craving the rumble of his bike and his woman squishing herself against his back. 'Okay boys, last time. The fucking Slasher. Has anyone found anything on this guy?'

'I had a talk with Override about scouring the web for anyone bragging about these killings, but no dice. Hammer, Creep and I have also been hanging around a few biker bars to see if anyone has gotten drunk enough to claim responsibility. Nothing there either,' Ghoul, the club's secretary, said. 'We'll keep working though, Prez.'

The man crossed his arms and leaned back in his chair. One of these days, Ghoul was going to fall back and land on his ass. Rooster just hoped that when that day came, someone would film it.

'What about you, Diablo?' Rooster turned to his enforcer. 'Got anything on this guy?'

'*Nada.* We're looking into whether anyone saw Amanda or Naomi before they were killed. The badges know fuck all,' Diablo said before crossing his arms as well.

'Fuck, okay, keep on it all of you. If that's all?' Rooster waited for a moment before he pounded the gavel for the final fucking time.

He watched as his brothers filed out of the room, all of them at their own pace. Ghoul and Hammer gave Rubble shit about his new custom. The man had ridden on it this morning, and no one could mistake that the colour was the exact shade of Rooster's sister's eyes.

Rooster swerved around his men and walked toward his office, Gunner not too far behind him.

'What's been going on man?' Gunner slouched into the leather couch, as Rooster walked over to his desk. He had finally moved everything into Patriot's space, merging most of his father's memorabilia and his paperwork with his own.

'What are you talking about?'

'You've been acting fucking weird since that teacher dropped Daisy round here. Not that I blame you, she's one hot fucking piece of ass, but pussy is just pussy… right?' Gunner raised his eyebrow, failing to hide his smirk.

Rooster knew what his VP was trying to do, but he couldn't stop his rage from boiling over. His hands landed on his desk with a powerful slam. As he leaned over, Rooster could feel his face turning bright red.

'Don't you ever fucking talk about Minx like that again! Do you fucking hear me?' Rooster growled, realising his mistake as a smirk crawled across Gunner's stupid face.

'You done?'

Rooster's hands left the wooden desk and landed in his hair as his feet took him around the room.

'What the fuck is wrong with me?' His hands gripped his hair, trying to create as much pain to focus, but all he could think of was Minx's soft hands instead of his. Fuck!

Rooster always thought that he would be content without an ol' lady, that the sweetbutts and occasional citizen would be enough to satisfy him until he rode the Harley's in the sky.

Clearly, Rooster had been fucking wrong.

'I would say you're almost as bad as Rubble, but you don't have Mila's eye colour on your custom... do you?' Gunner mocked, making Rooster want to glare at his brother, but he knew that the VP was right. There was something about his Minx that made Rooster throw all the rules out the window.

What was it about this woman that made him so crazy?

'She's already under your skin, isn't she?' Gunner's smirk increased.

'Fuck off,' Rooster said, fixing up his cut and continuing to pace behind his desk. His fingers grazed his chin as he thought about what to do next.

'Just remember what Patriot used to say.' Gunner shrugged before he walked out of the office. Rooster didn't even have to think hard, he could hear his father's words in his ear.

'When you meet the right woman, she'll take up your every thought. She'll be everything to you, your heart, the very air you fucking breathe, and if anything happens to her... it feels like the devil himself has ripped out every organ and left her heart for last. You make sure that you take care of her. Claim her. Protect her.'

Rooster knew his father wanted him to be happy, and to be with a trustworthy woman. Mila Rice was Rooster's every thought, she was his every breath, and his every sexual desire. *Fuck!* He'd already given her a road name for fuck's sake.

Rooster sat behind his desk and ran his hand over his face. The papers in front of him needed his attention, maybe some mind-numbing office work would help restart his brain and get Rooster thinking about what the fuck he was going to do next.

The club owned some legit businesses that allowed them to keep the coffers fat, and it also kept the do-gooder badges off their backs. Many of the brothers worked at these businesses to pay rent at the clubhouse. Except for those brothers that lived off the compound, or the officers of Black Alchemy. Since they already did so much for the club, they didn't have to spend anything on board.

Rooster glared at the papers in front of him, adding up the pays and deducting what he had to from each member. He really had no idea how much actually went into being the president. He was sure that this was something that Creep could be doing since he was the treasurer of the club, but Rooster needed the tediousness of the paperwork.

He went through each business, making sure that each place was staying in the black. Fuck, he was going to be riding the desk for the rest of his day.

***

By the time Mila walked out of the school building it was closer to five, but there he was. Waiting for her, Rooster in all his cocky glory, leaned against his gorgeous bike with arms folded firmly over his chest and not looking too pleased he'd been left waiting. Mila threw him a smile to try and ease the frown etched on his beautiful face, but it took the opposite effect. She had a feeling she was going to be in for a spanking later.

That thought made her slightly warm inside.

'Hey, Rooster!' she called out, and she skipped the last few steps in front of him.

'Minx. I told you that I don't like waiting,' he spoke. His words might have been warning but his honey gaze bore more relief than anger.

Mila opened her mouth to defend herself when Rooster chuckled and pulled her into his strong embrace, his lips claiming hers, with a promise of the punishment to come. She shivered with anticipation, but Rooster pulled away too quickly for her liking.

Rooster climbed onto his bike and waited patiently for her to mount the beast. Loose rocks from the parking lot flew up around them as he took off. The world flew by them as they rode through town and towards the mountains. Mila tightened her arms around Rooster's waist, the Harley let out a loud purr.

She watched from behind Rooster's back as the green of the trees blended with the blue of the sky, creating an amazing colour that she wished she could replicate.

They rode for about an hour, riding through the mountains, and back to their small town. When Rooster passed by the clubhouse Mila tapped on his shoulder to ask him what was going on, but he just squeezed her knee. His way of asking her to trust him. Mila tightened her grip around his waist again and rested her head on the club's insignia on his jacket.

Rooster took a sudden turn, causing Mila to let out a surprised gasp just as they pulled off to the side of the road, towards a clearing. There sat a lake, water almost the same shade as Mila's eyes glistened in the afternoon sun.

'Wow,' Mila whispered as they slowed to a stop. Rooster kicked the stand up and shut the beast down. He dismounted with grace and helped her off the bike. She wobbled for a moment, but he was right there next to her, his large hand grasping hers, keeping her steady.

Mila finally took a step towards the shimmering water, the soft grass folding under her shoe-encased foot.

'This place is amazing. How did you even know about it?' Mila marvelled and turned towards Rooster. For a moment, she watched a sense of sadness fall over his face. Knowing what he needed, Mila went back to him, wrapped her arms around his waist and pressed a kiss to his presidential patch. His strong, tattooed arms wrapped around her shoulders before he continued.

'Pop used to bring the family here. You wouldn't know it by looking at her, but Ma loves to picnic.' Rooster stood with her, swaying to the music of the wind in the surrounding trees. 'You should have seen it, Minx. My pops, the biker king of North Carolina, sitting on a homemade blanket. His four children spread out across the clearing, his Queenie in his arms. I don't think I've ever seen a man as content as he was during those picnics.'

Mila couldn't stop the small smile that spread across her lips as she thought of her own father and mother. She would have loved to be introduced to Rooster's father, to have the two families picnicking together.

Mila had to wonder what her father's reaction to Rooster would be. Would he have accepted the biker? She knew that her dad would have always wanted her to be happy, and she knew that he would have loved this lake.

She walked down to the lake's edge, and sat on a rock, urging Rooster to join her. He propped up on the rock behind her. His strong arms wrapped around her tighter. Mila had never felt so happy in her life.

'I was just thinking about my dad,' she said. 'He would have loved this place. He was an avid fisher.'

'You don't talk about your family much,' Rooster said. He had shared so much about himself the previous night, and she wanted to share more about her past with him.

Mila wanted him to know everything about her.

'Tell me about them.' Rooster pressed a kiss to the side of her head and rested his chin on her shoulder. The wind swayed them slightly, but it wasn't chilling.

She was warm in Rooster's embrace.

'My dad. He was my absolute favourite person in the world. It was just him, my mom and myself for so long. My mom always wanted a very big family, but she and my dad had an extremely hard time trying to conceive. Mom almost died giving birth to me and they didn't try again after that. So, it was just the three of us, we were happy. Dad would work a lot of long hours as a restaurant manager with Mom doing more of the school hours. She was always home to see me and ask me about my day.' Mila was very fond of her mom when she was younger, memories of freshly baked cookies, mugs of hot cocoa on winter days, and her homework out in front of the both of them. 'She was a teacher.'

Mila had wanted to be just like the woman when she grew up.

'I worked really hard in high school. Focusing more on my studies than on my social life. I think that made my parents happy. When I got a scholarship to UNC, my parents were definitely relieved. I didn't want them to worry about sending me to college in a different state. We lived on a tight budget. One night my dad was coming home from a particularly long shift, it was early Saturday morning and he had a green light at the intersection. A drunk driver ran the red…' Mila sucked in a deep breath. Sharing this triggered more emotion than she expected it would. 'I didn't even get to say goodbye.'

It had been years since her dad's death, but she could still remember waking up in her dorm room, her phone ringing and her roommate cursing up a storm. The one phone call had changed Mila's life forever.

Losing her dad, her best friend, was a pain unlike anything she had ever experienced. He had left a gaping hole in her life, and she never wanted to feel that way again.

Burying herself in risky behaviours was the only distraction and kept the grief at bay, but that wasn't a part of her life she was ready to share with Rooster.

She didn't have much left of her dad, apart from the good memories and his class ring. Mila never told her mother that she took it, she didn't want the fight that would go with explaining why. So instead, she kept the ring tucked away safely and only took it out when she was feeling particularly lonely.

A sudden realisation crossed over Mila. She hadn't taken her father's ring out of her jewellery box since the day Rooster rescued her from Foghorn. She wasn't so lonely anymore, and it was all thanks to the biker who wouldn't leave her side.

CHAPTER 21

'Was dinner always like that?' Rubble asked Angel as they lay in bed together. Her left hand lay on his chest, feeling his heartbeat for her and only her.

'You have no idea. It was worse when Pops was around, the arguments were legendary, but last night was something else. Steven and Rooster have always been these polar opposites, but Rooster was *beyond* pissed. Like to the point where I'm pretty sure the vein in his forehead was about to burst.'

Rubble chuckled at his woman's description of her brother. He was all too familiar with that vein. He knew she wasn't exaggerating.

'How the hell did Steven think it was okay to just take the seat at the head of the table?' she wondered. 'I mean, Rooster put up a small fight about sitting in Pop's chair. Then Steven just comes out of nowhere and takes the seat? It was so weird. Not to mention he barely spoke two words to you the entire night, it was honestly fucking rude. I mean I haven't seen the guy since I was thirteen but nothing about him now is who I remember from when I was a kid. He just doesn't seem like the same Steven anymore.'

Rubble shook his head. 'Yeah, it was pretty intense there for a bit.

I think it's going to take your brothers some time to get reacquainted with each other.'

They lay in silence, knowing between them that it was going to take more than 'some time' for Rooster to welcome back his blood brother. The Bates family weren't too kind toward deserters, something Rubble agreed with. He'd had to deal with enough of those when he was in the military. He held tighter to his Angel knowing that he wasn't going to make a similar mistake anytime soon.

'Are you sure you want to push back the date?' he asked. The only way he knew how to distract her nowadays, without taking their clothes off, was with their wedding plans. Not that there was much for them to plan left. The only reason they were even having a ceremony was to appease his grandmother.

'Yeah,' Angel sighed before a beautiful smirk crossed her gorgeous face. 'I just want to wait until all this family dust settles.'

'I'll wait, as long as my granny is still alive to see you make an honest man out of me.'

Angel giggled and rolled closer to his side. 'I promise.'

Angel was his, and he was Angel's. Nothing in this world could make him feel this whole.

'I love you, Angel.' His hands ran through her dark hair, and her blue eyes sparkled.

'I love you too, Rubble.' Her lips met his softly, but it wasn't enough for Rubble. Rolling his woman over, he increased the passion and the urgency in the kiss. Her hands went to his chest, her nails scratching against his bare chest in a way he loved.

The zing of her touch went straight to his cock. He knew she felt his hard-on. Her lips curved into a smile against his. Rubble's hands went to Angel's plump ass and squeezed just as a vibration rang through the air.

The both of them groaned but knew that Rubble had to answer the phone. He climbed off her, and he watched as she pulled her hair to the side. Letting out a deep breath, he hated that he had to leave her while she needed him to cool her fire.

She knew the MC life, she knew the score.

'Yeah?' Rubble asked, looking at his Angel. God, he loved the hell out of her. 'What's up, Rooster?'

'Where the fuck are you? We have a charity run next month and I've seen fuck all about it! I've heard your ideas and the brothers talk about it, but I've got fucking nothing in writing about when, how and where this run is happening,' Rooster shouted over the phone and Rubble winced at the man's tone. He was pissed. Rubble had really thought that his prez having a regular woman in his life would calm Rooster down a little. That obviously wasn't the case.

As much as he didn't want to let down his president, he couldn't bear to leave his woman. One glance over at Angel, he knew that he had to do the right thing. They would be married soon and when that happened he was going to take her on the best honeymoon to make up for all the times he'd had to run off for the club.

'Sorry, Prez. I'll be there.' Before Rooster could respond, Rubble hung up, pulled on his jeans and walked into the walk-in closet, grabbed his cut from where it hung with Angel's property patch.

'Well…' He shrugged causally. 'That was the prez.'

***

'Ah fuck my brother and his shit timing!' Angel groaned when she saw her man dressed in his cut. 'You still look hot even with clothes on.'

He was so handsome, how in the world had she gotten so lucky with Rubble?

'Be safe,' he said, as Angel tilted her head up to meet his kiss. He lingered, she knew he wanted to stay. Rubble grabbed the papers that he had put together for the charity.

'You too! Love you!' she called out and waved at his retreating back.

'Love you, Angel.' She couldn't keep the smile off her face, he was special, different. He was everything she had ever witnessed in her own father and he treated her the way Patriot had worshipped his Queenie. Rubble was a keeper.

Rolling over, Angel grabbed her laptop that had been a present from her man when she started doing online classes for a college course in business and accounting. She hadn't told anyone except for Rubble, she knew her pops was upset about her decision not to go to college like Daisy had planned to. Angel didn't regret anything, she loved being Rubble's ol' lady.

The assignment in front of her was only half finished, but Angel had no desire to even type a damn word. Instead, she gave in to the insane urge to finish off what Rubble couldn't.

After, she skipped down the stairs, a smile on her face before she saw her lounge, dining room and kitchen. There was a mess. Goddamnit, her post orgasm glow disappeared. She loved her man, but he needed to learn how to pick up after himself. With a sigh Angel plugged her phone into the high-tech speakers Rubble insisted on buying and cued up her playlist. With a swipe of her finger over the volume, Angel set about cleaning her house.

The loud vacuum took over the music, as Angel shimmied and shook her hips to the small snippets she was able to decipher. It was honestly a miracle she heard the knock at her door.

Without checking the peephole, she answered the door. Mentally rolling her eyes at the lecture she was sure to have from Rubble later... maybe she would leave that part out.

'Oh hey! What are you doing here?' she said, confusion coursing through her as she tried to understand why this man had come to stand at her door. Had something happened?

The hairs on the back of Angel's neck stood on end and, in that moment, she wished for the weight of her gun in her hands. She went to take a step back, but dizziness took over her and her legs went weak. Grabbing on to the door for support, Angel took in the way the shadows cast over the figure of the man before her. How the hell had he gotten her address?

'What are you doing here?' she repeated, trying to be firm in her voice.

'Woah, are you okay?' he asked and stalked towards her, his arms wide open to take her into a hug. He was on her before she could protest and her confusion was so intense that by instinct she hugged him back. Angel instantly regretted it.

He held a cloth over her mouth and nose. She struggled against him, but none of the self-defence techniques Angel had been taught over the years were effective. He kept that handkerchief over her face with the top of her head secure in his hand. She swung and kicked, connecting but without affect. He kept her close to his chest. So close, she could feel something pushing into her stomach.

Oh god, she was going to vomit. Bile rose in her throat just as her eyes grew fuzzy, and finally darkness overcame her.

Something was holding her down.

Angel's eyes were heavy when she tried to pry them open. A pounding in her head reminded her of those times when she gave in and drunk more than her body weight, but she couldn't remember touching a drop of alcohol. Angel tried to shift and felt only a cloth over her bare breasts, a coldness crept over her feet and up her exposed legs.

What the hell was going on?

Angel tried to move, to sit up, but the tight, rough rope prevented her from moving. A muffled squeal came from her mouth. She was gagged. She rolled her wrists to see if there was any chance of escape.

The heat and sting of a palm striking her cheek froze her instantly. She wasn't alone in this nightmare.

'You went and got yourself involved!' Angel could tell the scream came from the blurry figure of the man beside her. What the fuck was he doing? She tried to focus, but the drugs still kept her from being able to see too much around her. Somehow, she focused enough to see a familiar looking dagger glinting in his hands.

Where the hell had he gotten that?

Without a word, the man bent his knee into her mattress and straddled her hips. He started to yank the cloth draped over her chest, which was when she realised it was her property patch. That's when her fight reflex really kicked in. No one was going to disrespect her or Rubble like that, she would rather die before that happened.

She wiggled and tried to lift him off her, but he was too heavy. With a grunt and a flying fist, Angel cried out as he punched her already burning cheek.

'You don't fucking move!' The spit from his rage flew from his mouth and hit her face. The familiar looking blade by his side glistened in the afternoon sun.

She could no longer hide her terror.

'That's right... good girl,' the man whispered into Angel's ear. She flinched away and received another punch of her face. 'I told you not to fucking move!'

The look in his eyes spoke of horrors that Angel had only read about in the papers and, in that moment, she knew she wasn't going to make it out of this alive.

That thought alone brought about one of the last tears she would ever shed.

***

Rubble held his phone to his face. It wasn't like Angel not to answer his calls, she always managed to at least send him a text if she couldn't answer.

Voice mail again.

'Hey, it's Angel slash Heather. Leave your number, 'kay bye.' Rubble grumbled at the cheery voicemail answering him yet a-fucking-gain. The stone in his stomach somehow got heavier.

Something was wrong.

He still had to get a few more pieces of information to Creep and Rooster about the charity run, but in that moment, he couldn't give a fuck.

He had to get home.

Rubble called her one more time as he walked briskly through the clubhouse. He waved a dismissive hand at Ghoul and Hammer when they called him over for a game of pool.

'Hey, it's Angel slash Heather. Leave your number, 'kay bye.'

Something was seriously fucking wrong, he felt it.

Mounting his electric blue bike, he sped away from the compound to the home they shared.

Rubble's heart was in his throat. The organ threatened to fall out his mouth when he saw that Angel's car was still in the driveway and music was blaring from the windows. It would have been a picture of normalcy if the front door wasn't wide open.

He didn't even bother with the kick stand. He left his expensive custom on its side and ran into the house.

'Angel!' Rubble called out, as he stood in the middle of the lounge room. Half the room was spotless, and the vacuum cleaner was leaning against the sofa.

He waited a moment to see if Angel was going to come bounding down the staircase and greet him like she normally would.

The house stayed silent.

Rubble pulled his gun from the back of his jeans and started searching the house. She wasn't downstairs, so he turned down the music, and carefully stepped up the carpeted stairs.

The only door open was their master bedroom, every other room in the hallway was closed off. Rubble closed his eyes for a moment and hoped that he would find Angel sitting at her desk, with some brilliant excuse as to why she hadn't answered.

He swung the door open more, and Rubble's heart was physically ripped from his chest.

His Angel lay on their bed, where not even five hours before they had been sitting and talking about their future together. Her hands were bound and so were her legs, her body was bruised to all hell, her cheek was cut, and her full-of-life blue eyes were dull.

Rubble dropped the gun and ran to her. Nothing mattered, only Angel. His Angel. Her gorgeous face was cut beyond recognition, and her beautiful hair was splayed across the pillow. He prayed for the first time in his life to whatever God was out there, that he would see her blue irises sparkle with life again.

'Blink, baby! Blink!' he screamed and shook her limp body.

'Angel…' Rubble choked out, his hand grasping his mouth. The patch he had given her when he was finally a member of Black Alchemy and could claim her, was cut open in spots. Her name was shredded to pieces and the back of the property patch was completely in tatters on the floor.

He pulled out his burner phone and dialled his president's number. Rubble couldn't do this by himself.

'Rooster!' he screamed. 'Fuck! Fuck! Fuck!' Rubble was completely lost in his panic. He continued to scream into the phone. 'It's Angel.'

CHAPTER 22

'It's Angel.'

Those two words rocked Rooster to his core. He stared at the phone, the dial tone mocked him.

'Rubble hung up,' he said to himself, confused.

'You okay? What's going on?' Minx's hand grazed his arm.

'It's Angel. Something's wrong with Angel…'

'Okay, let's go then.' Minx's voice pulled Rooster from his shell shock. He dialled Stone's number.

'Meet me at Minx's… get there now!' His command left no room for interpretation.

Rooster dropped Minx back to her cottage without much more of an explanation and Stone was already waiting for them. She tried to convince him to take her with him, but Rooster didn't know what he was walking into. He didn't want to put her in any danger. He couldn't risk her getting hurt, he'd rather cut his own arm off first.

He pulled up to his sister's home, Rubble's bike laying on the ground and the front door wide open. He called out both his sister's and Rubble's names, but only a deafening silence followed.

Rooster raised his gun and moved with precision through the

house. Taking slow steps up the stairs, he found himself outside the master bedroom.

Rooster cracked open the door a little. The sight before him had all the air leaving his body. His Angel's lifeless form lay in his road captain's arms on the bed, blood coating the sheets, some even dripping to the once spotless carpet.

'What the fuck have you done, Rubble?!' Rooster cried, raising his gun to shoot his own brother if he had to.

'She had to have known him,' Rubble struggled out a strangled sob, shocking Rooster. 'The front door wasn't broken, and neither were any of the windows. The alarm didn't even go off.'

Rubble lifted his head, finally meeting Rooster's glare. The pained expression told Rooster everything he needed to know. He lowered his weapon.

Rooster glanced at his sister one last time before he turned away and took out his burner phone. This was going to break not only his family but the entire club.

Heather Jean Bates, also known as Angel, had been killed by the Bryson City Slasher, and the fact that she knew the killer was all new information the brotherhood had to deal with.

But first he had to make sure that his family was going to survive this latest horrible tragedy. Goddamn he had no idea how he was going to deal with any of this.

The gut-wrenching scream that came from his mother almost made Rooster cry, as she clutched at his forearms. Tears continued to roll down her sunken cheeks. He had no idea how Queenie was going to come back from this.

First Patriot, and now Angel.

Daisy buckled into a ball; her arms circled her middle as she let out a loud sob. Steven had tears running down his own cheeks as he cradled their youngest sister in his arms, rocking her back and forth. Rooster could see it was no comfort to Daisy.

The sobs from his sister made him want to hold her and never let go until the grief that took over her small body left forever. Looking at his older brother, Rooster wanted nothing more than to take the two women and hide away, to deal with their grief alone. Steven hadn't been a part of this family for so long. He didn't deserve to be now. Rooster wanted to mourn without him. His brother's presence in this moment felt unnatural.

Queenie's sobs turned into mumbled prayers as she crumpled to the floor. Her hands were shaking as she held them together. Rooster knelt with her, not to pray but to offer comfort. There was no merciful God as far as he was concerned, no family should have ever had to go through the loss of not just one murdered family member but two. All in the span of a few months.

Rooster rubbed at his chest. Hours had passed by in a blur, and he had no idea what the hell he was going to do with himself. He vaguely remembered his mother asking to be left alone, while Daisy had cried herself to sleep and had been tucked away in her bedroom.

Rooster hung his head and rested his hands on his hips. What the fuck was he going to do? The smell of vengeance was palpable, but the uncontrollable urge to break down or even scream for his lost family was just as profound.

His mind was in a fog. Anyone would have been able to sneak up right behind him. He felt weak and vulnerable and Rooster didn't like it.

Rooster reached for the medicine cabinet beside his head and searched for the pain pills. Anything to relieve this stress headache forming.

'Dylan?' Steven broke through the silence, Rooster didn't turn to his brother. Instead, he froze and waited to hear what his long-lost brother was going to say. 'Why would someone hurt Heather?'

Rooster wished in that moment to correct Steven about Angel's name, but he had to remember that the oldest Bates had left long before Angel had ever met Rubble. He so desperately wanted to say something, anything, to his brother. But Angel's death was club business. It wasn't something an outsider like Steven would be able to handle.

So, Rooster did the only thing he could do.

'I have no idea,' he lied.

***

A song was playing in the background of Mila's wonderful dream. She and Rooster were back by the lake, kids were running around and laughter was filling the air. They sat under that same tree, Mila in front of Rooster's hard chest, his strong tattooed arms encircled around her waist. She glanced to her side for a moment and saw her mother fully sober and her father sitting with Queenie and another man who had to be Rooster's father. Her heart was full as she continued around the picnic and saw not only Angel and Rubble but Daisy and Tank.

Mila had never had a big family and yet, being with Rooster, he gave her exactly what she had always wanted. She watched as a little boy and girl, both with blonde hair, ran around with lots of other children.

Music travelled around Mila and for a moment she thought it was from a speaker behind her...

Light was blaring beside Mila, causing her to curse whoever was calling her at this stupid hour. Suddenly the memories of the call about her father's death bombarded her, and Mila bolted up out of her bed. She reached for her phone with a shaking hand.

'Hello?' Her blonde hair was covering half her face and her mouth felt dry, as she dragged a hand across her nose and eyes. She pulled away strands of hair stuck to her skin.

'Minx.'

'Rooster? Babe, are you okay?' Mila covered her mouth with a trembling hand as her muscles released all the tension she hadn't realised she was holding, but something was wrong. She could hear it in his voice.

'I need you.'

That was all he had to say. After getting the address for Rooster's childhood home, Mila sped across town to the small ranch-style home. It wasn't exactly something she would have expected Rooster to have grown up inside.

She knew she shouldn't judge a book by its cover.

Mila clutched her arms to her chest and dragged her feet up the driveway towards the lit-up house. It was well after two in the morning.

She knocked softly at the door, before it swung open to reveal her man. He hadn't shaved during the day and his leather jacket was draped across a nearby chair. His white shirt and jeans were askew on his body and his hair was a mess, like he had been running his hands through it all day.

'Baby, what's the matter? Are you okay?' Mila went straight into Rooster's open arms and ran her hands over him, feeling for any injuries he might have been trying to hide from her.

'Angel… she's dead.' Rooster's normally strong voice cracked with emotion. No more words needed to be said, her strong man was broken.

'No…' she said, as she hung on to Rooster for dear life. His hand cradled her head against his chest, and she felt him let out a long deep breath. One that shook and threatened tears. Mila held on to him and stroked down his back, as he rested his head into her shoulder.

They stood still in the open doorway.

Mila glanced over Rooster's shoulder and saw a man in a suit standing in the hallway. Watching them. Rooster must have felt her stiffen because when he raised his head and looked behind him he shook his head.

'That's my brother,' he whispered, and Mila had a good look at the man in the suit. She couldn't believe that the man who had the face of a dog, could be related to a man like Rooster. They definitely didn't look alike. Mila opened her mouth to say something, but Rooster just shook his head slightly.

Now was not the time for questions.

'Head up the stairs, I'll meet you in the room on the right,' he said, before letting her go and heading over to his brother. Mila stared at the two men for a moment, but eventually did what Rooster asked.

She opened the door and was greeted by what could only be described as a teenager's bedroom. A twin bed sat in the corner with a dark blue comforter, posters of nearly naked women and motorcycles donned the walls, and she even spotted the odd Aerosmith and Def Leppard poster as well. She smiled slightly at the small insight into a teenage Rooster.

Mila sat on Rooster's old bed, waiting for him to come back from talking with his brother. She remembered his name was Steven from the conversation at the lake. He definitely wasn't the type of man that Mila expected the oldest son of an MC president to look like. She really needed to stop judging this family by how they looked.

The door creaked open and she watched as Rooster slipped through. For a moment, he looked like a man who had lost his sister in the most tragic way possible, instead of being the badass MC president she had grown to love…

That's right, she said love.

'Hey, are you okay?' Even though it was the dumbest question to ask, Mila couldn't stop it from slipping past her lips.

'I should have protected her,' he whispered, his voice cracking slightly. His entire body slumped on to the bed, his hands on his head.

'What happened?' Mila knelt on the bed and wrapped her arms around his neck, trying to give him all the strength she could provide. 'I didn't want to ask before… but what happened to Angel?'

'The fucking Slasher got her.'

Mila gasped slightly. For that monster to have hit so close to home…

'I should have protected her. I should have had the whole club put on lockdown.' Rooster broke, and Mila watched as the strong man crumbled before her. She knew what playing the *'What if…'* or *'I should have…'* game did to someone's mental health.

She said the only thing that came to her mind. 'You couldn't have known that Angel was even a target.' Mila rested her head on his shoulder. 'We all thought that Angel was safe. You can't punish yourself for the horrors of the monster.'

'I hate feeling this helpless…' Rooster admitted and sucked back a sob. Mila had never seen him look so defeated, and so crushed under the weight of what had happened. She wanted to take all his pain away, but instead she pulled back and turned his head to look at her.

She pressed a kiss to his forehead and guided him up the bed. She lay down on her back and pulled his head to her chest, her hand running through the windswept strands while the other just held him close to her body.

Mila felt his tears coating her arms and staining her shirt. His body shook with every ragged intake of breath, but she didn't say anything. She just let the man grieve for his family.

'You will find this monster, Rooster, and you'll make him pay for hurting your family,' she finally said. Never in her life had she condoned violence before, but this was different.

'Our family,' he croaked and sniffed away some stray sobs. 'You're part of this now, Minx.'

He wrapped his arms around her waist, pulling her in tight.

It felt like he would never let her go.

CHAPTER 23

Four months.

That's all it took.

He never thought he would fall for a woman, let alone a fucking citizen. And yet, there Rooster was. He stared at the sleeping form of Mila beside him. In the two months since Angel's murder he had been forced to put the entire club on lockdown. Mila had taken the whole change in such amazing stride. She still went to the high school to teach but Rooster insisted on her taking at least one prospect with her.

That had been an argument for the ages, but eventually she agreed.

So, there she was, laying in his bed at the clubhouse. Sunlight streamed through his windows and mixed with the blonde in his woman's hair.

His woman.

The thought made Rooster smile, Mila had been by his side every step of the way since Angel. She rode with him to the funeral, helped a crumbling and drunk Rubble to his room and had made sure that his mother ate something.

His Minx was fucking made for his world.

Minx snuggled her face into his chest and her lashes fluttered until her stormy sea eyes were shining. The blue depths reflected the sleepy smile on her face. God-fucking-damnit she was gorgeous.

'Good morning,' she breathed out.

'Morning, Minx,' he replied. Not being able to deny himself of her gorgeous lips any longer, his kiss joined the greeting. Trying to keep any lip lock simple was impossible when it came to his woman.

When she tried to climb up higher on his body Rooster regrettably pulled back.

'Hang on, baby, I need to talk to you about something.' Rooster watched as her eyes turned from raging desire to a dull blue. He sat up and made her straddle his body. Rooster gripped her thighs, keeping her still. 'I want you to be my ol' lady.'

'What?' Minx's eyes widened, her head drew back from his quickly and her blue eyes turned to a sparkle of excitement.

'I want you to be my ol' lady, Minx. It's not going to be easy, babe, you are still a citizen, and you will be the matriarch, but I know you. I know you can do it.' Rooster's hands ran up his woman's legs. When Minx didn't say anything to him, a moment of insecurity raced through Rooster.

'Are you sure, Rooster?' Fuck, he could feel her heart slamming against his chest. It matched the speed of his own. Her eyes searched his for any kind of untruth, so Rooster threw a smirk in her direction.

'I wouldn't have asked if I didn't know I wanted you to be mine.' Rooster plopped Minx next to him on the bed and, in all his naked glory, he moved over to the built-in wardrobe. He pulled the large white box out from its hiding place, before he sat back down on the bed and handed her the box.

Rooster was never one for big romantic gestures, and he had thought of a million other ways for him to do this. But this felt right, the two of them in his room. There wasn't anyone else he wanted to share this moment with.

'This is my promise to you,' he began. Minx watched him, the box untouched in front of her. 'That I am yours and you are mine. Minx, you are my ride or die and I will never look at another woman as long as I have you by my side. You are my woman, my Minx.'

Rooster pressed a kiss to her luscious lips one more time and pushed her gift towards her.

'Are you ever going to tell me why you call me that?' she asked as she pulled away the lid. Minx peeled away the tissue paper to reveal the leather property patch. He watched as she raised it up from its resting place and studied the patches. He had not only had a road name patch sewn on to the right breast, but the matriarch patch his mother once had sat beneath it.

Tears welled in Mila's eyes.

'You've got to turn it around, babe,' Rooster encouraged, and watched as she discovered the white embroidery that claimed her to be Rooster's woman.

'I call you Minx because you enticed me from the beginning to break all my rules. You were trouble from the first moment I met you, and I wouldn't have you any other way,' Rooster said and pushed away strands of her hair.

'It's beautiful,' she whispered. Mila swung her legs off the bed and slipped the leather on over her skin. She wore nothing but the patch, parading it and pulling it closed over her ample bust in a poor show of modesty.

'Minx, I don't think I've ever seen anything more fucking beautiful.' Rooster crawled across the bed, his target in sight. She squealed as he pulled her closer to his body and she giggled at his pouncing hug. The feelings Rooster had for this woman were insane, and the fact that she had accepted his proposal made his heart swell in his chest. He held her face in his hands.

'My little Minx.' Rooster moulded his lips to hers and she opened to him. Their tongues danced together. He pulled her closer, the cold leather creaked against his chest – a barrier that now had to go. He let his hand slide down her body and grabbed at her firm ass.

Rooster pulled her up his body. Her toned legs wrapped around his waist. He nipped at her exposed neck, and his Minx threw her head back with a moan. He wanted to mark her entire body, to show everyone just who this woman belonged to.

He pushed the zipper aside, exposing one of her gorgeous breasts. With a growl of satisfaction, he took it in his mouth and sucked hard. The sound of her heavy breathing was fucking erotic. Rooster's cock pressed against the soft skin of her thigh. He wanted to test his gorgeous woman but fuck she was teasing him with her responding desire.

Rooster let Minx slide down his body. Her feet landed back on the floor and the loss of her frame wrapped around his hips gave him a moment to think, but it wasn't with his brain. Pulling open the jacket, the heady scent of leather and Minx, the sight of her bare breasts, the look of lust in her eyes, had him going to his knees. His hand ran the length of her torso on the way down. He loved the little quiver of her tummy as she breathed, a trail of goosebumps following in the wake of his touch.

With a final glance up at her face, he knew she was ready, wanting. It was all there in the way she looked at him. He smirked with pride. She wanted him, the anticipation and need clearly displayed. She grabbed a handful of his hair and guided him to his prize.

Rooster circled her sensitive clit, careful not to touch the prize, not just yet. She moaned her disappointment and moved her hips forward. He pressed a kiss to her thigh and slipped his fingers along her folds. Her legs buckled momentarily. The moan that came from her throat was deep. Rooster sucked on her thigh and stomach, teasing her with his hot breath on her clit. He slipped his fingers deep inside her, holding her ass. Mila's head fell back and she leaned into his hand. The tension in her legs grew to trembling heights. She released a choking moan as her walls squeezed hard around his fingers.

Mila's groans turned more and more desperate until she stiffened and screamed out her pleasure, grabbing a handful of his hair to steady herself.

'God-fucking-damn, you're gorgeous.' Rooster grabbed her hips and buried his face into her wet pussy, breathing in the scent of her pleasure. It sent her into another fit of tremors.

He wasn't done yet. Getting to his feet, he lifted his Minx and carried her over to the bed, his cock hard and desperate. Minx could see his need and bent over the bed, wiggling her pretty ass, her pussy glistening wet. He took the head of this cock and glazed it with her juices.

'Condom!' Minx's muffled voice cried out.

'Fuck, Minx, we used the last one last night.' Rooster groaned and made to move away, but his Minx sat back and pressed against his cock with all her glory.

'Stay where you are,' she moaned and he knew he wasn't going anywhere.

'I'm clean,' he said with a grind matching her movement. 'Club policy,' he managed to groan through gritted teeth.

'Me too… I'm on the pill.'

Rooster let out a growl and buried himself to the hilt in her soft, wet heat. At that moment, he was ruined. Forever. There was no way he was ever going to have this woman with a covered cock again.

He pounded into the stunning warmth, tight, slippery, and hot. She pushed back, deeper and deeper he sank into her, matching and surpassing her rhythm, lost in his own, lost to this feeling, this woman. Rooster held her hips, threw his head back, and closed his eyes. He let the feeling of warmth creep up his spine, spread across his chest, and finally rush his entire body.

'Fuuuck!' He moaned slowly and leisurely pulled out. Mila flipped herself over, a smug look of pride on her face. She wiggled out of her patch and flung it across the room. It landed on the wingback chair exactly where she aimed but Rooster was too busy watching her tits wobble about as she whooped up her perfect shot.

He climbed up and over her and she lay back, letting him lay his body weight on her. The trust she showed him pleased him. Mila pulled him close, wrapping her arms tight around his back, her legs around his hips.

The feeling of her bare skin against him was the best thing in the world. Rooster was officially claiming Mila Rice, with everything he had.

Rooster loved how Minx looked at him, those pools of blue bearing into his soul. They promised love, lust and begged with mischievous need. He leaned in and kissed her gently. She wanted none of that and it sent a shock to his cock when she pulled him back in for a hot, lustful smooch. Her hips slowly grinded against his.

'Again? You are a fucking Minx.' Rooster chuckled.

'Are you up for the challenge?' She hissed and tightened her thighs around him, pulling his butt down to meet her next thrust, rubbing her gorgeous heat along his shaft.

No further invitation required, he slipped into her with ease. She dug her fingers deep into the flesh of his ass and pulled him closer, deeper.

Kissing her hard, he obliged her and thrust fast and deep, her need for him more exciting than anything he'd known, as the intensity of his climax grew with every glorious stroke. He pound into her, she matched his greedy lust until she cried out and her legs shook and tensed around his hips. Mila dug her heels into his ass cheeks, if she had spurs on she'd be riding him like a horse. He was about to lose it like a fucking teenager.

Rooster thrust one final time, emptying into her. He came harder than he'd ever come before.

'Minx, you're mine!' he cried and buried his head into her shoulder, panting and gaining his senses again.

Just in time to hear her say, 'Yes, I am yours and you are mine.'

'Fuck me, Minx,' he breathed out.

'I think I just did.' Minx giggled under him. Rooster laughed at her sass and pushed himself off her, gathering her up in his arms. Rooster relished in the fact he was a taken man.

'What's the time?' Minx asked sleepily from his side. Rooster glanced at the clock and winced.

His woman was insanely late to work.

CHAPTER 24

Mila sat in her lounge room, a pile of papers in front of her and a sigh on her lips. Rooster had left in the early hours of the morning with a sweet kiss, and a promise to be back in Bryson City as soon as possible.

God, she missed him and it had only been a day since she saw him last. The grading didn't help, it was the most mind-numbing part of her job. That night was particularly difficult simply because of the grade she was marking. Most of the sophomores, the boys in particular, didn't give a damn about studying. The reports were very difficult to read at times, but she did love it when she found a diamond in the rough.

Mila slid one of those special papers towards her and read through it. She had tasked her students to write about what they had done over the summer break. It was usually a task she would set for her younger students, but she wanted to get them back into the swing of writing papers again.

Something that she wasn't telling her sophomores was that none of this was going towards their final grade. About an hour later, Mila placed the last poorly written paper she could stand to read down and stretched her arms above her head.

She needed some wine, and she needed it fast. Mila walked into her kitchen and immediately something felt very off. Everything seemed to be in place, yet the back door was wide open. She only left it open during the summer.

Almost as if a cold hand ran up her back, a chill settled on her spine.

Mila felt hard eyes on her, they pierced her skin, and her muscles tensed, she was ready to run.

Something out of the corner of her eye moved. She turned and headed towards her front door. Stepping quickly, she could feel another person following her. Shifting her weight, she caught sight of the ski-mask-covered man.

A scream came from her mouth, and she ran for the prospect stationed at her front door.

'Tank!'

The heavy footsteps behind her increased.

Mila was sure the man behind her was going to catch her waist when Tank opened the door and caught her as she launched herself at him.

'What the fuck!' Tank yelled, before shots rang out. One of them hit the door frame, shattering the wood above Mila's head. Both Tank and Mila sprang into action.

The prospect grabbed Mila's arm and pulled her out to where her car was parked on the driveway. In that moment, Mila was thankful that she was too lazy to try and pull her car into the tight-fitting garage.

Tank had placed her keys into her hand and opened her door. The engine turned over easily, and she drove out with Tank following closely behind her. Mila's eyes shifted to her rear-view mirror, the shine of the Harley behind her was an instant relief, the shadow that came out of her house was not.

Mila's heartbeat thrashed in her ears, and her pulse raced. Was this the same guy that attacked Angel? Fuck! How much danger was she in now?

She sped through Bryson City Main Street, knowing that the safest place for her to be was at the clubhouse. The only reason she was even at her own house was to get the grading done.

Mila pulled up to the gates and saw Stone already waving her through – guess it paid to be the president's woman. She pulled off to the side and parked her car near the side entrance. Mila stepped out of the car and was instantly greeted by Gunner and Diablo.

'Heya, Minx.' Gunner hugged her, his giant form comforting for a moment. His huge paw patted her back twice before he let her go. 'Where's your patch girl?'

'We were ambushed,' Tank said. Running up beside Mila, he shoved his hands into the pockets of his leather jacket and rocked back and forth on his heels. 'I had to get her out of the cottage. We didn't have time to grab anything.'

'My ring!' Mila cried out, her mind instantly jumping to the one thing she had left of her dad. It was still at her cottage. 'My father's class ring. It's still upstairs in my jewellery box! I need to get it, it's all I have left of him.'

'It's not safe to go back there, Mila,' Gunner said, crouching down to her height like she was a toddler needing to be scolded. 'Let's get you inside and we can see what we can do about your ring, yeah?'

Without a word, Gunner led Mila over the parking lot and into the safety of the clubhouse, a deep frown furrowed his brow. Tank and Diablo followed close behind, scanning the surroundings as they moved.

The common room was pretty empty, apart for a couple of the brothers that she didn't know. Mila glanced at Gunner, but he just shook his head. As soon as she was in the safety of Rooster's bedroom, Mila turned on Gunner.

'Thanks, Gun, but who are those guys downstairs?'

'Brothers from a different charter. They're good guys, they're from our Vegas chapter. You gotta watch out, Minx, you don't have your patch with you and Rooster hasn't made his official announcement just yet,' Gunner said. 'What the hell happened back at your place?'

'The back door was open, he walked right in like he knew the place... What am I going to do about work? I can't just stay in Rooster's shirts and sweats all day. Plus my classes, I've taken too much time off already, if I do anymore I'll lose my job.' Mila was spiralling, she knew it, but she couldn't stop thinking about what the hell had happened in her home. Mila had no doubt in her mind that the guy in her house was the same guy that took out Angel.

'We'll take care of you, Minx. I'll have Tank or Stone go through your place to make sure he's fucked off. They'll grab some clothes and look for your father's ring. As for your teaching job, I already know that I wouldn't be able to convince you stay at the clubhouse. So we'll send Tank with you for protection,' Gunner promised before he slipped out of the room, leaving Mila alone for the first time. She started to pace.

Her mind was running a mile a minute and she couldn't focus on anything. Mila kept pacing the room she had spent so much time in, looking in drawers and cleaning up the non-existent mess in his bathroom.

Finally, she pulled Rooster's favourite Harley Davidson shirt over her head and lay on the bed. The ceiling was the most interesting thing in sight and, before long, her eyes welled up with tears.

Mila could have been raped, murdered and left for someone to find. Why was this monster targeting Black Alchemy? Even though her fear was palpable, she couldn't bring herself to regret getting involved with Rooster. He was everything to her, and he came with a family. Not just a blood related one, but a big, loud, and crazy family that welcomed her into the fold.

For the first time in years, Mila wasn't lonely.

She rolled onto Rooster's side of the bed scrunching his pillow against her chest, breathing in his scent when her cell phone ran on the bedside table. Jerking herself up, Mila brought her hand to her chest. Leaning over, she checked the caller ID.

Rooster.

'Hey!' she said as soon as she hit the answer button.

'Minx! Baby, are you okay?' Rooster's voice powered through the speaker and Mila's eyes well up with tears again. This time the drops fell down her cheeks.

'I was so scared, Rooster,' she wailed, hugging herself and rocking back and forth. God, she wished her man wasn't on a club run, she needed his comfort. Mila needed his arms wrapped around her waist as she snuggled into his chest.

Mila's whole body started to shake, and she slammed a tremoring hand over her mouth to silence her uncomfortable whimpering.

'Baby, I'm coming home. I'll be back tomorrow, don't worry, Minx. I'm coming back.' Rooster's words barely registered in Minx's mind, her heartbeat was actually hurting her chest it was slamming that hard. *'Minx, baby. Did you hear me? I'm coming back.'*

Mila's voice didn't work, the tremors were too much, but she did manage a sound of agreement that Rooster must have heard.

'Get some rest, Minx, I'll be home before you know it. You're safe where you are.'

***

Mila straightened her white blouse and patted away any dust that might have landed on her pencil skirt. She stared at herself in the mirror and ran a finger under her eyes to get rid of any excess eye liner or mascara. Mila pulled on her ponytail and sighed. God she hated the idea of going into school that day, but she hadn't been lying when she told Gunner that she could lose her job.

The prospects had done a thorough search of her cottage and found the place ransacked. Luckily none of her clothes had gone missing, but her father's ring was no longer in the safety of her jewellery box. It was gone, and that had sent Mila into a fit of tears when Tank knocked on Rooster's door in the morning with a bag of clothes and no necklace.

She wished Rooster was back, but the president of the Dark Angel's had asked him to stay back another hour or so. Rooster had called her when she woke up and spoken to her about going to work. He wasn't happy about it, but at least he understood her need to go. When she told him about her father's ring, Rooster listened as she cried. He never once interrupted her, but when her sobs turned to sniffles, Rooster instructed her to go to his dresser and open the top drawer. There lay a sterling silver skull ring.

'It was my father's. It's not to replace the one you lost, Minx,' Rooster said when Mila started saying that she couldn't possibly take it. 'It's a reminder that you are not alone, that you have a family behind you who will protect you.'

Mila agreed when she heard his reasoning. She almost said those dangerous, three words over the phone but thought better of it. There was plenty of time for that when she saw him that evening.

Tank followed her to the high school. He wasn't allowed in because he technically wasn't a student anymore. It wasn't like Mila could just go to her boss and let them in on what was happening in her world. Mila knew she would be fired on the spot.

So, there she was standing in front of her freshman class. Mila had planned this lesson to be one of fun. They were coming up to

Halloween and she knew the teens would be more preoccupied with parties and costumes than what Shakespeare was writing about.

She was about to pick one of the students with their hands in the air to answer her question, when a sudden noise made time freeze and everyone turned towards the classroom door.

Pop.

Pop.

Pop.

Students jerked up from their seats and rushed over to the windows, faces pressed against the glass and murmuring about what could be happening. Mila was stuck in her spot at her desk.

God, she hoped it was just a fight or the sound was a car backfiring, but then those same popping sounds rang through the hallway. Two from what she could count. This was the real deal, there was someone in her school. They were under attack. The urge to protect those kids was instant and Mila jumped into action. No one was going to die on her watch today, she couldn't bear it.

'Get under the tables!' she instructed and moved towards the door to turn off the lights. 'Get away from the windows and get under the tables kids!'

Alarms started to blare, and the overhead speaker system crackled something that sounded like the 'Active Shooter' lockdown siren.

'Attention. Lockdown. Locks, lights, out of sight.'

Mila ran to the classroom door and was about to lock it, but then the sounds of screaming came from the room down the hall from hers. Her students were cowering under their individual desks, whimpers and crying sounds permeated the silence.

Gunshots sounded. Whoever was shooting up the school had a semi-automatic by the sound of it and suddenly the room erupted into absolute chaos. Mila watched as the students at the front of the room bolted from their hiding spots and ran right into the supply closet at the back of the classroom. She reached for her cell phone.

Mila's mind hovered over *911*, but she didn't call that number. Instead, she pulled up Rooster's number and dialled.

'Hey, baby, I'm almost at the high school. I hope you're ready for an early lunch. You've got the first lunch period, right?'

'Rooster,' Mila whispered into the phone when the shooting stopped. 'We're in trouble.'

'What's going on, Minx? What's happening?'

'There's a shooter in the school…' Mila snuck under her desk, just as the door handle creaked, turned, and swung open with a bang on the wall. Mila jerked in fear, she could have sworn she locked that door. She leaned over and stole a peep at the attacker.

Attackers… there were two of them.

Both wore all black, including leather jackets and combat boots. If Mila hadn't been spending so much time with bikers, she might have mistaken it for some sort of body armour.

'Where are you, Mila?' one of them said, his voice sounding familiar, but in her terror-stricken brain she couldn't place it.

'Minx! Minx!' Rooster's voice was muffled through the speaker. Her heart sped at the thought of the shooters finding her, this was probably her only chance to tell Rooster how she truly felt about him.

'Rooster… I love you,' she whimpered into the cell phone and hung up.

'Miss Rice, if you don't give yourself up now we will shoot every child in this room until you do,' the other shooter warned before cocking his Glock.

She couldn't have any of her students in danger, so Mila quickly scurried out from under her desk and put her hands up in surrender. Both the shooters were wearing ski masks, but Mila could clearly make out the deadly smile of one of them behind the fabric.

'Don't hurt any more kids,' she begged.

The shooter with the assault rifle held it up to her as the other one told her to get in front of him. 'Walk,' he commanded.

Mila did what she was told, but then the voice of Jason Wright came from the hallway.

What the hell was he thinking?

'You need to let her go!' Jason yelled but didn't get to say another word. The attacker with the rifle turned it on him and shot the maths teacher in the face. Students screamed and the attacker who still held her was yelling at them all to shut up or he would open fire.

The attacker behind her grabbed her wrists behind her back before whispering in her ear.

'You will be mine, Mila. All fucking mine...' With those final words, he pulled the Glock toward his partner and shot him in the back of the head.

The butt of the gun introduced her to the darkness.

CHAPTER 25

Rooster rushed towards the police tape but was stopped by a street badge. The pig's hand touched his president's patch and Rooster had to fight the urge to lay the bastard down.

'I'm sorry, sir, this is an active crime scene. I can't allow you past,' the rookie recited, his hand rested on his gun holster.

'Who the fuck do you think you are!' Rooster yelled, not being able to keep his rage contained. 'My woman is in that school. I need to know she is safe!'

'Adams.' Police Chief Phillips waddled his way over to his subordinate and gave Rooster a nod of respect. 'Stand down. Rooster, come this way, we need your help.'

Rooster ducked beneath the police tape, glaring at the badge as he stalked towards the high school. There were cops everywhere, he even spotted a few federal agents milling around in their groups.

'What happened, Phillips?' Rooster asked and pushed his hands into his pockets. He needed to keep his hands occupied, there was no telling what he would do if he found his woman amongst the victims. Phillips stopped in his tracks, his face red with emotion.

'You ready for this, Rooster?' Rooster felt the blood leave his face, balled his hands into fists to avoid their trembling and struggled to comprehend the chief's meaning. 'It's pretty bad.'

When Rooster nodded his head robotically, the police chief continued. 'From what we've been able to tell so far, there were two guys,' Phillips said and led Rooster through the carnage. 'They shot their way through the glass panel next to the front entrance doors. The principal and Mrs Teller – a history teacher – confronted the attackers and were both shot before they could speak, the gunmen then headed towards the classrooms. The first one they entered was manned by a substitute teacher, Miss Clark, who was helping several seniors and juniors of the drama club. No one made it out of the classroom…'

'How many were in there?'

'Fourteen students plus Miss Clark.'

Chief Phillips led Rooster to the room. It was guarded by two uniforms and taped off. The forensic team were already in full swing. They passed two covered bodies in the hallway. This was absolute carnage if he had ever saw it before. Rooster stepped over the body of one of the masked gunmen and squatted next to Jason Wright.

'That's Miss Rice's room,' Phillips said, nodding towards the door. 'Mr Wright ran out of his classroom, according to a few of his students and called out to Miss Rice. He was shot as a result of that.'

'Where is Mila?' Rooster asked, his woman's real name feeling foreign on his lips, but there was no way Phillips would know who he was talking about if he called her Minx.

'We don't know.'

Rooster jerked his head up to the police chief. Phillips picked up the assault rifle beside the dead attacker with his gloved hands. Rooster noticed that the dead man had a Jokers Ace patch sewn onto the back of his leather cut. He was sure that if Phillips took off the mask, it would be Foghorn beneath it. The police chief tilted the gun and ran his finger along the serial number that had been ground down.

'What the fuck are you showing me?' Rooster muttered, his head filled with the chiefs last comment.

'The fucking gun, Rooster!' Phillips snapped.

Looking over the gun, Rooster hated to admit it, but the rifle looked familiar.

'This is the reason I brought you in here, Rooster.' Phillips' tone was solemn and low. 'I've been good to your club, Rooster. When my old man made the deal with your grandfather and his buddies all those years ago, you promised to keep this shit out of the county, and we would turn a blind eye to the shit you guys ran,' Phillips seethed. Rooster had never seen the man so angry before. 'Kids are dead, Rooster! They're dead because of your guns, and now we have a woman missing. I hope you have a plan to find her and fucking soon.'

***

Rooster paced his office again. His walk through of the high school shooting was playing on his mind as well as his conversation with the police chief but fuck if that was the thing that was taking all his focus.

Minx had told him that she loved him in her final moments, before she was taken. Rooster pulled at his hair. He knew he loved Mila Rice, he had known since their first night together – maybe even fucking earlier than that – but the fact that she didn't give him the chance to tell her back was fucking with him.

Rooster didn't care how far he had to go, he was going to have his woman in his arms and he was never going to let Minx go again.

He lapped around his office for what felt like the hundredth time, when a knock sounded through the room. Rooster called out to whoever it was to enter. The door swung open to reveal Gunner standing behind Tank, the prospect too afraid to meet Rooster's gaze.

Fury like he had never felt before raced through Rooster as he charged at the prospect. He grabbed Tank by his vest and rammed him against the closest wall.

'What the fuck happened! Where is my woman?' Rooster's hand held the young man's neck, he didn't give a fuck that Tank was clawing at him. Nothing was going to stop the rage flowing through his veins. 'Where is she?!'

Tank choked out, and Rooster let go only to let him speak. 'I heard the shot, Prez. I ran towards the school. The principal wouldn't let me on the campus, I watched as the two shooters barged through the doors and killed those ladies. They were dressed like us, but one of them had a Jokers Ace patch. I called Gunner, I didn't know what to do.'

'Why were you not protecting my woman!' Rooster yelled in the kid's face. When he didn't get an answer, Rooster asked a different question. 'Do you have any idea who the surviving guy is?'

His patience was wearing thin, he had to find his Minx. Rooster would never forgive himself if she ended up like Naomi or his sister. When Tank shook his head, Rooster shoved the prospect aside. The kid steadied himself and rubbed at his neck as Rooster returned to his desk.

The once impersonal surface was now covered in family photographs, from both Rooster's old office and Patriot's presidential office. The photos used to be comforting, now they mocked him. Why hadn't he thought to put at least one up of him and Minx together?

'You thought prospecting was hard before? You have no idea what's headed your way, Tank,' Rooster grumbled, dismissing the young man. He didn't want to let the kid go from the club, not only was Tank the son of an original, but he was keen to learn. Plus, they had no seasoned hang arounds lined up to take his place.

Tank ran out of the office, but Rooster really couldn't bring himself to care. Where the fuck was Minx? He sunk down into his desk chair, his hands rubbed his temples.

'What now, Prez?' Gunner asked. Rooster glared at his VP around his hand. His friend scraped a hand through his hair and flexed his fingers at his side. Gunner's nervousness was oddly comforting for Rooster.

'Call Override, there has to be something he can do. Get Diablo and Creep to have a look around Minx's house, maybe the asshole who took her has her there.' Rooster shook his head. There had to be something, some sort of clue as to where his Minx was being held. God, he fucking hoped to whatever higher power there was out there that Mila Rice would be found alive.

Rooster sat at his desk for well over an hour, just staring at the computer screen, catastrophising of what Minx might be going through. Did his club now have a third villain that they had to look out for? Did Minx have some crazy stalker she had never mentioned before?

The questions were never ending, and he was well on his way to a migraine from the stress. Rooster was about to lose his shit when his phone pinged on the table.

Override: I might have something.

Without replying he bolted up from his seat and out his office door. Gunner followed close behind down the stairs. Rooster was glad to have the extra backup.

They bypassed the bar and jogged down another set of stairs to get to Override's den. The overly secure door faced them as they hit the basement landing, but the stench of cheap perfume, and the shrill of feminine laughter hit them all at once.

Rooster didn't bother knocking, instead he punched in the code and the door swung open. Multiple high-tech computers lined the wall in front of the desk, which held a top-of-the-line keyboard and so much paper that it rivalled Rooster's own desk. The top of Override's blonde head was visible over the leather chair.

A light hung over the only other table in the room, maps and other diagrams spread across the surface.

'Talk to me, Override.' Rooster stood behind his brother and glared at the screens like they personally offended him.

'We were fucking lucky, Prez. Police have officially identified one of the shooters as Jye Sullivan, also known as Foghorn. He was shot by friendly fire, but that's not the lucky part.' Override pushed off from his screens and rolled his fancy leather desk chair over to the lit-up table.

'I managed to find camera footage of someone fleeing the high school. Followed it down Main Street but lost it when they left the city limit, but here's the weird part. Look at who was driving.'

Override slid a picture across the table and crossed his arms. Rooster picked it up and a cold chill ran down his spine, it was like someone had their hand around his throat and was choking him. The face in the photo was clear as fucking day.

'What the fuck?' Gunner said from behind him, Rooster couldn't have put it better himself. Suddenly, his entire world was turned upside down.

'Call everyone!' Rooster commanded, throwing the photo down on the table. This wasn't fucking happening! 'We need all hands on deck for this one. My brother has her… my brother has my Minx!'

CHAPTER 26

Mila woke and groaned as she tried to stretch out her sore muscles. Her legs tugged against something as they pulled. She glanced at her wrists and realised that she was tied to the bed, but that wasn't all.

Her best lace bra and panty set adorned her body, Mila knew that she hadn't put them on this morning. Where the hell was her comfy set that she wore when she was teaching? Fear took over her.

Mila squeezed her eyes shut for a moment, trying to control her breathing. There was no way she was going to hyperventilate. She would not panic. Yet, even as she was saying those words, Mila's chest started to tingle and tighten.

She turned her head slightly and took in her surroundings. The carpets looked to be once white but were now threadbare and a filthy grey. The paint was peeling off the walls in large flakes, and the springs from the bed were sticking into her body through the thin sheets. There were multiple locks on the door, and she swore she saw a line of ants travelling over the walls.

The floor creaked under the weight of someone else in the room. Mila jerked her head towards the sound, doing a double take at the man at the end of the mattress. For a moment she was relieved.

Steven stood, watching her with an intensity much like his younger brother, but there was a sense of danger that hung around him. Mila didn't know a better way to describe how he was staring at her with the blue eyes he shared with his mother.

Mila's breathing didn't get any better. Her limbs started to shake harder with each passing moment.

'Steven?' Mila finally found her voice, even if it was a little shrill. 'What is happening? Where's the shooter?'

The memory of Mila in her classroom with all those children ducking under their tables... God, please let them all be safe.

She took in the man glaring at her, finally noticing that he was wearing the same clothes as the shooters. Oh shit! Was he one of them? Where was the other guy? The images of the high school hallway bombarded her mind as she watched Jason rush towards her before being shot, and the shooter – who she now knew was Steven – turning his gun onto his accomplice.

The other guy was shot.

Steven killed him.

'You don't have to worry about that biker scum anymore my beautiful Mila. He's not going to bother us again. I saved you from him.' Steven grinned, but it did nothing to comfort Mila. It was too wide, too many teeth. It was way more threatening than any smile should be, and it turned her insides.

What was going on with him? This wasn't the same man she met two months ago.

'Where is Rooster?' she asked.

'Don't you fucking say it!' Steven screamed, spittle gathered in the corners of his mouth and his nostrils flared. 'Don't say that ridiculous name... What the hell was my father thinking? Giving him that cute nickname. Dylan didn't deserve a road name. I did! The oldest son!' Steven started to march in front of the bed, his hands coming up to scrub his chin. His eyes were bloodshot, and he began to mutter to himself.

'How could he have been so surprised that I didn't join his precious gang. He and his fucking queen, my mother. They cast me out!' Steven turned back to Mila suddenly and launched himself on top of her. She let out an oof but was quickly shut up with a slap to her cheek. 'It had just been the three of us. For so many years, and then they had Dylan, and then Heather straight afterwards. Why the fuck would they want to replace me? I thought I was a good boy, obviously I wasn't good enough for them. They made sure I knew that by having an entirely new family, right in front of me!' Steven shook Mila and she cried out in pain as her shoulders pulled against the tight ropes.

'I'm sure that's not true, Steven,' Mila managed out. She had no idea how Steven could believe that, based on what Mila had already witnessed amongst their family. Queenie loved her oldest son and hated that he lived so far away.

Steven grabbed her face in his hand, his fingers burying into her skin.

'Shut up, you stupid bitch!' Steven screamed before he aimed another sharp slap towards her. Mila's cheek burned red, and tears sparked in her eyes. 'You don't know a fucking thing.'

That's when he produced the knife and began twisting the sharp point against his forefinger, not quite drawing any blood.

'So, you know why I cut cheeks? Because they are so soft and plump. They're the same as ass cheeks and tits, and fuck me, Mila, you have a great set of both.'

Mila's eyes widened and her whole body went into momentary shock. Oh god she was going to pass out, the room was spinning. The truth hit her square in the face, Mila shook her head uncontrollably as she squeezed her eyes shut. She couldn't bear to even look at him. It couldn't be Steven, he had been in California since he was eighteen.

He couldn't be the Bryson City Slasher.

Before she could say anything, the cold blade sliced through the material of her bra and cut the skin between her breasts. Mila couldn't do anything, she couldn't move, she definitely couldn't escape. All she could do was scream.

Her cheek burned and stung as salty tears dropped on to her damaged skin. Mila let out a hiss when Steven traced the cut with his finger, motherfucker was enjoying this.

'That's it, babe, scream for me. You're making me so hard.' Steven rubbed his growing crotch against her bare leg, and Mila whimpered into the motel room.

***

Rooster bent his bike left and right down the winding roads. He had to save his Minx before she ended up being another girl in the newspapers. The fact that the man who took his woman was his very own brother, fuck, it was all just too crazy for Rooster to comprehend.

Why the fuck would Steven even go after Mila?

He sped through the peaceful neighbourhood of his childhood, pulled into his mother's driveway, and left his bike on the concrete. Rooster didn't even bother to knock as he shoved the front door open.

'Ma!' he shouted, walking through the house. He found his mother in the kitchen, wearing her old property patch and one of his father's t-shirts, boiling a pot on the stove.

'Don't you yell at me like that, Dylan Bates, I don't care that you are an adult and the president. I am still your mother.'

'Sorry, Ma... Where is Steven? He's staying with you right?' Rooster tapped his foot to the floor but didn't say anything else as he crossed his arms. He didn't want to lose his shit in front of his mother, but Rooster was done, his patience had been left behind at the clubhouse.

'No, no. Your brother said that he didn't want to stay in this house. I think he's staying in a motel outside county lines.' Queenie shrugged her shoulders. Rooster's entire body tensed up. He grabbed his mother's shoulders and made her face him.

'Where?'

'My god, Rooster! Why are you acting like this?' Queenie's eyebrows drew together, and she tilted her head, holding Rooster's gaze.

'There was a shooing at the school. Minx is missing... Steven has Minx!' Rooster finally admitted to his mother. The former matriarch's face went from straight up horrified to terrified.

'What? No. He wouldn't do that to you, Rooster, he's your brother, after all. Are you sure it wasn't just some Joker trying to make you turn on your brother?' Queenie stepped away from Rooster, but he couldn't let her keep living a lie.

'Did he tell you were he was staying?' he begged.

'No, but he did take your father's truck.' As the words left his mother's mouth Rooster grabbed at the sides of his head as a sudden rush of warmth covered his body. Patriot's old truck had a fucking tracking device!

'Thanks, Ma!' He pressed a kiss to her cheek and bolted out the still open door. Rooster picked up his bike, not looking at the marks that were left on his tank and called Override.

'You need to find a location for Patriot's truck,' Rooster said without a greeting.

'Roost, that information had been wiped from the system when the old prez died,' Override said, the typing of his flying fingers barely audible over the phone. Rooster recited his father's license plate number and registration code. 'I'll have what you need in five minutes.'

'Make it two, Override.'

***

Mila screamed again, earning herself another whip from the fucking riding crop Steven had hidden in his nightmare motel room.

'That's it sweet, Mila, scream for me. Look at how hard you're making me.' Steven dropped the cane and unzipped his dirty suit pants. 'You see it, don't you. You want it too, don't you, Mila?' She tried to shake her head but as soon as she moved, her breasts were whipped again.

'I knew as soon as I met you. I knew that you had to be saved from that life. I always wondered why someone as beautiful as you, someone with such a respectable and honourable job, would be with someone like my little brother. A motorcycle bastard. Why would you want that? You should have been with someone like me, a respectable man with a good job and a great reputation.' Steven leaned down and tried to kiss her, but Mila wasn't going down without a fucking fight.

'Murdering women isn't a job asshole,' she spat, before she was punched in the cheekbone. She heard it crack before she felt the pain.

'I'm not a murderer, you stupid biker whore. I'm an advertising executive. Why did you have to get involved? You tainted yourself by being with him. How could you do that to me, my sweet Mila?' Steven ran another finger down one of her new cuts, this time making sure to scrape his dirty nail into the blood. He lifted his hand and studied the crimson liquid before sucking it off his finger.

There was so much overwhelming pain Mila thought she was about to pass out again.

'Now take what I fucking give you,' he seethed, before forcing her mouth open with a squeeze of his fingers and stuffing his dick inside. Hitting the back of her throat, Mila gagged and tried to jerk away but the monster had her head locked in place. 'You even think of biting me, and you'll die a hell of a lot more painfully.'

Steven surged forward and pinched Mila's nose, stopping any kind of air flow instantly. She choked trying to scream again and strained against the rope now cutting into the flesh on her wrists.

Darkness crept into the corners of Mila's vision, as the door to the room of horrors slammed against the wall. Air hit her lungs, and she coughed against the sudden change. The hard stomp of boots, grunts of effort and the hum of a blade being swung in panic played out a scene she was too weak to watch. Her head hung as she coughed and heaved air back into her lungs. Curses and threats bounced off the walls around her. A figure crouched next to her head and for a moment she was afraid, but then the comfort of Rooster's honey eyes settled her heart.

'Thank fucking God!' he said as he rested his head against Mila's. They stayed like that for a beat, then Rooster went to work untying her hands. He carefully avoided any place that might injure her more.

'No! Stop!' Steven cried out. 'She's mine! You're ruining–!'

A hard kick to his face put that thought to bed.

'Call Stitches!' Rooster barked his orders. 'We'll use Pops' truck to get Minx back to the clubhouse. Creep, call Tank. Get him to bring the van.'

Words started to muffle around her as she lay still on the bed and let her relief sink in. She was going to be safe. Her hero had come to rescue her.

CHAPTER 27

Rooster watched as Mila slept on their bed at the clubhouse. Stitches had made sure that Minx was going to be okay, at least physically. The club's doctor had given him an ointment to rub into her cuts and welts. Her worst cuts had been stitched and thankfully the majority of them were not deep enough to leave a lasting scar.

Leaning over, Rooster pressed a kiss to Minx's forehead, he was going to be gone for a few hours, but he couldn't wait any longer to tell her exactly how he felt about her.

'I love you,' he whispered into her ear, and pulled away. Rooster was met with his woman's open ocean eyes. They swam with unshed tears. He pushed away strands of hair from her forehead, needing to touch her. 'Minx. You're awake baby.'

'You love me?' Her whispered voice broke under the realization.

'Yeah, Minx.' Rooster smiled and brushed his lips against hers gently. 'I'm so fucking in love with you baby.'

Minx's arms circled around Rooster's neck and pulled his head down just enough for her to whisper into his own ear.

'I love you too, Dylan.'

'I know you do, baby.' Being careful of her reddened and swollen cheek, Rooster cupped her face and kissed her tenderly one more time. 'I'm not sure how you found out about my real name, but we'll have a talk about it later. For now, I'm going to send Ma up to keep you company. I've got Tank on door duty, while I take care of business.'

'He's the Slasher...' Minx said softly, tears rolling down her cheek quickly.

'What was that, baby?'

'Steven... he's the Bryson City Slasher. He told me how he liked to take a knife to cheeks because they reminded him of... of... o–' Rooster grabbed Minx's hands and pressed his lips against them, not doing anything but breathing her in, letting the new information roll through his brain.

If what his woman was saying was true that would mean that not only is his older brother the murderer of fourteen children, four teachers and his fellow school shooter, but he killed six other women, including his own sister, and that wouldn't even be the sickest part.

'Make him pay, Rooster,' Mila whispered. Rooster was taken back to the night when his woman held him while he grieved the loss of his younger sister. Those same words had once felt like wishful thinking... now they were a vow he was going to keep.

Rooster kissed her hands quickly one more time before standing up and leaving. His mother was already standing by the door and, judging by the look on her face, she'd heard everything.

'This can't be true, Rooster,' Queenie begged. 'Steven lives in California, for fuck's sake! He didn't even come to your father's funeral. How could he be there and here?'

Rooster took his mother into a hug, feeling her trembling. She was about to become panic stricken. He couldn't have her like this, not if she was going to be looking after Minx.

'I'm going to find out the truth, Ma, I promise you.' He squeezed her tightly and held her a little longer than usual. He walked down the stairs and into the main room. Brothers stood around the pool tables and the bar, but no one was playing, shooting the shit or drinking. The room was buzzing with a quiet murmur of voices.

Rooster slipped behind the bar and tugged open the trap door that led to the cube. The cold concrete cellar had once been a wine cellar but when the Originals ran into trouble with the Jokers and discovered that the room underneath was relatively soundproof, it became the unofficial holding for enemies of Black Alchemy.

Rooster climbed down the ladder and listened as his older brother's screams became louder and louder with every step. He turned when he hit the concrete floor, and saw Steven strapped to a metal chair. Half his fingers were laying on the ground, his left cheek was cut up and his whole face had turned black and blue. Diablo was cleaning the blood off his sheers when he raised his head.

'He awake?' Rooster asked, stripping off his cut and hanging it on the hook. His enforcer nodded his head and stood back against the cold wall. Rooster grabbed the other metal chair in the room, swung it around and sat in front of the man he had once considered his blood.

Steven gave him a stupid grin, making his ugly face even worse. The split in his lips dropped with red ooze and one of his eyes was closed.

'Hello, little brother,' Steven spat.

'Was it you?' Rooster asked, completely ignoring Steven's effort to form a familial bond.

'Was it me what? Did I try and set your woman free from this life? Did I want her for myself? Why, little brother, you saw us in that motel room. You saw how she wanted me, Rooster, how does it feel to be the second best brother now?'

'Did you kill Angel? Did you kill all those girls? Amanda, Naomi? Did you kill them?' Rooster felt Diablo tense up behind him. Since he hadn't let his brotherhood know about the latest information from Minx, it wasn't a surprise to Rooster that his enforcer was taken off guard.

'I didn't do anything they didn't enjoy. They were weak women, Rooster. You need strong ones in your club, especially when I take over. It's my fucking birth right! I'll have Mila by my side and club whores who don't beg for mercy like a little bitch.' Rooster jerked out of the chair and threw it to the side. He reared back his fist and was about to make contact when Diablo came out of nowhere and tackled the tied-up Steven to the ground.

'You sick, twisted bastard. She was your sister… and you, you raped and murdered her!'

'She was nothing but a motorcycle whore. How our father allowed her to become that way is beyond me, that's why I was never going to allow Daisy to end up like that,' Steven defended himself, completely sprouting off nonsense.

'Were you going to kill Daisy too?' Rooster asked. His anger froze him in place at the need to protect their innocent baby sister. He no longer recognised the fuck in front of him, there was no way in hell Rooster was related to that thing.

'No!' Steven's lips curled back in disgust at Rooster's question. 'I was going to convince her to go to school in California. She would marry a respectable man just like myself and stay away from ever becoming what her older sister was.'

Rooster couldn't hear another word that came from Steven's mouth. Nothing could have ever prepared him for the fuckery that was happening before him.

'Call Rubble, Creep, and Gunner in here. They're gonna wanna hear this,' Rooster commanded Diablo, it was time for this shit to be over with.

His brothers all filed into the cube one after another. Diablo had even managed to find Rubble surprisingly sober. Rooster's brothers all stood in a line, giving him their full attention and respect.

'Boys, we have a situation here,' Rooster said, his hands on his hips and his head hung on his shoulders. He needed to keep his cool for what was to happen next. 'It seems as though we didn't just catch the Bryson City High School shooter... Steven is also the Bryson City Slasher.'

The silence in the room was chilling. Rooster watched as Rubble planted his feet wide apart and his hands started to shake. The road captain was going to take blood tonight, but Rooster was going to get answers first.

He called for Gunner to strip the monster naked and hang him on the wall. The chains hanging down were old, rusted and would hopefully cut into the Slasher's wrists.

While his VP was dealing with Steven, Rooster picked out his weapon. The steel softball bat was heavy in his hands and would be the perfect tool to get the man to talk. He needed answers, but he also wanted to make sure that they would never hear from this monster again.

'What kind of sick animal rapes and murders his own sister?' Rooster asked before he swung. The sound of metal against bone reverberated through the soundproof dungeon. 'Then you kidnapped my woman.' The ping of the bar rang in the air again. 'The pain that you put her through...' Another ping. 'You're going to spill your guts before Diablo cuts them out of you. Talk now!'

Steven didn't say anything, his head was hanging low on his shoulders and his breath rattled. Rooster nodded his head towards Gunner who was manning the cold hose. Water sprayed from the pipe and Steven squealed back to life.

'Well, answer me.' He listened as his brother continued to wheeze. 'Since you don't feel like answering, we'll just whip it out of you.'

Rooster moved to grab the same riding crop that had been found in the motel room. He flexed the crop and watched the fright in Steven's eyes. 'Aww, are you getting scared, little man?'

He didn't wait for a reply. Instead, he just thwacked the man's penis, another pig-like squeal came from him. 'Are you going to talk now, little man?'

Steven still said nothing. Rooster went to town, whipping and scaring the man to the point where, even if he was pleading for Rooster to stop so that he could talk, Rooster just stuffed a dirty rag into his mouth.

An hour had passed and several riding crops lay broken to the side. After giving the man a bloodied body and a penis that would be lucky to work again, Rooster asked him if he was ready to talk.

'Fine!' Steven yelled, surprising Rooster. 'I just wanted revenge.'

'Revenge for what?' Rooster asked, his anger subsiding at the sight of the man's pain. He tapped the man's penis with the barrel of his gun softly, causing Steven to howl.

'They replaced me! Everything that you have is because they replaced me with you! Dad always liked you better and so did Mom! Dad gave you the road name, he trained you for the club, I wasn't needed anymore. And now that Dad is dead, I was going to make sure that everything you had would be mine! I fucking deserved everything he gave to you and everything you have, including your woman. She's mine!'

Rooster just stared at the man who was his brother for twenty-six years. 'Creep and Rubble, you're up.'

'You're the one who killed her?' Rubble screamed as he rushed at Steven. 'You killed my Angel.'

Rubble's fists were clenched. Rooster was going to let the man get his anger out on Steven. It was fucking time to kill the monster. Rubble continued to scream and clock Steven in any place he could find, there was not going to be a single inch of skin that wasn't going to be bruised or cut up.

Had Creep not pulled the rabid Rubble off Steven, he'd have finished him before the treasurer got his pound of flesh.

Creep wasn't about fists, he brought a knife to this fight. The filthy mongrel deserved exactly what he'd dished out. Creep cut and slashed, opening up the squealing pig. Steven begged for mercy. Creep asked him how it felt and the asshole cried like a fucking baby.

When he was close to losing consciousness Rooster turned around and walked out of the cube. He didn't want to listen anymore. 'Finish him off,' he said. 'Tank and Stone can clean up the mess.'

CHAPTER 28

'What have you got for me, Override?' Rooster asked, leaning over the back of his friend's luxury desk chair.

'How the fuck were you related to this monster, Roost?' Override mumbled and pulled up a dozen different articles. Some from the *Bryson City Bugle* and others from different towns between North Carolina and Los Angeles. All of them reported different crimes, from arson and petty theft to the mutilation of animals. Each of the articles ranged between when Steven was a pre-teen to just before he came to Bryson City.

'How did you connect all this to Steven?' Rooster asked. He pulled up one of the only chairs in the room and stared at one of the articles that described the brutal rape of a girl in Los Angeles. She'd survived but her attacker was never found.

'It wasn't easy. It's not like we can take this information to the cops, but all of them had the similarities that I just couldn't go past.' Override enlarged one of the articles about a fire that happened in Bryson City when they were kids. It had been big news when it happened, since they were such a small town the newspaper was more of a gossip column than anything else. These past few months, the reporters had finally had something juicy to sink their teeth into.

'I remember this. That old warehouse behind The Honey Pot went up in flames and almost took out the building. Fuck, Pops was furious when that happened,' Rooster commented and read through the information. No one had been hurt, but it was suspicious enough that the police opened a full investigation into the fire. They turned up nothing, only that it was deliberately lit. They found accelerants but the case remained cold to this day.

'Yeah, well. Turns out that Steven was found only a couple of miles down the road from the fire. He smelt like lighter fluid. They didn't have enough to charge him, so he was released into the custody of your parents.' Override pointed to a line where Steven's name was briefly mentioned. Rooster read ahead and a frown started to form in his brow. He never remembered his parents bailing his brother out of jail, not once, but the timeline did match up with his brother and parents fighting more and then Steven suddenly announcing that he was going to attend college in LA.

All those missing pieces from the past few months were coming together, and Rooster wasn't sure how he felt about it.

'What happened while he was in LA?' Rooster asked. Steven hadn't been back to Bryson City ever since he left for LA, not even to visit for their birthdays or the holidays. He would always say that he was just too busy at his advertisement firm to come home for a break.

'It's not any better man.' Override clicked his mouse, and he watched as more articles created a timeline of crimes. Along with some police reports, all of them were by women reporting that someone was stalking them and breaking into their homes. Some of them even reported that their underwear was missing along with jewellery.

'There are at least a dozen reports about a man that sort of fits the description of Steven, stalking or loitering around their windows.

They were always on the ground floor apartments, and each time the police came by the check it out he would be gone, but there would always be a stain left by the windowsill.' Override shook his head and continued down the timeline, each offense was followed up with a bank statement or some other kind of proof that Steven was still in LA during the time of the attacks.

Rooster couldn't believe what he was seeing. Steven wouldn't stop bragging about having the perfect life, about not being tied down to the club and not having a family to answer to when he was here after Angel's murder. Fuck, Rooster had been taken for a fool and he didn't like that one fucking bit.

'Roost…' Override interrupted his thoughts. His face said that he had more bad news. Great, Rooster didn't know how much more of this he could take. 'There are pictures of some of the girls, it seems as though stalking wasn't enough for Steven. He started raping some of the girls he stalked and, according to social media, this happened right around the time his girlfriend of a few months dumped him.'

The sound of a click filtered through the air and three pictures appeared on Override's screens. Rooster had to suck in a breath because he couldn't believe what he was fucking seeing. All of them stared back at him, with pained blue eyes and dirtied up brown hair that was the exact shade of Angel's. Rooster knew that he wasn't seeing pictures of his sister but they all bared such a striking resemblance to her that Rooster had to double take.

'What the fuck am I looking at here, Override?' Rooster growled. His heart was thumping in his chest, and sweat was building at his hairline. Override scrolled down through the police photos, Rooster was about to throw his damn chair at the wall. Fucking hell, their sister was Steven's target all along. That knowledge brought up the coffee and the small amount of breakfast Rooster had managed to ingest that morning. He thought back over the women that were

Steven's earlier victims. They all looked similar... the blue eyes, the brown hair, all of them described as though their smiles could 'light up a room'.

Each of the women who were assaulted by Steven had a large cut over the swell of one of their breasts, deep angry marks that would take a seriously good plastic surgeon to cover up. Rooster couldn't imagine not only having the mental scars of what Steven had done to them but also the physical ones as well.

He had already spoken with his woman briefly about what she had been through in that motel room. The few times she repeated her story, Minx would break down and have to stop completely. Rooster was worried as any partner would be that his woman was bottling up her emotions too much.

'There's also this...' Override didn't even try to cover his wince when Rooster shot a hard glare at his friend. 'I wasn't sure if I should show you this, but I got photos of all the Bryson City Slasher victims... They all look the same.'

Override clicked his mouse a few times and Rooster stared at the screens and almost fucking lost his lunch. All the women had blue eyes and brown hair like Angel. All of them except for Minx.

'There's one more thing...' Override muttered as he pulled up more information.

'You need to be fucking faster at giving me this information, man!' Rooster fumed.

'I didn't want to overwhelm you with this at once. I thought that if I gradually got to the worst of it, it would be easier for you to process...' Override shrunk back into his chair and clicked on the last file on the screen. Whatever his brother was going to show Rooster, he knew it wasn't going to be good.

Rooster leaned forward and glared at the computer screen. The photos of a girl – who again looked just like Angel – lay dead on the slab in the coroner's office. She had a slice over her right breast and finger bruising around her neck. Her face was pale blue under the harsh light and, if it wasn't for the horrific mutilations to her body, she would almost look serene. Peaceful. But Rooster could only imagine what her last few moments on this earth was like.

'He killed the last one, raped her and strangled her as well as cut her up like the other women he raped,' Override said, skimming the report attached to the photos. 'She fought him though, the coroner noted that she had skin cells under her fingernails and the cops were able to link that DNA sample with the rapes happening. One detective even noted down that they could now be looking for a serial killer, not just a serial rapist.'

Rooster couldn't take any more of this.

He needed to get away from all of it.

The fact that he shared blood with the Bryson City Slasher hadn't bothered him until he realised just how fucking sick Steven actually was. He had hurt so many women, changed their lives and ruined them beyond repair. Rooster knew that he would never lay a hand on a woman, especially his Minx, but even the idea of sharing blood with Steven was making him physically ill.

He jumped up from his seat, scaring the crap out of Override and booked it out of the computer geek's den. Rooster needed some time to himself, he needed to be able to process all the fucked up things he had learned about his biological brother.

Brothers called for his attention as he stomped through the clubhouse, but Rooster didn't stop. He didn't know how he was going to react to anyone asking him if he was okay because, in that moment as thankful he was that Steven could no longer breathe, he wasn't okay with all the new information.

His office door burst open. He didn't bother to close it, the idea of being in the room by himself was almost suffocating. Rooster slumped into his office chair and let the evidence swirl around in his head. He leaned forward and hung his head in his hands, the shame of Steven's transgressions drowning him.

'Rooster? Honey?' Minx knocked softly on his office door. He didn't look up to answer her, but he knew she wasn't going to leave as she stepped inside and closed it softly behind her. Everything about his woman was soft, but at that moment, Rooster wasn't feeling very soft towards anybody.

'Minx, not now.' Rooster rubbed his hand over his eyes, trying to get that last image out of his head. She had looked so much like Angel, the brutality of the rape and abuse that followed made Rooster want to bring his brother back from the dead just to kill him again.

Minx didn't listen to his warning, and slowly came over to his desk. She planted her hip against the wooden edge. Her delicate hand splayed out on the dark wood, as she ran her other hand through Rooster's hair. 'Override said that you might need me.'

'Override overstepped his bounds,' Rooster shot back, immediately regretting his words. Minx's fingers paused in his hair, the slight comfort that he was experiencing in his chest evaporating. He covered her small hand that was still on the desk with his own, squeezing it slightly to give her reassurance. 'I'm sorry, Minx. Override just showed me some stuff. It was… a lot.'

'I know.' Minx sat at the edge of his desk and Rooster's hands cupped her hips. The need to touch her was so strong that he couldn't deny himself even if he wanted to. 'Override didn't tell me what he showed you, just that you didn't react well to it.'

'You can say that again.' Rooster traced his thumb over the seam of Minx's jeans, enjoying the way her hands went back into his hair. Without a word he pulled her off the desk and onto his lap, cradling her in his arms. Minx's hand rested over his head, his father's skull ring glistening in the low light of his office. Rooster held her close and whispered in her ear just how much he loved her.

He felt Minx relax into his arms and, for a moment, they were both silent. He knew that his woman could feel his heart beating for her under her palm. Rooster kissed Minx's pretty blonde hair and sighed into the fresh peach shampoo.

'He did more,' Rooster finally said, into the dead air. 'Steven hurt so many other woman before he came back to Bryson City. I never knew. How could I never know the monster that was my brother?'

'How could you have known, Rooster?' Minx's soft voice brushed against his neck.

'We share the same blood, Minx.' Rooster flexed his arm and showed her the veins running down his skin. 'I share blood with that monster of a human.'

Minx placed her hand over his forearm. 'Are you saying that you could commit those horrible acts, Dylan Bates? That you would hunt down and abuse women who offended you or reminded you of something that you hate?'

His woman's words caused Rooster to think about how similar the other women looked to Angel. Needing the comfort, he nuzzled into Minx's hair again. 'I could never do what he did to those women, Minx.'

'That's why you're the hero here, Rooster. Not the monster.' Minx leaned up and kissed him quickly. Rooster wanted to take it further, but he knew that his woman was still dealing with the trauma from that day. Minx looked up at him with those large eyes he had fallen so in love with and said the words that he didn't know he needed to hear. 'Because of you, the world has one less monster in it now.'

CHAPTER 29

Rooster knew that he shouldn't be here, but he had no fucking choice. He needed to put the fucked up crimes of his brother behind him, and the only way Rooster was going to be able to do that was by being confronted with the lair of a serial killer. The information from Override had been spinning in his head for days, he knew he needed to see inside the Bryson City Slasher's lair and burn it to the ground.

The motel outside of Bryson City was rundown and neglected. He glanced around, probably looking more suspicious than anything else. He hadn't returned since he rescued Minx from Steven's clutches. An eerie air permeated throughout the entire motel. It was abandoned, which was why his monster of a brother chose this as his home base.

The double-storey building had a large vacancy sign that only partly remained, signs of it having been shot up many times. The ground had unkept weeds growing through the cracked pavement and parking lot. Doors hung off the hinges of some of the rooms, and the ones that did have the doors attached were missing room numbers, but Rooster didn't need a map to remember where he rescued his woman from. It was etched into his brain.

Slowly he took the stairs to the second floor, the wind picking up and whistling through the dead air. A couple of rats were eating something dead in the corner of the staircase, they didn't move as he approached. Rooster had to avoid them and continued towards the motel room of terror.

A faded shape of the number four was branded on the door that might have once been a rich dark green but was now the colour of vomit. The door lay on the floor where he had kicked it down in desperation. Rooster could still remember the adrenaline rushing through his system that night.

He was determined to get his Minx back in his arms again, seeing the way Rubble had deteriorated after Angel's murder had painted a vivid picture of how Rooster would react to finding his woman in the same position.

Even though he'd found his Minx alive, she had emotional and mental scars that would haunt her for the rest of her life. Rooster was doing everything in his power to chase away her fears, but it still broke him when she would wake in the middle of the night fighting off his arm in fear of being back in this very motel room.

This was the place that housed his woman's demons, but it also housed his own as well. Rooster stepped over the door, which let out a loud crack beneath his riding boot that echoed through the abandoned motel.

He probably should have brought Gunner or one of his other trusted brothers with him, but Rooster needed to do this alone.

The air hung stale, and dust particles danced in the dirt-covered window. It was the only source of light in the room, the warm glow of the sunset casting a weird orange glint in the evil space. It was not a source of happiness, instead it was warning of horrors that occurred here.

The bed was only a mattress mounted on an iron frame that sat along the furthest wall. The image of his Minx tied to the metal headboard, her body bruised and abused, would never leave Rooster's mind for the remainder of his days. The way her terrified eyes had met his as he kicked the fucking door down, how her body was contorted in a way that would cause her pain for days afterwards. The tears in her eyes when his brother had his disgusting cock shoved in her mouth, Rooster wanted to bring Steven back from the dead just to cut off his cock again and stuff it in his mouth.

Even though it had taken hours, and multiple brothers taking their pound of flesh, Rooster was now hoping for more time to teach the monster a lesson. No one messed with the BAMC women and lived to tell the tale.

He continued through the room, kicking at a lamp that had fallen during the scuffle to free his Minx. The once white, now grey threadbare carpet stuck to his riding boots. Rooster's hands were thrust in his pockets to stop himself from touching anything that would leave evidence. The lighter he had stolen from Override grazed his fingers, but it wasn't time to use it yet.

The time would come soon, but not yet.

Rooster could hear a faucet dripping from the bathroom and he followed the noise, pushing through sliding door that became stuck before he used his brute strength to shove it open.

Discoloured ceiling tiles from a past leak threatened to cave in on the bathroom. The floor to wall tiles were cracked with dirty grout lines with mould. Next to the rust-stained basin of the sink was a wall with exposed piping. Rooster stepped into the disgusting bathroom with the warped mirror, rat droppings covering the disgusting floor.

He wasn't sure what he was going to find in this room, but what he did shocked him. Panties covered with vacuum sealed plastic sat where the usual complimentary shampoo and conditioner would be.

So many panties, but seven of them had blood as well as other stains that Rooster didn't want to identify.

Something also caught his eye in the stalker's haul. A thick, silver class ring sat next to the leaking faucet. Rooster picked it up and, much to his satisfaction, read the name of his Minx's father. His woman had been losing her mind since this ring had gone missing and now he could bring it back to her.

Then the realisation crashed over Rooster.

Minx had this ring stolen while she was staying with him at the clubhouse. Steven had been stalking his woman, but for how long? It wasn't like Mila was the Bryson City Slasher's type according to Override's research — it was incredibly rare that his techie brother was wrong. If what Override had uncovered was correct, then his woman had the wrong hair colour, which, yes, could have been easily fixed, but Rooster got the sense that Steven didn't have that kind of time.

Rooster hated the way his brain was thinking, he didn't want to be exploring why his woman had been taken. He wanted to put the whole fucking ordeal behind them. With the renewed idea of burning the place to the ground, Rooster turned to leave.

He was stopped when he spotted a bit of paper sticking out behind the wall where the sliding door was hidden. Carefully, he pulled it open and immediately the food he had consumed before going on this ride threatened to make an appearance.

Photos, so many fucking photos, of his sister Angel.

Rooster scoured the entire fucking shrine to his sister. There were photos of her walking down Main Street, a smile on her face as bright as the engagement ring on her finger. Some had close ups of her pushing her hair out of her face, but her ring was blacked out with permanent marker. Other photos had her eyes scratched out, where others had lip marks. Rooster couldn't believe what he was seeing. There were photos here from before Steven even came back into town. Before the killings started.

He noted some of them had Rubble in the frame, but his brother had large crosses over his face and body.

There were other photos that didn't look like Angel at all but that, as he looked closer, Rooster realised were of all the murdered women. They were gory pictures, Amanda still had fear in her lifeless eyes. All of them were barely dressed or had ripped lingerie on their bodies and there was blood. So much fucking blood.

Rooster couldn't physically look at the hundreds of photos that were stuck haphazardly on the door, but one did catch his attention. It was further away from the rest of them, but Rooster would recognise his woman's face from a mile away. She stood with him at Angel's funeral, her hand holding his while they had a moment of silence to remember their fallen sister. Rooster had been scratched out, and words were written over Mila.

MINE

Rooster had seen enough. He stormed out of the lair, his woman's ring in his pocket and the one photo of his woman in his other hand. He pulled the lighter from his pocket and flicked it to light. He burned the edges before letting it fall on the stained mattress and walking out of the room.

Rooster mounted his bike and took off for home, back to his woman as smoke rose from the back wheel. Someone would find the motel burned down and wonder what had happened, but no one would know what hid in the ashes.

The Bryson City Slasher was killed and his lair would never be found.

With that thought Rooster pushed his bike harder and smiled under his bandana. His woman was waiting for him.

CHAPTER 30

Thanksgiving, Christmas and New Years passed by Mila, or Minx, as she'd rather be called these days. Slowly her sense of safety was coming back, but she still hadn't returned to the high school. She hadn't gone to any of the funerals, something she felt incredibly guilty for, but she couldn't bear to face the parents of those fourteen students.

Minx was the reason their children were being buried in the ground.

The new school principal had offered her old job back, but she had turned him down. There was too much trauma in one room. Maybe one day she would return to the job she loved so desperately, but right now she couldn't.

Which brought Minx back to the present, as she lay in Rooster's arms, dressed in one of his favourite Harley Davidson t-shirts and a pair of sweatpants. Her man was shirtless but wore those jeans that hung low on his hips. They were doing an exercise her therapist, Dr Wilson, had suggested. It was so that Minx could get used to the feel of Rooster's skin against hers.

Her mind often drifted to Queenie.

When the former matriarch went to Rooster about selling the

house he had grown up in, Minx thought her man was going to completely explode. But once his mother explained that there were just too many memories for her to live in that place every day, Rooster seemed to understand.

Minx knew exactly how Queenie was feeling, she had moved out with Rooster about two weeks after the incident. She tried to stay in her bed for one night, but she couldn't stop thinking about the fact that Steven had been in her house. Minx knew her man had taken care of her nightmare, but she couldn't deal with the idea that her cottage wasn't safe anymore.

Queenie had been teaching Minx everything that she knew about being the matriarch ol' lady. It was a lot easier now that they were both living at the clubhouse.

At first, she was worried about living within the walls of the club, but Minx quickly discovered that it was quite the opposite.

She loved it!

Minx was living with one big family of men, women, and children. She couldn't believe how wide they all held their arms open for her but, as much as she loved the club, she didn't want to live in the clubhouse for the rest of her life.

The alarm Rooster had set earlier brought Minx out of her thoughts. It was time for her appointment.

'You okay, baby? You still want to do this?'

'I need to do this,' she replied.

Nodding his head, Rooster held Minx's hand and helped her off the bed. That first night had been tough for the both of them. Minx would wake up multiple times during the night, fighting off Rooster's arm or anything that she felt was tying her down.

Mama Bear, Grizz's ol' lady, came to her with the number of a therapist when she found Minx sitting on the counter in the kitchen late one night. It didn't take much for her to break down, admitting to the older woman that she hadn't been sleeping. After a long chat and the first colours of the morning creeping over the horizon, Mama Bear came back with a post-it note and a number. Minx had been seeing Mrs Wilson ever since.

Mrs Wilson was simply amazing. She had not only been helping Minx with her PTSD, but also with the problems she faced after her father's death and her mother turning to the bottle after she lost her great love. Navigating all that grief took a lot of patience and heavy-hearted tears, but those cathartic sessions were seeing her on the mend.

Minx watched as Rooster moved around their room, throwing on a shirt and tying up his riding boots. As if he could feel her eyes on him, Rooster looked up and smirked that gorgeous smirk of his. Minx could honestly feel the love in his stare.

Even though neither of them had said the words since the night he had rescued her, they knew how they felt about each other. She dressed quickly in a black tank top and jeans, his father's skull ring still adorned her finger, but now she had her own father's class ring back. It hung on a necklace around her neck, never to be left at home again.

Minx pulled on her own boots and adorned her precious property patch. The smooth leather comforted her in a way that she had only felt in Rooster's arms.

'You ready, babe?' Rooster asked. Minx took in what her man looked like. Dressed in his tight white shirt and his cut, Minx felt herself fall more in love with him and she hated that she wasn't able to show him. The few times she had thought that she was ready to be intimate with him again, Minx freaked out before he even got her top off.

'Yeah, let's go.' Minx followed her man through the clubhouse, holding his hand tightly, loving that she was able to feel so comfortable here. Just being around the brothers who loved her like a younger sister, Minx knew that she could live the rest of her life in the Black Alchemy Motorcycle Club world.

Minx sat on the old floral couch in Mrs Wilson's office. The sun streamed in from the atrium window, painting the room with a mellow glow. Her therapist sitting across from her was a woman of bright coloured dresses and soft, sweet words. Her white hair was pulled away from her face in a grandmotherly bun. Behind a set of thin, rose gold frames resting on her button nose, a pair of kind eyes and a simple smile welcomed Minx. Neither of them said a word as she took a moment to bathe in the comfort of the sunlit room.

'What are you feeling, Minx?' the doctor finally started when she sensed Minx was ready.

'I'm still not sleeping properly,' Minx admitted. 'Even though I know I'm in Rooster's arms, we've been doing the exercises you've been tasking us with, and I know I am safe with him. I just feel like when I close my eyes, if I open them again, I'll be back in that motel room, and I'll have to go through everything again.' Minx grabbed one of the decorative cushions and hugged it to her chest as she rocked back and forth.

She was desperate to feel safe again.

'Have you spoken to Rooster about this?'

Minx just shook her head behind the pillow, she didn't know how to talk to Rooster about what she was feeling. Not only was the man who hurt her his fucking older brother, but Steven was also the man who killed Rooster's sister. Really, what did Minx have to complain about? At least she was alive.

'Why not?'

'Because I'm terrified. I know that Rooster loves me, I do know that, but we haven't told each other since the night he rescued me.

I'm scared that he just said those words because I was almost killed.' Minx wrapped her arms tighter around the pillow.

'And how do you feel about him?' Mrs Wilson continued. The question surprised Minx.

'I love him. My fucking god! I love him, I've never had feelings like this for any man before.' Minx smiled slightly, it felt so good to finally admit her feelings out loud.

'Minx, I'm going to say something to you, something that you might already know. Sweetheart, you need to tell Rooster how you feel. It's the only way you are going to be able to move on with this man.' Mrs Wilson pushed her glasses up her nose again.

***

Rooster stood outside Minx's shrink's small farmhouse. He liked Dr Wilson, she seemed to be helping his ol' lady. He hated that his woman wasn't comfortable sleeping next to him just yet, Rooster was almost desperate to fix Minx's problems but he knew this was a battle she had to fight herself. All he could do was stand by her side.

Rooster watched as Minx walked out of the front door, lost in her own thoughts. He wanted to pull her out of her mind and into his arms so badly. He would never let her go, but he also knew that Minx wasn't ready for that just yet.

'You doing okay, babe?' Rooster asked, throwing her the smile that made her roll her eyes but her lips twitch upwards.

'Huh?' Minx blinked. Her blue eyes, while red and puffy, focused on Rooster immediately. Fuck, he hated that his Minx had to go through all of this because of his good-for-nothing brother, but even he had to admit how proud he was of his woman.

'Are you doing okay?' he repeated.

'Yeah...' Minx sighed and walked towards him, surprisingly she wrapped her arms around his middle. Rooster couldn't stop his own arms from circling around her as he pressed his lips to her blonde hair and breathed in her cream and peach scent. 'I just really want to go for a ride before we go home.'

Rooster knew the perfect place. He helped her on to his bike, and they took off. Normally, the ride back to the clubhouse was about thirty minutes, but as they passed the driveway that would have taken them to the club's compound Rooster felt Minx's arms tighten around him. She had obviously thought that they were going to go back to the clubhouse, but Rooster had something to show his brave woman.

They rode for another ten minutes until he pulled up in front of the clearing where Minx had first told him about her father and where he had felt something inside him shift. The clearing was just how Rooster remembered it, only this time there was a beautiful lake house.

'Where are we, Rooster?' Minx asked. He felt her mood had shifted and turned to see a spark in her eyes and a smile grace her lips. Rooster loved her smile and he hated that he hadn't been able to see it in full force for so long.

'We're home.'

Minx climbed down from the Harley and stood in front of the house. The brick complimented the dark roof while windows lined the lounge room wall, giving the whole house natural light that Rooster knew Minx would love.

'What is this place?' Minx turned her head back and looked at him as Rooster hopped off and stood beside his woman.

'I wanted you to have a home that wasn't the clubhouse. A place where we could grow old together, and where we could raise kids.' Fuck, the ring had been burning a hole in his cut since he put it in the pocket earlier that morning. It was a simple ring, but he knew that

Minx would love it. The diamond was pear cut and set in a modest gold band. It was finally time. He took a step back and knelt down beside her. 'Minx…' Rooster cleared his throat, as Minx turned to face him. Hands went to her mouth and tears shone in her blue eyes.

Fuck! Had he messed up? Had he read the signals wrong? He had already claimed her, and she was still around despite his brother's fuckery. Rooster knew the next step would be to bind her to him legally. He was internally freaking out when he heard a small chuckle break through her tears, and Minx's delicate hand landed on her chest.

Rooster took that as his cue to continue.

'Babe, before you I was incomplete. I always thought I was going to live the biker life that my grandfather did before he was caught and now… now I can't imagine a life without your smile; your eyes when I make you mad; your beautiful blonde hair splayed out on my pillow after I've fucked you oh so thoroughly. Minx, I just can't live without you. Your warmth when you cuddle into me in the middle of the night is what helps me breathe easy, your smell when it clings to my shirts… fuck, Minx, I love you with everything I have. Marry me.' The last words that came out of Rooster's mouth sounded more like a command, but it didn't stop his woman collapsing into his arms with a watery laugh.

'I love you too,' she mumbled before kissing the crap out of him.

'Marry me, Minx?'

'I didn't think you would really need an answer since you practically told me that I was going to marry you.' Rooster just looked at his woman, he loved seeing this playful smile of Minx again.

'Yes! Of course I'll marry you!'

Rooster slipped the ring on her finger, and it fit fucking perfectly.

CHAPTER 31

Minx sat across from Mrs Wilson yet again. She had been making amazing progress since agreeing to meet with the psychologist, and the proposal was the clincher. Everyone could see it, including Minx. She was feeling strong again, feeling powerful and independent, while also learning that it was alright to rely on her family for when she needed support.

She and Rooster had been getting more and more comfortable around each other. They still had a lot to learn, and sometimes butted heads when it came to their differing opinions, but overall, Minx was feeling secure and loved in her relationship. Which was not something she had experienced in the past. Her man's arms were a source of comfort, now especially when she fell asleep every night. Minx was still plagued with nightmares but they didn't visit her nearly as often. The idea of becoming more intimate with Rooster again had been playing on Minx's mind for the past week, but she was still nervous.

Stitches had done an amazing job fixing her up after the motel room, but the deeper cuts had left behind faint, permanent reminders of what could have happened to her. Minx was worried that, because of those scars, Rooster wouldn't find her as attractive anymore or, even worse, would remind him what could have occurred if he hadn't rescued her in time.

Minx glanced up at Mrs Wilson's kind eyes. She smiled and waited patiently for her to start. Her therapist was like the grandmother that she never had, and Minx was impressed that she was able to just blurt out what had been playing over and over in her mind. 'I want to have sex with Rooster again.'

'And what has brought this on, Minx? Just the other day you were saying that you didn't know if you felt ready for that step yet,' Mrs Wilson said. She leaned forward and rested her chin on her hand, her legs were crossed and a yellow legal pad sat in her lap.

Minx thought about Mrs Wilson's question. She knew what had brought about her wanting to be with Rooster again. Minx had caught him in the shower that morning, and even though he was just cleaning himself, she'd seen his cock, thick, long and hard. That sight almost had her whimpering in pleasure and want. It had been so long since they had been together, but she wanted him so badly. Then when he reached down to touch himself, Minx almost lost the fight within, but the sight of Steven's crazed eyes came into view and she quickly left the room.

That was what she wanted to talk to Mrs Wilson about. Minx wanted to be with Rooster again and needed to know how she could get around her emotional block. 'Yeah, I want this. No, I *need* this, Doc.'

Mrs Wilson nodded her head, listening intensely. Mrs Wilson tilted her head and looked up towards the bright roof. Minx could see that her shrink was trying to formulate her response. 'You need to talk to Rooster about how you're feeling, Minx. I know the both of you had said that you love each other, and you both seem to be communicating better, but there also seems to be a distrust. You don't have anything to be afraid of Minx. That man out there thinks the world of you.'

Minx smiled at her therapist, she knew that Rooster loved her. She turned her head and, just like every session, he was sitting outside doing some work on his phone. He always waited for her, maybe he wouldn't have to wait too much longer.

Minx nodded and took in everything that Mrs Wilson was saying, banking it to her memories. She glanced down at her engagement ring and smiled. She and Rooster had been slowly furnishing their home, starting their lives together. All his actions were supporting everything that Mrs Wilson had been saying – that Rooster thought of her as his world. There was no doubt in her mind that he was Minx's.

Later that night Minx and Rooster were laying on their bed. Minx was curled up against his chest, listening to his heartbeat. The rhythmic thump-ka-thump and the soft touches of his hand in her hair was almost putting her to sleep.

'How would you feel about some of the brothers coming over for a housewarming soon?' Rooster asked, breaking the silence of the room. He had been amazing trying to understand the techniques that Mrs Wilson had been teaching her. The need to entertain and have her family around her outweighed the pressure on her chest.

'When were you thinking?' Minx asked, looking up at her man. His crazy gorgeous honey-coloured eyes sparkled with desire that she felt right down to her core.

'Sometime next week?'

'Perfect,' Minx said, getting up from her comfortable spot and straddling her man. A simple kiss on his lips caused his arms to go around her body and hold her close to him. 'Rooster,' Minx said, pulling away slightly. 'I need to talk to you about something.' Her eyes met his, and for a moment she lost all thought. But then she saw the confusion and maybe even a little fear behind the honey eyes. 'It's nothing bad, I just need to get something off my chest.'

Rooster nodded and placed his hands on her thighs. Loving the feeling of his touch, she covered his hands with hers.

'I want to try having sex again, you know that.' She winked, causing a chuckle to come from his chest. 'But you also know that it is proving more than difficult at the moment, so I was thinking that maybe we just go really slowly. I don't want to stop trying. And babe, I need you. I'm so horny.'

***

Rooster didn't know what to say. Bringing her head towards his, she gave him a scalding kiss. His hands moved from her thighs to her back, crushing her body against his. Shifting her, he lay her slowly on her back. He hovered over her, careful not to put too much weight on his woman. With light and slow kisses, he made his way from her mouth, giving her cheek special attention and moving down her neck, leaving small marks and nips. Rooster knew that his Minx was squirming with lust but also with nervousness. He was nervous too. He loved her with every part of his body, and he wanted to make sure that she trusted him enough to go through with being intimate again. He moved slowly until his rough hands grazed her soft skin under her shirt. It pebbled and caused her to shiver in his arms. Sitting her up, he slowly took off her shirt, making sure to keep eye contact with her the whole time, so that she knew who she was with.

Her bra followed quickly, her breasts still had traces of the abuse that she had endured and she tried to cover them. Gently Rooster moved her hands, replacing them with kisses, soft and light. His faint touches made Minx's body react in a way that was new to him. His mouth continued south, slowly unbuttoning her jeans and removing her underwear with deliberate touches to her skin, peeling back the plain cotton so as not to alarm her. She responded by lifting her hips, allowing him to pull them under her butt. He let his fingers trace the taught skin of her mounds. Her breath quickened and Rooster knew he'd started to lose her. He saw her blue eyes glaze over. He couldn't have her drifting into a nightmare, not when he was here to make her feel safe. When she closed her eyes, he knew he had to pull her back into reality. And fast.

Moving up her body, he hovered over her, pushing his weight off her.

'Open your eyes, Minx,' he commanded. When she didn't do it, Rooster felt deflated. But he couldn't give up on her. 'I need to see those baby blues. Open your eyes. Please.' His voice held a bit of pleading that normally he would be ashamed of, but he needed Minx back with him. 'Look at me, Minx. It's me, stay with me babe.'

She opened her eyes and he held her gaze.

'It's us, Minx. You and me.'

He felt her hand caress his arm, moving slowly over the muscles, up over his shoulders and along his neck to trace the chisel of his jaw. With an open palm she caressed his cheek. He watched her explore his features with an intensity that made him feel her love. He knew she was seeing him, he felt every bit of her love and he had never felt so turned on. Afraid his hard cock might announce its presence against her, he moved his hips to the side, and she stilled. She grabbed a handful of his hair.

'Don't move, I want to feel you, Rooster.' She reached down and grabbed his ass and guided his body back into position above her. 'I want to feel your weight on me. I want the feeling of you and only you. I want you, Rooster. I need you.'

Settling his whole body down against her, unsure how she would react, she pulled him hard up against her and buried her face into his neck. She took a long breath in, drinking him in.

Letting her slowly discover him again aroused something deep in him that went beyond anything physical. He was afraid to speak for fear of frightening her in this moment or ending the intensity of his own arousal.

He was sure she felt it, heavy between them. She moved beneath him, lifting her hips and parting her legs, rubbing against his hard cock. He felt the heat of her core and leaned in to kiss her, rocking in rhythm with her.

Minx opened to him, letting her tongue explore his. He melted into her need and she clung to his body, writhing against him. He felt like an excited teen, the heady lust between them banished all the fear.

'I want to feel your skin against mine,' his Minx breathed between kisses. 'I want you inside me, Rooster.'

Loathed to break the spell, Rooster continued to kiss her.

'Rooster! Get these off now.' She pushed at the top of his jeans.

With a chuckle, he broke away and rolled to her side, and in one swift motion, lifted his hips to unbutton his fly. His hard cock was soon free of its constraints. She grabbed at him, hungry for his flesh as he tried to kick them off his feet.

'Give me a chance, babe.' He laughed at her enthusiasm.

'Come here and fuck me, Rooster!' She pulled at his body and he didn't wait for a further invitation, she was ready. He slipped into her hot wet pussy with ease. She pulled his ass into her. 'Deeper,' she groaned and threw her head back.

Rooster, lost in her lust, pounded into her, his Minx matching his energy. She cried, 'Yes' as she dug her nails into the flesh of his ass. He growled as her nails dug in, the pain had him spiralling in sensation. They moved as one towards a fast-approaching abyss of pleasure. Riding each other hard, a sweaty heat plastered skin to skin, the scent of sex filled the air and Minx's moans fell to the back of her throat, each thrust announcing her impending orgasm and sending Rooster hurtling towards his own.

Minx's body tightened with a slow, deep moan. Her hot pussy clamped down on his cock, over and over. Rooster thrusted against her energy, bringing his own sensational climax.

Through gritted teeth he groaned her name as his body shuddered to a slow stop. A moment of pure love and joy enveloped him and he allowed his body to relax into his Minx. She wrapped her arms and legs around him, holding him close and tight. Her short breath and quiet sobs told him she was crying, her words putting his mind at ease.

'I love you, Rooster. I love you more than life itself,' she whispered through tears of pure happiness.

Peeling away from each other, they lay spent looking up at the ceiling. He reached out to hold her hand, grieved not to be touching.

'I love you too, Minx,' he said to the room. With a chuckle she wiggled up against him, pressing her clammy body to his. She propped herself up on his chest, and pulled his face towards hers and made sure he was looking at her in the eyes.

'Now… say that again.' She had a lazy sexed up grin that made him bean with pride.

'I said I love you, Minx.'

She leaned over and pecked his swollen lips and snuggled into his chest, her hand over his heart. They lay in silence for a moment. Soaking each other in, Rooster felt himself slipping into a peaceful endorphin induced sleep. His Minx's soft breathing announced that she'd already found hers.

EPILOGUE

Two lines.

Minx checked the box in her hands and then back at the stick that she just peed on.

It had been three months since she and Rooster had that magical night of making love, and they hadn't exactly been careful those past months either, but now she was pregnant. There was no denying it, even if one smiling stick could sometimes lie, four tests definitely didn't. That with her tender breasts, her constant dizziness and nausea added to the confirmation.

Minx moved over to the sink and stared at herself in the large mirror. She didn't look any different, but she still cupped her stomach and was immediately brought to tears. She smiled as ecstatic, anxious, joyful tears streamed down her face and ridiculed herself. Damn those pregnancy hormones.

They had created something so spectacularly beautiful. Minx wondered what their baby would look like. Would it be a boy or a girl? Would they have Minx's blonde hair or Rooster's dark? She hoped that they inherited Rooster's honey-brown eyes.

They were too stunning not to be passed on.

'Minx...' Her husband-to-be knocked on the bathroom door,

bringing Minx out of her thoughts. She turned around and was about to open the door, but she was stopped. What was Rooster going to say? They hadn't exactly discussed children apart from Rooster mentioning it in passing during his proposal. 'You okay in there, baby?'

'Yeah!' Minx called back, her voice breaking slightly. She winced at her reaction. She knew that Rooster wouldn't believe her words, but she was thankful that he let it go. 'I'm good.'

'Okay, baby. Some of the brothers and I are going to go to the clubhouse to get some last-minute details sorted.' Rooster called out that he loved her, which Minx returned. She wiped at her eyes and poked her head out of the bathroom door and puckered her lips. Her man brushed his against hers, before saying that he will see her later. They were originally going to spend the night apart from each other, but the more Minx thought about it, the more she hated the idea.

Minx ducked back into the bathroom, wrapped the sticks up in toilet paper and grabbed her phone. She paused for a moment on the best person to call. She wanted to call her mother, but she hadn't spoken to Meg for years. So, she called the only other mother she knew.

'Hello, dear.'

'Queenie… I need your help.'

Minx paced the front room of her house and waited impatiently for the ten minutes that it took for her future mother-in-law to show up. She hadn't given a lot of information over the phone, but Minx was sure that Queenie had a suspicion as to what was going on. Minx heard the car door slam shut and she rushed outside and smiled at her future mother-in-law.

Minx covered her stomach with her hand absentmindedly. Queenie smiled back and hurried over to the front porch, pulling Minx into a hug. 'How long have you known?'

'I just found out,' Minx admitted.

'So, what has you so scared?' Queenie asked as Minx led her through to the kitchen area. It was still in the process of being furnished with the kitchen essentials, but there was enough to make a cup of coffee, or tea for Minx now. The question had Minx stopping and thinking. Her and Rooster's communication skills had gotten a lot better since they'd first started dating.

'I guess, I thought we would have started a little later. I'm not sure we're ready for this.' Minx shrugged as she poured water into her white kettle. She had always loved kids, it was one of the reasons she had become a teacher. Which was something that she would have to put off going back to if she and Rooster were going to have this baby.

'I'm going to tell you something,' Queenie said as she sat down on one of the bar stools by the island bench. The view of the lake was stunning in the afternoon sun. 'Patriot and I were not married when we had our first son. We weren't even married when we had Rooster. It wasn't until I found out about Heather that Patriot finally asked me to marry him, and by that time we had already been together for almost fifteen years. I was committed to him, I was his ol' lady and matriarch of the club that we both loved so much. Minx, you may still be relatively new to this life but know that my son would never have taken you as an ol' lady if he didn't think that the two of you wouldn't be together forever, youngin' included.'

Queenie's words calmed Minx down some. She wasn't scared of having a baby, she was scared that Rooster would change his mind about them. When she truly thought about it, without an instant reaction, Minx knew that not only was she going to love this baby but that Rooster was going to be an amazing father. Her fears were instantly calmed. Now all they had to do was get through the wedding.

Minx stood in front of the clubhouse the next day, her hands resting on her stomach as she looked at the amazing transformation that the dusty parking lot had gone through. Baby's breath hung along strings of festoon lights that stretched across the lot, the brothers had set up mismatched chairs that offered an eclectic feel and created a makeshift aisle. The whole courtyard was the perfect metaphor for their pairing.

The biker and the teacher.

It was almost time. Brothers, family and a few friends were all sitting waiting for her to make her grand entrance. Since Rooster was the national charter president, many of their guests were from the other charters around America. She hadn't met many of them yet, but the few that she did meet were family to her now too.

Minx didn't have a father to walk her down the aisle, but when Gunner had volunteered to do the job, Minx immediately agreed.

'Well look at you, Minx,' Gunner said from behind her. She jumped and turned around to face him, her dress flared out around her. The short lace dress was perfect for her, Minx didn't want a long wedding dress. Especially since Rooster planned on the both of them riding off on the back of his motorcycle. The sweetheart neckline and the straps were her favourite part of the dress. They connected at the back making it look like angel wings, a tribute to her fallen sister. When Minx noticed the details of the dress, she couldn't stop crying. She wanted so desperately to have Angel there with them today and she knew that Rooster did too.

'Thanks, Gun.' Minx smiled. She and Gunner had gotten to know each other really well in the short time that she was living at the clubhouse. The man wasn't much of a talker, choosing instead to grunt as most answers, but Minx knew that she could trust the man with her life.

'You are missing something though,' he said, pulling her

property patch out from behind his back. 'You can't get married without your patch.'

Minx had never thought about wearing her patch because of the details of her dress, but as soon as the familiar leather graced her shoulders Minx thought of the leather as protecting the memory and the love of Angel. Minx fought to hold back the tears as he held out his arm.

Damn hormones.

'You ready, Minx?'

With a nod of her head, Minx and Gunner started the slow walk thought the clubhouse front doors. The speakers softly played Elvis Presley's 'Falling in Love with You'. It was the same song that Queenie and Patriot had danced to at their own wedding. Minx couldn't hold in her tears, they fell down her face and she silently thanked the angels for waterproof makeup.

Her eyes scanned the crowd of bikers and ol' ladies, Daisy had even come down from New York to watch her brother get married. Ivy and some of her other favourite students also sat on the outskirts of the crowd.

Minx's eyes finally went from the crowd to her future husband. Rooster's normal blank face was holding the biggest smile that she had ever seen. From his boots to his jeans, he was dressed in his normal biker getup. Instead of his regular upper half, he had put on a white button down and his cut, but he looked fucking perfect to her. She couldn't believe that this day was happening.

The ceremony flew by her in a blur of cheers and beautiful words. Minx barely remembered all of it, except for her husband's honey gaze telling her that he loved her with every breath he took. When the both of them said 'I do' brothers roared in celebration and immediately started moving chairs out of the way for the reception.

The celebrations continued well into the night, only a few times

Rooster mentioned her not drinking any of the champagne they had bought for the occasion. She had been avoiding anything more than a tiny sip to keep him in the dark, but the bushes that surrounded the clubhouse were getting drunk for her. She had been sneakily throwing her drinks into the plants all night.

By the time they rode off to cheering brothers and sisters towards the cabin in the mountains where Rooster's parents had spent their honeymoon, Minx was beyond exhausted and wanted nothing more than to be alone with her new husband.

Her whole world had just become so unfamiliar, but oh so wonderful.

Rooster carried his wife over the threshold, sat her on her feet and kissed the absolute crap out of her. 'I love you, Mila "Minx" Bates,' he said as he pulled away.

'I love you too, Dylan "Rooster" Bates,' Minx said, loving the face that he made when she called him by his law-given name. She hadn't said it since that night and she was never going to say it again because, just like her, his name wasn't what he was born with.

He was Rooster.

President of Black Alchemy and her husband.

'I have something to tell you,' she said, jumping up into his arms. She was thankful for the short skirt as she wrapped her legs around his waist. 'I'm pregnant.'

Rooster froze and Minx's heart dipped before his mouth found hers and kissed her with a ferocity that she had only felt a few times. 'I can't believe that you are mine,' he said. 'And that you're carrying my baby. Minx, I fucking love you.'

ACKNOWLEDGEMENTS

To my mama, Brooke – You've shown me what being a strong female character is like. You've helped me with my writing and have been my sound board for so many things. Thank you so much.

To my papa, Tim – You have always supported me through every goal I wanted to achieve in my life. You've helped me with the MMC perspectives. Thank you for being an Alan in a world full of Kens.

To Brigid – Thank you for being there for me, for answering my midnight phone calls and for the snacks you bring to our sleepovers. And most of all for being one of the most loyal friends I have ever had.

To Marjorie – Thank you for dealing with my erratic messages, for helping me find my head when I'm losing my mind over an idea and most importantly, thank you for dealing with my crazy.

To my grandparents – Thank you so much Nanny and Grandad for everything you've done for me. For being that ear when I needed it.

To my little sister, Eden – I'm putting you in here because Mum said I had to include you ;)

Shawline Publishing Group Pty Ltd
www.shawlinepublishing.com.au

SHAWLINE PUBLISHING GROUP